THE LOST BOY

JANE RENSHAW

INKUBATOR
BOOKS

Published by Inkubator Books
www.inkubatorbooks.com

Copyright © 2022 by Jane Renshaw

ISBN (eBook): 978-1-915275-74-5
ISBN (Paperback): 978-1-915275-75-2
ISBN (Hardback): 978-1-915275-76-9

Jane Renshaw has asserted her right to be identified as the author of this work.

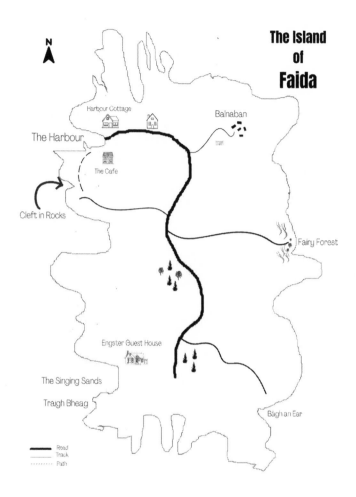

The Island
of
Faida

PROLOGUE

The boy had been bad.

That was why he was in here.

That was why he was hot and thirsty and his back hurt and his legs ached. Even though he wasn't big, there wasn't enough room for him to sit up or lie down properly, so he had to half-lie and half-sit with his knees up against his face.

By twisting one shoulder, he managed to bend his arm so he could push his hand into his pocket and feel around until his fingers touched one of Yoda's ears. Spiky. He whispered, '*Yoda*,' and carefully brought him out, making sure his finger and thumb gripped the little guy tight.

If he dropped him, he might not find him again in the dark.

Yoda was his lucky mascot, but usually the boy kept him hidden in his pocket because people might not understand – they might think he was a big baby, carrying a tiny plastic *Star Wars* figure around with him everywhere he went.

He couldn't see Yoda, but he could hold him in his hand and feel his sticking-out ears and his funny walnut face. Yoda always helped him stay calm. If the boy panicked now, in this small space, he could really hurt himself.

His shoulder was sore from pressing against something hard.

How long was he going to be left in here for?

His breathing had gone funny. It was like he was running hard, even though he wasn't moving at all.

'Soon,' croaked Yoda, 'get out we will.'

Yoda always spoke his wise words in a weird order.

'Yeah,' whispered the boy, pressing his thumb against the point of one of Yoda's ears. 'We'll soon be out of here. But then what?'

Yoda was silent, but the boy's voice seemed to echo back at them from the dark.

Then what.

Then what.

Then what?

1

ANNA

The sea was a gorgeous Mediterranean blue, but the north wind coming off the Sound of Jura whipped at Anna's face, making her glad of her cashmere hat and scarf. It was always cold at the harbour, her least favourite place on the island, and she'd been standing here a while. The boat should have arrived quarter of an hour ago.

If she'd been a spiritual kind of person, she might have been tempted to wonder whether the delay had been contrived by a higher power to give her time to reflect. To search her soul. To reconsider. At this, the eleventh hour, doubts would only have been natural.

But Anna had none.

First thing this morning, she'd stood in front of the mirror in the bathroom and looked into her own eyes, searching for – what? A trace of the old Anna? A flinching from what she had to do? A little human feeling, perhaps? In almost every culture on every continent on Earth, the crime she was about to commit was held to be most abhorrent.

But Anna felt nothing.

No pang of guilt, no shiver of horror, no *cràdh*, as they said in Gaelic.

No anguish.

The rhythmic slapping of water against concrete at the edge of the slipway kept drawing her gaze. There was something unsettling about a rising tide, something sneaky about the way it crept up over the land, as if it were hoping you wouldn't notice. The sea was cold at this time of year. It took forever to warm up after a Scottish winter, even in the relatively mild climate of the Hebrides, and in May it was often colder than in December.

She pushed her hands into the fleecy pockets of her jacket. Was the harbour really the coldest place on the island, or was there something so grim about this point of departure, the scene of so many goodbyes, that it triggered a sort of psychosomatic cold shock response?

And now she could see *Venus*, finally, labouring round the reef of Sgeir Eskernish, pitching and yawing in the standing waves that tended to mass there whenever there was a strong flood tide running up the Sound into the teeth of a north wind.

Anna had told the Clarkes that the crossing from Tayvallich would be fun.

'You'll probably see seals and maybe dolphins, or even a basking shark!'

She smiled as she imagined them huddled in the cabin, spray streaming down the windows. *Venus* wasn't even a proper ferry; it was just a scruffy little tourist boat that stopped off at Faida on Sundays, Tuesdays and Thursdays from April to October – once in the morning, and again in the late afternoon. It was also one of the boats that was chartered for the 'school run' to pick up kids from the islands on a Monday morning and deposit them home on a Friday afternoon. There were no facilities on board apart from a rudimentary toilet that the young guys who crewed it seldom bothered to clean.

As *Venus* approached the harbour, the skipper gunned the engine and they picked up speed, slamming headlong into each wave. Anna was sure he did this deliberately – he was one of those locals who seemed to despise the tourists who provided him with his living. Once past the quay, he swung the boat around in a too-tight circle, and the tall blonde woman exiting the cabin staggered against the rail. After a bit of manoeuvring, *Venus* bumped up against the side of the slipway. The skipper had positioned her too far down the slope, which meant that the disembarking passengers would have quite a step from boat to concrete.

First to make landfall was Rod Clarke, jumping down with a cheerful 'Oof!'

Anna recognised him at once from their Zoom sessions, although the grey in his hair was more obvious in natural light. Tall and lanky, he was dressed in a good-quality khaki jacket, navy walking trousers and sturdy boots, all of which had a patina suggesting he spent a lot of time in the great outdoors. The pair of binoculars slung round his neck completed the look.

He was a lot more animated than she'd expected, given the boat trip he'd just endured and the impression she'd received in their Zoom sessions that Rod Clarke was not exactly the life and soul of the party.

'Oh wow, Anna, this is *amazing!*' He beamed at her, pushing his glasses up his nose, and then turned back to the sea, flapping his hands at the view – the rocky coast of the island, the blue sea, the little white clouds scudding over the Paps of Jura. 'Thank you *so much* for this! It's *so kind* of you! And it's great to meet you in person at last!' He had a booming, rather attractive bass voice.

'It's surreal, isn't it? From two dimensions to three?' Anna returned his smile with what she hoped was convincing warmth. 'I'm really glad you could come.'

Penny Clarke didn't seem to be quite so thrilled to be here. She was almost as tall and slim as her husband and had a natural elegance about her, enhanced by her choice of outfit: a tailored white jacket and pristine skinny-fit grey walking trousers that showed off a great pair of legs. Anna was sure those boots had never seen mud, and her hair had probably started out the crossing in a carefully styled sweep of blonde bob. Now, the wind was flipping it up like a comb-over as she struggled to lift a large suitcase from the side of the boat onto the slipway. The young guy whose job this really should have been was standing with a rope in his hand, pretending to be busy and watching her with a slight smile.

Anna hurried to help.

'Thanks!' gushed Penny as Anna grabbed hold of another large case. 'I don't know where half of this has come from – I'm sure it can't *all* be ours!' She made a comical face, but the jollity seemed forced. 'It really is *very* good of you to have us, Anna.'

It really was. Surely the Clarkes should be questioning this largesse, the offer of a free holiday from a woman Penny knew not at all, and Rod only from a Facebook group, some brief exchanges on Messenger and a few Zoom sessions?

Anna smiled. 'You're more than welcome. A captive audience with which to talk birds – my idea of heaven, although possibly not yours!'

Penny laughed. 'Don't worry – I'm used to it, with this one and his birder mates.' She nodded at Rod, who had joined them, although he made no move to help his wife lug another bag off the boat.

'How was the crossing?' asked Anna.

'A bit lively!' Rod was practically jumping up and down like a kid in a sweetie shop. 'Exhilarating! The boys got soaked! The skipper told them not to stand at the back of the boat because that was where the spray from the bow landed – so of course that's where they insisted on stationing themselves for the duration.'

Anna turned an indulgent smile on the boys, who were running screaming to the end of the quay. They were both skinny little things, having inherited, she assumed, their parents' body shape. Even in their bulky coats, you could tell that they had almost impossibly narrow pelvises – no bums. Not an ounce of fat on them.

The three seagulls that had been dozing at the end of the quay suddenly took off, wings beating the air. The younger boy snatched up a stone and flung it after them, while the older swaggered back towards the adults in that strange way some small boys had, as if in the throes of a fit, torso contorting as he walked, arms and legs flung out exaggeratedly.

'It's the middle of bloody nowhere!' he shouted. 'This place is *crap!*'

Anna expected his parents to tell him not to say 'bloody' and 'crap' and not to be so rude – they must surely be aware that Anna's family owned the island – but Penny Clarke just threw him an exasperated look, while Rod boomed, 'Oh Freddie, Freddie! Look around you! Have you no soul?'

Freddie looked from side to side and made a disbelieving face, turning up the palms of his hands to convey, *This is all you've got?* He shot a look at Anna. 'There's *literally* nothing here. Now we know why we were the only people on the boat.'

From poring over the Clarkes' social media accounts, Anna knew that Freddie was ten years old and 'a character'. He was rather a beautiful child, with big blue eyes, a Cupid's bow mouth and honey-coloured curls. In contrast, six-year-old Alfie – 'a cheeky monkey' – was not what you'd call easy on the eye. He had the same curly hair as his brother, but if Freddie was a cherub, Alfie was more like an elf or a goblin. Or maybe gargoyle was nearer the mark. He certainly had the sort of classical ugliness a medieval stone-carver would have delighted in – very close-set eyes, a funny, squashed button of a nose, and a receding chin.

Both boys were wearing suede baseball caps with 'Burberry' emblazoned on them. Freddie's cap was blue and Alfie's was terracotta, but their puffer jackets were an identical beige with a black and red check across it. Also Burberry, presumably. Why waste time parenting your kids when you could throw money at the little buggers?

'I need crisps,' stated Alfie, grabbing his mother's arm and pouting up at her while blinking rapidly in what Anna assumed was an attempt to be cute.

'Oh, darling, I don't think I have any.' Penny picked up a rucksack and began unzipping pockets. 'How about an apple?'

The pout morphed into a moue of distaste, into which Alfie put all the disgust of a vegan who'd just been offered veal. He looked up at Penny and enunciated, as if to an idiot: 'I – want – crissssssps! Mum! You haven't forgotten them, have you? Mum? Mum? Mum!' He tugged down sharply on Penny's handbag, yanking it off her shoulder and making her wince.

'All right, Alfie, hold your horses. I'll check the other bag.'

Alfie sighed theatrically, rolling his eyes at Anna as if to say, You can't get the staff.

Freddie ran up to Penny and shouted in her face: 'I want crisps too!'

As Penny continued unzipping compartments, Anna looked from her to Rod. What would they say, what would they do, if they could see inside her head? She imagined their gasps of shock, their looks of bafflement, of disbelief, of horror. Their panicked shouts as they bundled the boys back onto the boat.

Rod finally hefted one of the bags. 'So how many people live on the island?'

'Tam, Broc and I are the only permanent residents.' Anna took a leather holdall in each hand and began walking up the slipway to where she'd parked the Land Rover. 'But Tam works on his brother's trawler – he's away out in the Atlantic at the moment, off St Kilda, last I spoke to him – and Broc is at school on the mainland and stays with my sister and her family in Oban through the week, so I'm on my own a lot of the time. There are the guest house punters, of course, as well as the day-trippers and holiday let guests, although we're refurbishing the holiday cottages, so they're empty just now.' She had, in fact, blocked out the whole of May as 'unavailable' for both the guest house and the holiday lets, as she hadn't known which week the Clarkes were going to choose.

The carrot to tempt them here had been a story about an extended family from the USA who'd booked out the whole guest house for the month of May and then had to cancel at the last minute, leaving a gaping hole in Anna's schedule.

The offer of a free holiday, of course, had been too good to resist. *They've already paid for the whole month and will get the money back on their travel insurance*, Anna had assured Rod on Messenger. *Why don't you pick a week in May and come and stay at their expense? We'd love to have you all. Broc will soon get the boys away from their screens!*

'Broc had a football game yesterday, so he's staying on the mainland this weekend,' Anna told Rod now, 'but he'll be back on Friday. He'll be able to spend a bit of time with the boys before you leave.' The holiday was Sunday to Sunday.

Rod smiled. 'Well, that's a treat in store for Broc! Broc MacLean – you know, Anna, your son sounds like a character in an old western!'

'He does, rather!'

Freddie, giggling manically, was now chasing Alfie with a dead crab, and Alfie, screaming at the top of his voice, was running straight for the edge of the slipway.

'*Alfie!*' yelled Penny. '*For goodness' sake, look where you're going!*' She dropped the case and rucksack she was carrying and ran back down the slipway. She was fast – very athletic, actually – but she wouldn't reach him in time.

Anna held her breath.

But Alfie skidded to a halt a good three feet from immersion, and Freddie took the opportunity to slip the crab down his neck. As his little brother writhed and wailed, Freddie looked at the adults with a smug grin that said, *My work here is done.*

'Freddie, mate,' said Rod mildly. He shook his head and turned back to Anna. 'I'm hoping for corncrakes. There definitely are some on the island, yes?'

'Oh, yes! Heaps! They arrived a couple of weeks ago. Just head for the nearest patch of yellow flag irises and you're pretty much guaranteed to hear them, although catching a glimpse is another matter.'

'I've only ever seen one corncrake, and that was from behind as it ran away from me,' Rod said wistfully. 'I'd disturbed it – unwittingly, I hasten to add – going for a pee behind a wall on Iona. That would be … oh, ten years ago now, at least.'

Penny was left with the unenviable task of removing Alfie's coat and attempting to locate the crab – not easy, given that the boy was writhing about in apparent agony. As Freddie gyrated round his brother in a victory lap, Alfie yelled at Penny, '*Get it off me!*'

The kids were even worse than Anna had hoped – archetypal spoilt brats, straight out of the pages of one of those cautionary tales for children. Each seemed as bad as the other, but she'd have to choose. It was going to be difficult enough contriving a tragic fatality for one boy, let alone two.

So which was it to be?

Freddie or Alfie?

Which child would she kill?

2

PENNY

Everything in Penny was screaming: *Get me out of here!*

A whole week. A *whole week* stuck on this bloody island! Freddie was right – there was literally nothing here. Through the expanse of glass that made up one wall of the massive guest living area, all she could see was scenery.

Suddenly, at her elbow: 'That's Jura, across the water.' Anna MacLean smiled up at her. 'Sorry – didn't mean to startle you.'

Rod's little friend Anna was one strange cookie. The woman seemed to glide silently about the place. And she always had a big false smile on her face, like the Cheshire Cat. She should wear a bell round her neck.

'Jura,' repeated Penny, although she couldn't care less.

Anna pointed out of the floor-to-ceiling windows. 'The conical hills are called the *Paps* of Jura because they're meant to look like boobs.'

Penny supposed she should attempt a smile of her own. And maybe an amusing remark. 'They could certainly give the Kardashians a run for their money.'

Anna flung back her head and laughed, revealing little white teeth. She was in the Kardashian mould herself: long, dark, straight hair, oval face, neat waist, man-friendly curves. Relatively long legs for a short-arse. Penny had only seen her once during Rod's birder Zoom chats, and then only from the shoulders up.

She looked like she could live off the hump for a few days, anyway, if she got stuck up a mountain or down a gorge. Or up to her neck in a bog.

Penny would be willing to bet that the Isle of Faida did a nice line in bogs.

On the five-minute drive from the tiny harbour, Rod had waxed lyrical, of course, about the scenery. 'That's the machair – look, boys! One of the rarest habitats in the world!'

Alfie had glanced up obediently, but Freddie's eyes had remained glued to his screen.

'It's just grass.'

'And that, Frederick, is where you couldn't be more wrong! It's a very special kind of grassland packed full of native species, all kinds of wild flowers, even some rare orchids ... The soil it grows on is enriched by tiny bits of shell from the sea, and in wonderful places like this it's managed sensitively, just lightly grazed – Look, Highland cattle! You wouldn't want to get on the wrong end of those horns, eh, Alfie? – And once a year, it's cut for hay. Good old traditional, wildlife-friendly farming practices. You get all kinds of birds in the machair. Lapwing, snipe, golden plover ...'

Penny had tuned out at that point. Partly because she was bored out of her mind, but also because an email had just arrived on her phone from Lisa in Procurement. Last month, Rod had ordered new tyres for the entire fleet of intercity coaches – without, of course, running this by Penny first. Or Frank, their head mechanic, who had assured her that all the old tyres were still well within the legal tread allowance, and even the worst of them would have done another three months. Four at a pinch.

Fifteen coaches.

Six tyres each at two hundred and twenty pounds a pop.

And just like that, Rod had pissed twenty thousand pounds up the wall. The tyres had already been fitted before the matter had been brought to Penny's attention, so returning them for a refund wasn't an option. And Rod had had all the old tyres disposed of, even the ones with plenty of wear left in them, so they couldn't even swap them out and wait until they were on the cusp of illegality before changing to the new ones.

Sometimes Penny felt like she was the only one in the whole company who ever thought about the bottom line.

And now the supplier was hassling Lisa for settlement of the invoice. Well, they could whistle. Get in line, my friend, behind the dozen or so other creditors they had accumulated in the last two years. Penny hoped the takings over the summer would make a dent in their debts, but she wasn't holding out any great hopes. Passenger numbers were well down on last year. Which had been well down on the year before that.

Remortgaging the house was looking like the only option.

And who knew what Rod would decide to splash out on next? Maybe he'd decide the whole fleet needed replacing.

She wouldn't put it past him.

He was out of control.

There he was now, tramping along the beach in front of the guest house. Rucksack on back, binoculars in hand. She really hoped that this holiday would give him a chance to recharge his batteries. If anything, his depression, and the unpredictability that seemed to come with it, had got worse over the last two years rather than better. Maybe this time away with his beloved birds would help him get a bit of perspective and move on, as she'd had to do, for the sake of the kids, if nothing else.

Even a week on a nature reserve would be worth it if it helped Rod recover his bounce. Which, to be fair, he already seemed to be doing. There was definitely a spring in his step, and he was holding himself more upright.

'You have a lovely home,' Penny felt she should say, turning to look at the room. It was vast. There was a dining area with a long, sociable table overlooking the yard at the back of the house. But most of the room was taken up by groups of sofas and armchairs in tweeds and antique-look leather, with a big log-burner pumping out much-needed heat against the far wall. On the wall opposite was a floor-to-ceiling bookcase filled with Rod-friendly stuff – books on nature, history, archaeology ... And what was it with nature buffs and silly fantasies about going off on intrepid adventures? She'd be willing to bet there'd be at least one autobiography of some masochist well chuffed with himself for surviving four months on a raft in the Pacific with the loss of only a couple of appendages to shark attacks.

On the plus side, she had no complaints – well, not many – about the guest accommodation. It was high-end and modern, housed in a big wood-and-glass extension tacked onto the side of the original Victorian farmhouse where the MacLeans had their own digs. Rod and Penny's bedroom was palatial, with great views out to sea and a super-king bed. Even the kids' room was spacious, and the en suites were very sleek and sparkling clean, with pristine white towels and good toiletries.

But in this living area there were things like fish made from driftwood and faded old watercolours. A pair of stag's antlers. A sculpture of an otter. Penny would have chucked out all the tat and replaced it with some funky abstract seascapes and maybe some modern art glass in blues and greens.

'Thank you,' said Anna, with her Cheshire Cat smile. 'I hope you'll be comfortable. Lunch will be at one, but can I get you tea or coffee, and some cake? What would the boys like?'

Oh no.

Where were the kids?

It was always a bad sign when they went so quiet that you forgot about them.

'Uh, thanks, tea would be great.' Penny edged across to the door that led to the stairs. 'Black, please. No sugar. And I try to keep sugar to a minimum with the boys, so ... just water for them – and actually, if you have crisps, that would be fantastic? Thanks, Anna!'

She took the stairs at a run.

And not a moment too soon.

Freddie and Alfie were grappling in the doorway to their en suite – or rather, Alfie was jumping up at Freddie, and Freddie was fending him off with one hand. Both the en suite and the large, sunny bedroom were full of steam.

Alfie was whining: 'Let *me* have a go!'

Freddie had the shower fitting pulled out as far as it would extend and was holding it high above his head, angled through the en suite's doorway so that the blast from the power shower pummelled the white duvet of the nearest twin bed.

When he saw Penny, for a split second he looked at her with completely unchildlike – what? She could never decide. Coldness? Indifference? Contempt?

And the usual traitorous thought jumped into her head: *Why can't you be like other kids?*

Then the moment had passed, and he was an ordinary little boy again. He pushed Alfie away and scampered back into the en suite. He quickly turned off the water and shoved the shower fitting back in its holder.

'Look what Alfie's done, Mum!'

When Penny eventually returned to the big living area, she found Anna setting a tray down on the coffee table in front of the wood-burner. On it were a big mug of tea, a piece of carrot cake, two glasses of iced water and two bowls of crisps.

'Anna, I'm *so sorry*, but the boys have somehow managed to spill water on one of the beds. I'll change the sheets. Where do you keep the fresh linen?'

Anna straightened, grinning at Penny manically as if this was the best news she'd had all week. 'Oh, don't worry! I'll do it. You relax with your tea.'

No way could she let Anna go up to the room and realise what had happened. Penny wasn't about to let the boys sabotage this for Rod. Not again. Last summer, they'd been thrown out of a gorgeous boutique hotel in Guernsey just twenty-four hours into the holiday.

'I'm sorry, Mrs Clarke,' the hotel manager had said unsmilingly, actually holding up a manicured hand to indicate that Penny should stop speaking. 'We have to think of the health and safety of everyone, and that includes your sons. I suggest you find somewhere that specialises in accommodation for children with special needs.'

The cheek! *Special needs?* Freddie was top of his class, and Alfie was also a very bright child.

They'd had no choice but to check in to a Premier Inn.

Which wasn't even an option here. Anna would probably pack them off to one of the mid-renovation holiday cottages, where living on what was basically a building site would provide the boys with unprecedented opportunities not only to cause damage but to get themselves killed while they were at it.

'No, Anna, I insist. If you just give me a spare duvet and a fresh cover, I'll see to it. And do you have a drying room or somewhere I could put the wet duvet? It's only water, thankfully, so no harm done.'

'Okay!' Anna was still in Cheshire Cat mode. 'The linen cupboard for the guest rooms is on the landing. I'll give you the key. The drying room is through the door under the stairs.'

The sheet and mattress protector under the duvet were also sopping wet. And the pillow and pillowcase. And the mattress. Just how long had Freddie been soaking the bed for?

Penny turned the mattress and sneaked all the bedding downstairs and into the drying room. But if Freddie ended up having to sleep in a wet bed, maybe it would be no bad thing. She knew that part of the problem was that she was too soft with them – trying to compensate, she supposed, for being a busy working mum. She did try to be firm when necessary, but it wasn't easy with a couple of very lively, very headstrong boys, particularly as Rod seemed to consider himself their best buddy rather than their father, and left all the tough stuff to her.

Maybe she should turn the mattress back over, wet side up. Actions should have consequences, as Penny's dad had always said. But she knew what would happen – Freddie would make Alfie sleep in the wet bed.

As she left the drying room, she heard high, excited screams and giggles coming from the living area. She got there at the same moment as Anna, who was coming through the door from the owners' accommodation. Freddie and Alfie were jumping around on the furniture as if they were in a soft play area, throwing carrot cake at each other.

'*Freddie! Alfie!*' she yelled. '*Get down now, please!*'

Freddie launched himself from a leather armchair onto a

tweed-covered sofa like he was one of those parkour people, turning a somersault as he landed.

'*Freddie!*'

She felt like weeping.

But Anna was still, thank God, smiling. 'It's just high spirits. Eh, boys? Being in a new place is always exciting, isn't it?'

Freddie jumped down off the sofa and grabbed a crisp from one of the bowls. As he munched, he looked around him, hands on hips, before turning to Anna and wrinkling his nose. '*That's* cool.' He waved a hand at the wall of glass. The doors that formed the middle section now stood open to the decking, on which plantation chairs were arranged to take in the view. 'But *this*' – he indicated the room – 'is all, like, *really* old-fashioned and *eeeww*? The chairs look like they smell. Like the chairs they had in Great-Gran's old folks' home. They all wee-ed into them.'

'Freddie!' snapped Penny.

Anna laughed. 'Well, I'm sorry if the furnishings don't live up to your obviously high standards, Freddie.'

'It's not *high standards* to want to sit on a non-wee chair. That's just, like ... probably a basic human right.' And he snatched a whole handful of crisps and ran out of the open doors, followed immediately, of course, by Alfie.

Anna started to examine the furniture. 'Freddie's quite a character, isn't he?'

'You could say that. I'm sorry – you're right, they're hyper with excitement. They'll calm down in an hour or so, hopefully.' *She wished.* 'Your son's a bit older, isn't he? Broc?' Probably good to emphasise that her kids were younger and so required more leeway.

'He's fourteen.' Anna's smile had slipped a bit. She was using her fingernail to passive-aggressively pick ground-in cream cheese icing off one of the chairs.

Penny rushed to help. 'So he's past the jumping-on-furniture stage. But I suppose once they're over that, you're into the teenage years, and I'm sure they're just as challenging.'

'Actually, Broc has never been a problem in terms of discipline. Possibly because he was home-schooled until he was eleven – obviously there's no primary school on such a tiny island. So I suppose he acquired adult manners from an early age.' Anna opened the door of the wood-burner and threw bits of cake and icing inside. 'He would see his friends on the other islands regularly, and his cousins on the mainland, but day to day it was just me, his dad and the wildlife, which he's become as obsessed with as we are.'

Thank God Broc wasn't here. Or wouldn't be, anyway, until the end of the week. Freddie and Alfie weren't good with other kids, no matter how tolerant and mature – in fact, the nicer they were, the more Freddie saw it as a challenge to pick a fight.

'It must have been quite an adjustment, going to school on the mainland and living away from home.' Penny followed suit and disposed of her handful of cake debris in the stove.

'For me, I think, more than for Broc.' As Anna said his name, a real smile curved her lips for the first time. 'He's taken it in his stride. I miss him terribly, of course, but he's fine with my sister's family. One of his cousins is in the same class, which helps. It's a home from home for him. And he's got lots of new friends. I think he misses his crows more than he misses us.'

'His *crows*?'

'A pair of hoodies – hooded crows – and their offspring that Broc has managed to semi-tame. The Hoodlums, as he calls them. I'm on feeding duties while he's away, so don't be freaked out if you see a crow pecking at the glass. They really can be little hoodlums.'

Oh, for crying out loud!

Penny hated crows with a passion. She always shuddered

when they flew up from the road and she saw what they'd been feasting on – the fresh corpse of a badger or hedgehog or bird. And they pecked out lambs' eyes while they were still alive, didn't they?

Nasty, evil things.

She stepped through the open doors to the decking. 'Talking of hoodlums ...' There was no sign of the boys. 'Freddie! Alfie!' She turned back into the room. 'You know, I'm beginning to think that packing your kids off Monday to Friday is the way to go.'

The manic smile was back. 'I'll just get a cloth to wipe the furniture.'

Penny walked across the decking and down a couple of steps to the short grass beyond it.

'Freddie!' she shouted again.

'Don't worry.' Anna was suddenly right behind her. 'They can't come to any harm. There's no one else on the island, and if they decide to go for a paddle, the beach is very gently shelving and completely safe. It's good for kids to run around outside.'

'Most kids, maybe, but Freddie ... He has a tendency to just take off. One minute he's right there with you in the supermarket or wherever; the next he's halfway to Leeds. And I mean *literally*. Once he got on a bus and ended up in Devon. We call it *doing a Freddie*.'

'Oh dear.' Anna grimaced sympathetically. 'Quite the adventurer, eh?'

Penny shivered in the breeze coming off the sea. 'That's one way of putting it.'

'There they are, look!' Anna pointed. 'Safe and sound.'

And there, indeed, were the boys, running along the sandy beach.

'Why don't you relax inside in the warm, and I'll bring you some fresh tea and cake?' Anna indicated a grouping of a sofa and two chairs near the glass wall with a view out over the beach.

Penny had just sat down on a very comfortable little tub chair when her phone pinged. No doubt another email from Lisa. What did she expect Penny to do about the unpaid invoices – find a hoard of buried treasure and return triumphantly, showering her with gold doubloons?

She swiped at the screen.

'And put the phone away for five minutes!' Anna touched Penny's arm. 'I know you've got worries – Rod and I do *sometimes* chat online about things other than birds! But this should be a break for *both* of you. Then you can return to the fray refreshed at the end of the week. Don't you think?'

Penny had to read that email. But she nodded. 'You're right – we both need to de-stress. Rod in particular. He's been – well, not himself lately.'

'Which means you've been shouldering most of it?'

To her horror, Penny felt emotions welling up at the unlooked-for kindness. She found that she couldn't speak.

And now, suddenly, Freddie and Alfie were back in the room.

Alfie grabbed at her sleeve. 'Mum, *Freddie hit me!*'

Freddie jumped straight back up onto a sofa.

'Get down, please,' Penny managed, but it was hard to force the words out. Tears prickled at the back of her nose.

She looked up at the high joisted ceiling and swallowed.

She wasn't going to let the boys see her cry.

'Now, Freddie,' said Anna firmly, 'if you don't want to sit on a "wee" chair, I don't imagine you'd be much keener on a "poo" one, hmm? You could have otter or bird droppings on the soles of your shoes.'

Freddie looked down at his trainers as if this were a completely bizarre idea. But he jumped down off the sofa.

'Do you mind if I join you for that tea and cake?' said

Anna brightly. 'It's so nice to have company. It can get a bit lonely when I'm here on my own.'

Freddie had grabbed Alfie and was forcing his face down onto the sofa where he'd just been jumping.

'*Please*, Freddie,' Penny begged. '*Please*, just *stop it*.'

Anna MacLean must really be desperate for company if she was enjoying this.

3

ANNA

'And God knows what we're going to do when the school fees fall due.' Penny set her mug down on the seagrass coaster and pursed her lips in what seemed to be her default sour expression. She hadn't bothered to lower her voice, but Freddie and Alfie seemed engrossed in their game of Buckeroo on the other side of the room, both of them stretched out on their stomachs on the rug in front of the wood-burning stove. They really were very skinny, cartoonishly so, like little stick boys a child might draw.

She couldn't resist asking, 'What's your local state school like?'

Penny's already rather prominent eyes boggled. 'Oh, well ... You know. It's Greater Manchester, not ...' She turned her head slightly to look out at the view. In the foreground was the short, sandy track through the machair, the fresh new grass studded with yellow primroses, always the first flowers to bloom in the spring. But the star of the show was the beach itself – Camas Sgiotaig, the Singing Sands – a long, curved, inviting expanse of pure white sand punctuated by clusters of boulders and lines of rocks stretching into the sea. One of the lines of rocks had a tiny lump of an island at the end of it, like an inverted exclamation mark.

Above the high-tide mark, the dry sand was searingly bright in the sun. Even the wet sand remained almost colourless, but where the shallow sea encroached it turned bright turquoise, like a magician's trick.

To right and left, concealing the coves to either side, were grassy headlands flanked by tumbled masses of black basalt boulders, and below them great slabbed pavements of limestone and sandstone scattered with more rocks. Further out, the sea turned cobalt, and then there was Jura, the paps rising up to close the vista.

Sunlight glanced off the exposed quartzite on the tops of the paps, the limestone pavements, the sand.

It danced on the water.

That same bright light was now falling full on Penny's face. The photographs on her social media accounts must have been cleverly doctored to conceal the dark circles around her eyes and the slack, pasty skin of someone who wasn't getting enough exercise or healthy food or sunlight. And her lips seemed thinner. Maybe the Clarkes were so hard up that she couldn't afford Botox any more. Anna knew she was thirty-five. She looked at least ten years older.

'She's nae bonnie,' as Tam's Auntie Jean would say. The word 'bonnie', in the sense Jean used it, had little to do with conventional beauty, rather conjuring up someone rosy-cheeked and sunny-tempered and blooming with health. The antithesis, in fact, of Penny Clarke. There was even a tangy, bitter-lemon smell coming off her, probably from an expensive hand cream or perfume with 'citrus notes', but it lodged unpleasantly in Anna's nostrils.

Penny lifted her arms above her head in a stretch. She might not be 'bonnie', but there was something fascinating about the woman's body, those long limbs and the grace with which she moved them, the elegance of her posture even when she was just sitting in a chair. Anna could imagine her being the star of her salsa dance group, her fluid movements and sinuous hip action drawing every eye.

A sudden crack made them both jump.

Alfie was sitting back on his heels, holding a piece of S-shaped brown plastic that Anna recognised as the tail of the Buckaroo mule.

'Oops.' Freddie grimaced.

Penny sighed. 'I take it that's not meant to be detachable. For goodness' sake, Alfie. These games belong to Broc. Have some respect for other people's belongings, please. Say sorry to Anna.'

'Sorry, Anna,' parroted the boy.

'If Broc's fourteen,' said Freddie, 'he's a bit old for Buckaroo, isn't he? I'm only playing it because *Alfie* wanted to.'

Anna got up and crossed the room to the boys. 'I doubt whether Broc even knows we've still got Buckaroo. You're right, Freddie – the toys in the cupboard are ones he doesn't play with any more.'

'So the kids that come here can wreck them and he won't mind.'

'Well –' Anna waited for Penny to jump in here, but Penny's sleek blonde head was bent over her phone. 'I'd rather you didn't wreck them, if at all possible.'

When Broc was little, if he broke one of his toys by accident, he'd be so upset that he'd sometimes smash it to pieces in a frenzy of grief and guilt. As Tam had once remarked, 'It's like he's a demented vet putting it out of its misery.'

Anna wanted to stamp on the poor, maimed Buckeroo mule – Bucky, as Broc called him. She wanted to smash every game in the place rather than leave them to the mercy of these brats.

There was no question that the world would be a better place without either Freddie or Alfie in it. She'd surely be performing a service to society if she could prevent one of them growing up to swagger about the bars and clubs of London, treating young women in the same way they treated their mother. Plotting dastardly business deals from their offices in the Shard. Appearing as candidates on *The Apprentice*.

So which should she go for?

Freddie or Alfie?

'We could glue it back on,' Alfie suggested, holding the tail back in place on Bucky's rump.

Freddie brightened. 'Do you have superglue?'

'No!' Penny finally looked up. 'Absolutely not, Frederick.'

Freddie, who seemed unable to sit still, picked up the Buckaroo box lid and balanced it on Alfie's head like a hat. 'So what does Broc do when he's here?' He stared at Anna. 'Hang out at the skateboard park? Oh no, forgot, you don't have one. Play football? Oh no, forgot, there's no football pitch, and even if there was, there's no one to play with. Sell drugs to the holiday kids? He could buy them on the mainland and then –'

'Freddie,' said Penny wearily.

Anna forced a bright smile. 'He's into birds and other wildlife, like your dad. So he's quite happy tramping about the island seeing what he can see.'

'Wow. It's going to be *so* much fun hanging out with Broc.'

Freddie lifted the box lid off Alfie's head and then brought it back down again forcefully. Alfie wailed and grabbed his brother's arm, making the sleeve of Freddie's sweatshirt ride up to reveal a purple bruise above his elbow that suggested this was a frequent occurrence, Freddie bullying the much smaller child and Alfie squeezing his arm in an attempt to fend him off.

Freddie.

It had to be Freddie.

'Stop that!' Penny suddenly yelled. 'Freddie, *leave Alfie be!*'

'How would you like to do some art, boys?' Anna suggested. 'There's paper in the cupboard ... See? All different sizes and colours ... And here's a box of shells and lichens, and dried flowers and seaweed and things, for making collages with. And before you ask, Freddie, no, I'm not going to give you superglue! But you can have ordinary glue as long as you keep it off the furniture and each other!' She grinned at stony-faced Freddie. 'I'll put newspaper down on the coffee table, and you can make some pictures to take home to remind you of Faida.'

'Fantastic,' said Freddie.

But Penny favoured her with a half-hearted smile. 'Thanks, Anna.'

When she'd sorted them out with their 'art' materials, Anna put the empty mugs and plates on the tray and left the room, closing the door between the guests' living area and her own kitchen and clicking down the snib on the Yale lock. As she did so, a yell suddenly rang out.

Freddie's dulcet tones?

She'd give the little bastard something to scream about. If possible, it would be good to do it today. Getting Freddie on his own was hopefully not going to be too difficult.

She crossed the flagstone floor of the farmhouse kitchen and set the tray down on the worktop by the sink. It always felt like stepping back in time, coming into the old house after being in the sleek new extension, which, despite her attempts to soften it with tweeds and rugs and books and pictures, could never be called cosy.

Her uncle Henry had lived in the farmhouse for decades before he'd retired to Glasgow and she and Tam had taken the place over, and they'd made a conscious decision not to mess with the period charm of the old place. They'd retained the original Victorian windows and shutters, and all the fireplaces and old doors, even the warped pantry one that didn't close properly in winter.

At first, they had lived in the house purely as their private home and just let out the cottages and run the shop and café as income streams to supplement Tam's earnings as a fisherman. But Anna had always longed to have a B&B. The sticking point had been that they didn't want to spoil the old house in order to create the high-end accommodation that her research suggested would provide the best return.

So, five years ago, the family trust had funded an extension, built to Anna's own design. She'd had lots of fun with that, spending hours online and flicking through magazines until she knew exactly what she wanted: a fishing lodge feel, lots of wood panelling and bookcases and delicate watercolours, but with a modern twist and quiet, natural colours. A big, sociable open-plan living area with a glass wall to the west for a panoramic view of the sea, but also lots of big windows in the east elevation, overlooking the farmyard, where she'd position the long table for sunny breakfasts. She had imagined the guests cracking open their boiled eggs while watching the free-range hens that had produced them pecking about in the cobbled farmyard.

Upstairs, a sea view for every bedroom. Top-of-the-range en suites.

They'd designed the extension to be pretty much self-contained, with its own hallway and door to the yard, so the guests need never set foot in Anna, Tam and Broc's private space.

'We're going to have to charge an arm and a leg,' Tam had kept saying as the building had taken shape.

And they did. A double room at the Engster Guest House cost over two hundred pounds a night, which was very expensive for the islands. Anna had secretly worried that Tam might be right, and they'd priced themselves out of the market, but they'd had a great write-up in *The Telegraph* just a few weeks after opening, and had been booked pretty solid ever since.

The kitchen was the hub, where Anna prepared all the breakfasts and dinners and, if required, packed lunches. The café was the only other place to eat on the island, and it was only open from ten till five on certain days, which meant that Engster was less a B&B and more a very small, very niche hotel.

After washing up the dishes, she opened the fridge. She had more decisions to make. First, lunch – they could have the vegetable soup she'd prepared yesterday and some home-made bread with cheese and chutney, followed by apple pie and custard. Second, the dastardly deed – where could Freddie most convincingly suffer a tragic accident? There was plenty of scope on a rugged island like Faida for a small boy to come a cropper. She'd gone over the pros and cons of the various options many, many times, but, as with the selection of her victim, she'd considered it sensible to wait until she'd sussed the boys out before deciding on the scene of the accident.

Where would be easiest?

Where would be safest, in terms of no one connecting Anna to what had happened?

Dumping the soup into a pan, she set it to heat on the Aga. Then she climbed the stairs to the landing and opened the door of Broc's bedroom. It wasn't a typical boy's room. He had no posters of Lamborghinis or fighter jets or characters from *Fortnite* or Marvel on the walls. Instead, there were his own drawings of birds and animals and aliens and strange imagined worlds, and the unintentionally comical portraits of friends and family. Tam's dad looked a bit like an angry turtle.

On the end wall was a big satellite image of Faida.

Sitting down on the bed to contemplate it, she found herself picking up Badger, running her fingers the wrong way up the back of his head to make his fur stand on end – 'punking' him, as Broc called it. Badger always went to ground at the bottom of the wardrobe when Broc had his cousins or friends to visit, knowing they'd tease him mercilessly for still having a soft toy.

She set Badger on her lap, and the two of them studied the image.

The basalt cliffs of Sgorr Gobhar, on the eastern shore, were unimpressive from above, reduced to a few meandering dark grey and brown lines, but the shadows they cast were like big black splodges of ink spilt on that part of the photograph – over the sea, the shore, the strip of temperate rainforest crouched under them. Once, most of the Hebrides would have been clothed in temperate rainforest, which thrived in the wet, relatively mild, oceanic conditions of the west coast. But when hunter-gatherers had become farmers, they had begun to clear the land for crops. Now, the ancient woodland clung on mainly in the places humans didn't want. The steep slope under Sgorr Gobhar was of no value for growing crops or even for grazing. At its southern extremity, it ended in another cliff, from which there was a sheer drop to the rocks of the beach fifty feet below.

An unsurvivable drop.

A sudden movement at the window startled her, but it was only Norman Hoodlum, flapping onto the sill. He brought his beak right up close to the glass, black eyes blinking. They were odd-looking birds, hoodies, without quite the gravitas of their cousin, the all-black carrion crow. Hoodies were more jaunty, with their grey tank tops, as Broc called them. The grey areas on their otherwise black bodies really did look as if they were wearing short-sleeved jumpers.

'Well, Norman,' she said, getting up from the bed and crossing to the window, 'are you hungry? Is it lunchtime?'

On the desk under the window was Broc's paint box and the watercolour he had been working on, a silly one of a fat fish dressed in a coat, scarf and boots. She smiled. Anna's mother, a professional painter, delighted in her grandson's talent and was always giving him tips, which he'd pass on to Anna, as if she only needed to know this one thing to make her into an artist too. 'If you look at the shapes of the spaces *between* the things, Mum, rather than the things themselves, that's a good way to get it right, because your brain kids itself that it already knows what shape the actual things are.'

She was trying to work out whether the fish was a real species or out of Broc's head when Norman lost patience and hopped off the sill, swooping down towards the front of the house.

As Anna left the room, she paused for a moment to look at the closed door at the end of the landing. She did this periodically, playing a terrible sort of game with herself.

Today?

Would it be today that she put her hand on the doorknob and turned it? Walked inside?

She turned away and descended the stairs.

Her decisions were made. All she had to do now was get the Clarkes to Sgorr Gobhar. But as she stirred the soup, her gaze kept being drawn back to the framed photo of Broc and his cousins on the wall next to the Aga. The kids were standing knee-deep in the sea, and Broc was staring right at the camera. Right at Anna, or so it seemed.

He was adept at making her feel two inches high. It was as if he looked straight into her soul. What would Broc say if he knew what his mother was about to do?

Even as a small child, this look of reverence would come over his face when he encountered living things in the natural world around him: a butterfly, a tiny beetle, a mushroom, even a daisy. He would solemnly drink it in. Ask questions. Carefully walk away without 'hurting' whatever it was. 'Don't hurt them, Dad!' he had begged Tam when he'd found a wasps' nest, or 'bike', as it was called in Scotland, over the back door of the building at the harbour that housed Faida's tiny shop and café. Much to the amusement of Tam's very unsentimental family – fishers and hunters all – Tam had allowed the bike to remain.

Poor Debbie and Sheena, the women who'd worked with Anna in the café that summer, had refused to use that door, and it had been Anna who'd had to run the gauntlet whenever there was rubbish to be taken out or something to be fetched from the store. After the third sting, she'd dressed head to toe in Tam's oilskins, got a broom and whacked that bike until it crashed to the tarmac below.

Broc had been inconsolable. When she'd pointed out that the wasps would make another, he'd rounded on her. 'It's too late in the year now! And all the wasp grubs inside will *die*, Mum! You've *killed them!*'

Broc was, of course, vegan, and this was one of the few things that he and Tam clashed about. Tam would point out that humans were designed to be omnivores, that it was natural for us to eat meat. He'd ask Broc if he thought the Hoodlums should be vegan.

'Of course not, but that's different!'

'Why is it different?'

'Because they're only doing what they have to do.'

'What's natural for them, you mean. So why should we humans go against *our* nature?'

'Because we've got a choice, Dad! Because it's better for the environment! And anyway, humans eating loads of meat isn't *natural* – and it's caused massive habitat destruction! It takes so much more farmland to produce calories from meat than from plants. If people ate vegan food even just a couple of times a week, it would help the planet a lot.'

Tam would agree that this was a good argument, but was that really why Broc didn't want to eat meat? Wasn't it more about not wanting to eat the poor little animals? That was silly nonsense, he would argue – the whole of nature was based on organisms killing and eating those lower in the food chain.

'But humans are the only species that destroys the habitats of everything else! How can that be right?' Broc, by this time, would be getting red in the face with zeal for his cause. 'We already do too much killing!'

Anna didn't look at the photograph again. She picked up the dish of scraps for the crows and opened the back door.

4

PENNY

Rod appeared wearing his old brown sunhat with the disgusting sweat stains that Penny had tried and failed to scrub out before they came away on holiday. She'd then sneaked the hat into the bin, but he'd spotted it and pulled it out, brushing off the eggshells and onion skins and having a go at her for buying into the 'throw-away culture'. Apparently it was fine to spend twenty thousand pounds on new bus tyres and throw away the perfectly good old ones, but suggest he might want to buy a new hat – and you could get those things for about ten quid – and *you* were the irresponsible one.

He immediately swooped on the kids at the coffee table.

'And what's this, then? Oh, wow, Alfie, that's very cool! Is that lichen?'

He probably wasn't even faking it. The kids taking an interest in nature was a dream come true.

Penny was already sitting at the big table, which Anna had set for lunch with pottery bowls and plates in swirly blues and greys, chunky glasses and a big jug of iced water. There was a plate of stodgy-looking wholemeal bread, but also some oatcakes. Penny broke a little off one to nibble while she waited.

'Okay, looks like we're eating soon,' said Rod. 'Wash hands, boys.'

He took a seat opposite Penny. 'I heard a corncrake! I'm pretty sure I did, anyway – in a clump of irises about a quarter of a mile down the road. We should all go out later and see if we can spot it.'

'And if we can't, at least we get to look at some pretty irises.'

'Exactly!' He beamed at her and grabbed a slice of bread. 'This looks homemade. Is there no end to Anna's talents?'

Penny didn't want to burst his bubble, but when the boys had left the room, she hissed across the table, 'Don't you think Anna's a bit ... odd?'

'No. In what way?'

Where to start? The woman was virtually a hermit on this godforsaken island. She was creepy. She had pet crows.

'She smiles too much,' she settled on.

Rod paused mid-chew. 'She *what*?'

'She goes around with this big smile on her face the whole time? Even you must have noticed.'

'Penny, listen to yourself! What the hell's wrong with *smiling*?'

'It's so fake. She reminds me of Lechy Leo.'

She hadn't thought of Lechy Leo in years, but suddenly she could see him as clearly as if he were standing right in front of them, his nicotine-stained fingers reaching to paw her arm, those gross whiskery ginger sideburns seeming to have a life of their own, to actually move on his face as it contorted in a wide toothy leer.

Rod was staring at her. 'You're surely not suggesting that Anna's some kind of ... *pervert*?'

She sighed. 'No, of course that's not what I'm suggesting. But she's –'

'Shhhh!' Rod hissed as the door from Anna's quarters opened.

He jumped up from the table to take the tray from Anna. Making out like he was the kind of man who didn't expect to be waited on by a woman.

'It's vegetable soup,' said Anna. As if to prove Penny's point, she had the usual simper on her face. 'I hope that's okay?'

'It smells wonderful!' And then, of course, he was giving Anna a blow-by-blow account of the corncrake almost-sighting.

Anna commiserated. Then: 'Broc has some motion-activated cameras set up covering a few clumps of irises – it's been a while since we checked the footage, but there may be something on there. I could take a look.'

'No, no, don't worry,' boomed Rod. 'It's not really the same, is it?'

Penny laughed. 'Apparently it doesn't count, Anna, unless he sees it with his own eyes.'

'According to the latest Birdspotter update,' Rod went on, 'a Richard's pipit has been sighted on South Uist, so there's a chance it might pop up here, yes?'

'A chance, yes,' said Anna. 'But don't get your hopes up too much. We're a pretty small target.'

Rod's face fell. 'How big is the island?'

'Just a couple of miles long and a mile wide. But don't worry – the whole place is a nature reserve, so we do have a good high density of birds!'

Alfie perched on his chair as if on a crazy fairground ride, slipping off to one side and then the other; grabbing the edge of the table and jumping up, feet dangling; throwing himself back down on the chair and making it shudder. He had so much energy, it made Penny tired just to look at him sometimes.

'Have you got ants in your pants, darling?' she asked with a grin.

'No,' said Alfie in his literal way, immediately sitting still.

'Sit nicely, please, Alfie,' said Rod. This was typical – on the rare occasions when Rod decided to exert a bit of discipline, usually when they were in someone else's company, he chipped in just after Penny had already dealt with the problem, but with such split-second timing that it looked as if he'd been the one to sort it.

Penny lifted the jug of water and starting filling the glasses.

'Would anyone like a drink of something other than water?' Anna turned her sickly smile on the boys.

Freddie gave her a long look. Was it possible that Freddie sensed something off about her too? He could be quite sharp about people.

'Coke!' shouted Alfie.

'Whisky!' shouted Freddie.

'Water's fine,' said Penny. 'Thank you.'

'Why do we always have to have *water*?' grumbled Freddie. 'She just offered us another drink, and you're all, *water's fine*, like me and Alfie don't even get a say? We're not even *paying* for this shit!'

'Freddie, don't be so rude and obnoxious!'

'*Don't be so rude and obnoxious!*' Freddie shot back.

Penny looked at Rod, who finally said, 'That's enough, mate.'

'Apologise to Anna,' said Penny, 'for being such a brat.'

Freddie put a sickly smile on his face, as if in imitation of Anna. Perhaps it was. 'I'm *soooo* sorrrry, Anna!'

'Apology accepted,' said Anna mildly.

Freddie was staring at Anna again. Finally, he said, 'You don't have a Scottish accent,' like an accusation.

Anna laughed. 'I do have an accent, but it's not strong.'

Rod had grabbed two more slices of bread and was digging into the butter. 'Generally speaking, Freddie, the higher up the social scale somebody is, the less obvious their accent. Anna's family own this whole island. They're probably aristocrats – eh, Anna?'

'Not at all.' Anna had a hand on the back of one of the empty chairs, settling in for a chat. 'We come from humble enough stock. Back in the 1800s one of my ancestors had a small ship-building operation on the Clyde. By the time my great-grandfather bought Faida – this was in 1905 – the family was quite wealthy, but he had three sons, and everything was split between them. Our branch of the family got Faida.'

'So you own it now?'

'A family trust owns it. I'm just the one who lives here and runs the business.'

Freddie spoke through a mouthful of cheese and bread: 'No one who was *really* rich would want to live *here*.'

'Probably not,' agreed Anna. 'It's not exactly bling, is it?'

'Thank God!' bellowed Rod.

'But the accent thing is a bit of a strange one in the Highlands,' Anna continued.

Penny took a spoonful of soup. It was tasty enough, but the lecture on Scottish history was hardly making for an enjoyable meal.

'My husband Tam would describe himself as solidly working class, but he doesn't have what you'd call a "strong" accent, either, when he's speaking English. Until relatively recently, English was taught as a foreign language up here, which is why the Highland accent is meant to be one of the most easily understood in the UK by people from abroad. There aren't lots of dialect words and differences in pronunciation, like you get in the rest of Scotland. Gaelic, on the other hand … When Tam speaks Gaelic, his fellow native speakers can tell from the words he uses and the way he says them that he comes from Jura.'

'Say something in Gaelic,' Rod encouraged her.

'*Bealach a' choin ghlais.*'

'Aaaah! Such a poetic language! Although now you're going to tell me that means something gross, like …'

'Stinky bum!' shouted Alfie.

'Stinky bum,' agreed Rod solemnly, and Alfie went off into peals of laughter, collapsing on the table next to his bowl.

'It means "the Pass of the Grey Dog".' Anna was grinning at Alfie. 'That's *pass*, Alfie, not *ass*.'

Cue more hysterical laughter. Even Freddie smiled.

'It's the name of the strait between the islands of Lunga and Scarba,' said Anna, 'just to the north of here. Boats often come to grief there because of the strong tidal race – according to Tam's family, who are all fishermen, the seabed is covered in wrecks.'

'Ah, *shipwrecks!*' gurned Rod, closing one eye in his cringy Long John Silver impression, which he'd insisted on doing on the boat over here – in front of the crew, who had pointedly ignored him.

He was so besotted with this bloody place that if Anna had told him the island had been the scene of a full-scale massacre, he'd no doubt have rubbed his hands in glee. Actually, there probably had been massacres. All those hairy-arsed Braveheart Highlanders running about with those big swords she couldn't remember the name of.

'Do you have a map of the island?' asked Rod.

Anna scuttled off happily to fetch one, and while she was gone, Penny hissed at Freddie: 'You were very rude to Anna just now.'

Freddie looked back at her defiantly.

'Anna has very kindly invited us here for a *free holiday*, so I expect you boys to be a bit more appreciative of that and a bit nicer to her. Okay?' She glanced at Rod.

'Mum's right,' he said at last, when he'd finished his huge mouthful.

Penny waited for him to say something more. But no, apparently that was it.

Anna returned with a map, moving the bread and the butter so she could spread it out on the table in front of Rod's place. 'There's only one tarmacked road, which goes inland from the harbour in the north and then returns to the shore here, where we are now, at Engster – which means "farm meadow" in Old Norse. Then there are dirt tracks ... The road is a bit like a spine, and the tracks are like ribs, you see?' She touched the map.

Rod pored over it. 'I was reading on your website about the fossil beds. They're on the north shore, yes? Apparently they've even found dinosaur fossils there. Alfie likes a dinosaur, eh, Alfie?'

'Yeah!' Alfie crowed. 'I'm going to find one! Freddie, I'm going to find a dinosaur!'

'No you're not,' said Freddie.

Anna smiled. 'I'm afraid that *is* very unlikely.'

'And there are Iron Age hill forts, Freddie,' Rod went on, peering over his glasses at the map. 'Dun Morval ... Is that one of them?'

'Yes,' said Anna, 'but there's really not much there to interest the boys. It's basically just heaps of earth.'

'But heaps of earth that ooze history!' Rod was poking at the map. 'And look here – Balnaban. That's the ruined village of blackhouses?'

'Mm. Again, there's really not much to see.' Like the weirdo she so obviously was, Anna seemed determined to talk the island down. 'Just heaps of stones. It's a sad kind of a place – abandoned during the Clearances, apart from one family who were kept on as shepherds for the sheep that replaced the people.'

Rod grimaced. 'That must have been disturbing for the family who were left. Like living in a ghost village.'

Freddie looked up. 'Ghost village! Can we go there, Dad? Can we go there now?'

'We'll do the ghost village tomorrow. This afternoon, Anna, I was wondering if you'd show me your "patch"?'

That sounded vaguely sexual, but for once Anna didn't crack a smile. She was nodding in that earnest birder way Penny knew all too well. 'Of course! The Fairy Forest, as Broc calls it, is probably the best place to start – I think you'd like it, boys. It's a remnant of ancient temperate rainforest over on the east of the island.'

So, basically, a damp wood.

But Rod was practically drooling. 'Fantastic!'

'The biodiversity is amazing,' Anna agreed. 'These forests are really insect-rich, so they're a bit of a magnet for birds. Wood warblers, pied flycatchers, redstarts, even things like hawfinches –'

'Now *there's* a bird!' Rod got out his phone and began googling. 'Look at this guy, Freddie. See the size of that beak! What a bruiser, eh?'

Freddie looked up from his bowl with a sigh. 'Yeah, Dad. Nice.'

'That sounds like a lot of fun,' said Penny brightly. 'But I'm afraid I won't be able to join you – I've a Zoom meeting early tomorrow morning, and I've a mountain of prep to do.' This was true, in a way. She hadn't actually set up the meeting yet, but she needed to get onto Wayne, their operations director, and talk strategy.

Tap tap tap. Tap tap tap.

The noise was coming from the other side of the room. Penny turned to see four grey and black birds – three on the decking and a big bastard perched on the handle of the glass doors. It was staring straight at her.

'Oh my *God*! Are they trying to get *in*?'

'Yeah.' Rod chuckled. 'You've seen the Hitchcock film, Pen? *The Birds*?'

'It's the Hoodlums, Broc's hooded crows. They just want more food.' Anna disappeared back into her own part of the house and came back with a plastic tub. As she approached the doors, the big bird on the handle jumped down casually and strutted across the decking to one of the plantation chairs, which it hopped up on. Anna turned to Rod. 'Norman and Daphne are feeding another brood now, of course, but it looks like Monty and Morag will be staying around as helpers. We don't know their sexes, really, but one's bolder than the other, so they're probably male and female.'

As Anna opened the doors, Rod tiptoed across the room to join her. 'I'll hang back – don't want to spook them. Do you think they recognise people?'

'Definitely.' Anna took a handful of whatever the tub contained and threw it onto the decking.

The big crow jumped down and began frantically pecking up the food. The others lurked at the edges of the decking, watching.

'If we stand back, the others will come for the worms,' said Anna.

'Mealworms?'

'Yep, their favourite. Apart from eggs. They would probably literally kill for an egg.'

'Interesting that Monty and Morag have become helpers.'

'They're learning how to be parents,' said Anna. 'Also, it takes a good long while for them to learn all the various aspects of crow behaviour and culture.'

Culture?

For crying out loud!

Anna was even worse than Rod. They were *birds*! And bloody sinister ones at that. The way it had stared in at Penny ... As if it was sizing her up and wondering if all that lovely flesh was worth the hassle of tackling such a large prey item.

This whole place was giving her the heebie-jeebies.

And maybe the kids were feeling it too. After lunch, Alfie climbed up on one of the sofas, curled up in a ball and closed his eyes, while Freddie sat down at the coffee table and contemplated the collage he was making in untypical silence. His 'artwork' was a mess, consisting of as much stuff as he could randomly cram onto the paper. Sometimes Penny wondered if Freddie could have some sort of syndrome, but always pushed the thought away. He was a handful, yes, but then so were a lot of boys his age.

Up in their bedroom, as Rod hunted through a case for his gilet, he started on about Penny not coming with them. 'We should be making the most of this quality family time together.'

Penny draped one of his shirts onto a hanger and shoved it into the wardrobe. 'I'm usually the one having the *quality time* with the kids, Rod. It'll be an unaccustomed treat for them to have your undivided attention for a few hours rather than being stuck with boring old Mum in their face twenty-four-seven. But don't worry, I'm sure that pattern will reassert itself soon enough.'

For once, *he* could wrangle the kids and see what kind of quality time he managed as they rampaged through the wood, clearing it of any wildlife that was reasonably mobile and had any sort of instinct for self-preservation.

He was looking at her with that weary, you-give-me-such-a-hard-time expression that really pissed her off. But she smiled sweetly. 'I'm sure you'll all have a lovely afternoon with Anna.'

'Actually, I'm sure we will.' He sighed. 'You're not thinking she has designs on my virtue, surely? She's happily married.'

'Oh, get over yourself, Rod!'

'So what exactly is your problem with Anna, other than that she "smiles too much"?'

'She's a bit of a weirdo, you must admit.'

'By which I suppose you mean she isn't obsessed with money and status and her appearance. She spends her time out in nature instead of sweating in a gym. She – shock horror – *reads books* instead of numbing her brain with soaps. Oh yes, Pen, by your standards she really is *a bit of a weirdo.*'

For a long moment, Penny couldn't speak.

And then it was all tsunami-ing out of her: 'If I wasn't "obsessed with money and status", the four of us would be living in the gutter – or at least on a council estate with a pit bull next door and yobs throwing eggs at the windows and pouring lighter fuel through the letterbox.'

Rod, of course, had no idea what it meant to be poor, to have none of the choices, the security that money gave you. She flashed on Dad, standing with his hands on his hips, facing down the group of youths who'd just trashed the flowerbed in the front garden.

'And I wish I had the time to go for a walk or read a book, but by the end of a day spent trying to save our business and stop the kids killing each other, all I have the headspace for is zonking on the sofa with a glass of wine and *Coronation Street* on catch-up. *I'm so sorry* if that makes me boring, Rod!'

'Oh, I'd settle for *boring* any day!' he hissed. '*Boring* is the last word I'd use to describe *you.*'

'And what's that supposed to mean?'

'You think you're saving this family? You think what you're doing is actually helping anyone but yourself? Who cares about the bloody business? Who cares that the kids get to attend some poncy private school? *You* do! Only *you*! You need to take a long hard look in the mirror, Pen.' And with that, he shoved his manky hat on his head and flounced out of the room.

5

ANNA

The quality of light under the trees was strange. At this time of year, when the canopies were fresh and new and just starting to close, the light was dim yet at the same time oddly luminous, the mosses on the forest floor zinging bright green in the gloom. It was almost like being underwater – there was that same feeling of disconnection, of having entered another realm.

The path hugged the contour, a damp, dripping green tunnel through a fairy-tale forest. The native trees – mainly oak, ash, pine, hazel and birch – were stunted by the wind and festooned with lichen. Everywhere were ferns of all shapes and sizes as well as a host of different species of mosses, liverworts and fungi.

'Ah, a little bridge!' exclaimed Rod.

'My grandfather made it, decades ago,' said Anna as the boys pounded across it and ran on ahead along the path where it crossed a sunny glade.

The bridge was made of wood, green and slimy with age, and spanned a peat-darkened stream that tumbled its way down the slope through mossy boulders and contorted tree roots. She paused on it, ostensibly to look down at the water, giving the boys time to move out of sight.

She stopped again in the glade and pointed up at the angle of a branch. 'Hazel gloves fungus.'

Rod went up on tiptoe to examine it. 'How very bizarre!'

'Isn't it! It's supposed to look like fingers in a kid glove, which is more obvious when it's freshly formed in the autumn. These are a bit dried and shrivelled by now.'

Rod poked at the fungus experimentally and smiled round at her. 'Skeleton fingers, Freddie would probably suggest.'

She smiled back.

She could hardly believe that the Clarkes were actually here, that everything was working out just as she'd planned. But it had all been laughably easy – to find Rod on social media, to join the Facebook group for twitchers – birders who were obsessed with sighting as many species as possible – and befriend him, to persuade them to come and stay on an island in the middle of nowhere with a complete stranger.

With their children, for God's sake!

The man had no clue how to look after his own kids. Off they'd gone, running into the forest like Hansel and Gretel – a forest on a *cliff face*, virtually, steeply sloping above and below the path on its wide ledge. What responsible parent would let his kids go off like that unsupervised? Especially when one of them had a history of running off and the other was six years old!

'Is it parasitic on the tree?' asked Rod.

'It *is* parasitic, but on another fungus that also grows on hazel trees – the glue crust fungus. That crusty black stuff underneath the fingers? It feeds on decaying timber and is even more interesting, actually – it sticks broken twigs and branches together and to the living ones, making ladders through the canopy so it can move from tree to tree. See up there, there's a branch that looks like it's floating in the air? It's actually stuck to the twigs of the tree with glue crust.'

'Wow!' Rod took off his glasses, polished them with the cuff of his fleece, and returned them to his nose. 'I can see that this place would be attractive to birds. Have you seen many vagrants here?'

Like most twitchers, Rod was less interested in ecology than in ticking birds off his list, in particular rare 'vagrants' that popped up in random places. Just along the shore, in the direction Freddie and Alfie were heading, was a cliff where seabirds nested, but she doubted he'd be interested in common old kittiwakes or herring gulls.

'Loads,' she lied. 'Last year we had a hermit thrush all the way from America.'

Rod's face took on a dreamy expression. 'A hermit thrush,' he repeated softly.

'Why don't you hunker down here – there's a good view across the glade – and I'll go after the boys?'

He nodded. The fact that the boys were now some distance away, judging by the faintness of the noise they were making, didn't seem to concern him. He didn't know about the abrupt drop in that direction, of course, but he could see the steepness of the slope this whole forest clung to, and how far below the rocky beach was.

'I really do envy you,' he said suddenly. 'I think I would be happy staying here forever. I wish I could just pack it all in and move to an island. Live off the land. Never see another bloody bus for as long as I live.'

Anna made her face sympathetic. 'The business is still in trouble?'

He gave a mirthless laugh. 'The business is going down the tubes – which is probably where it belongs.' He plomped himself down on a fallen tree trunk, long booted legs stuck out in front of him. 'All our problems are of our own making.'

'I'm sure that's not true.' Becoming a shoulder for Rod to cry on was no part of Anna's plan. She turned from him abruptly. 'I'd better make sure the boys are okay. You stay here and see what you can see.' She made her tone bracing and cheery. 'Who knows, another hermit thrush may be along any second!'

Rod smiled weakly. 'Thanks, Anna.'

The path was muddy and mossy and treacherous, even for the good treads of Anna's boots, but if you slipped and fell, you wouldn't tumble off it down the slope. It ran along the back of the ledge of level ground, which was about ten feet wide at this point. Even so, when she came here with Broc, she would always keep hold of his arm despite his moans that 'I'm not five years old, Mum!' He would pretend to make a dash for the slope, and she would snap at him not to mess about. 'This place is *dangerous*, Broc.'

'Yeah, if you're a lemming. Although, in fact ...' And off he would go on a lecture about how it was just a myth that lemmings threw themselves off cliffs.

Now she could see the red checks of a Burberry jacket through the greens and greys of the forest.

She'd have to think of some excuse to get Freddie off the path.

It was just Alfie, though. He had a stick in his hand and was poking it into the ground, flicking up moss. As Anna came along the path, he turned and looked at her. 'Where's Dad?'

'He's back at the clearing, hoping to see birds. Why don't you join him? I think he could do with an eagle-eyed helper. Where's Freddie?'

Alfie pointed up the path with the stick. 'I couldn't keep up.'

Doing a Freddie, no doubt.

Excellent.

'I'll see if I can find him. Off you go, back to your dad.'

She hurried on up the path, which now climbed steeply, the ledge narrowing. Gaps in the canopy gave glimpses of the high basalt cliffs above. At this point, the strip of forest was confined to a steep slope between two verticals: the cliffs above and below, from where the other-worldly calls of the nesting seabirds could be heard. This was where she and Broc always turned back.

But she could see red checks appearing and disappearing through the trees.

Freddie had already left the path.

Moving as silently as she could, Anna did the same, bent almost double to duck under the low branches and twigs of the trees, which were stunted by the wind in this more exposed area. Her feet slipped on the slick, rotten branches that littered the ground, slimy with decay. She found herself sliding and tripping on the rocks and roots concealed under the grass and the moss, all the while unable to stand up properly, obliged to force her way through a narrow space at the height of her midriff, always having to pick up her feet and lower her head. A couple of times she found herself slipping down the slope and having to grab onto a tree and swing herself round, like a bad dancer clinging to her partner.

Once, she lost him and had to throw caution to the wind, hopping and sliding from tussock to rock to treacherous patch of mud. But then there was the jaunty checked jacket, there he was jinking through the trees, hardly slowed at all, it seemed, by the steepness of the slope or the difficulty of negotiating the low branches. He was much smaller than Anna, of course. He probably hardly had to duck at all.

She would have had no chance of catching him if he hadn't suddenly stopped.

He was maybe fifty metres ahead, standing looking down at something. Anna crept forward, trying to keep as many trees as possible between them. Her heart was pumping as, she supposed, adrenaline flooded her system. She had never understood Tam and his family's love of the hunt. Often Tam would go off to spend a whole day on Jura, stalking red deer, and come back with tales of long treks across the moors, of subterfuge and stratagems, of lying in a hilltop hollow for hours waiting for the perfect shot.

'Patience,' he always said. 'More than anything, it's patience makes a good stalker.'

Anna kept low, glad she'd decided to wear her old khaki jacket and charcoal walking trousers. She blended well into the background.

Unlike her quarry.

He suddenly took off, jumping up the slope and darting off round the contour of the hill. Anna hurried after him as best she could, over and under the obstacles the forest seemed determined to put in her way. The ends of branches jabbed at her head, and the palms of her hands stung from the friction of the rough bark she kept having to grab to stay upright as her left foot kept slipping down the slope.

Had he seen her?

If he had, surely he would have no cause for concern? Unless a subconscious sixth sense, a primitive instinct buried in his DNA, had kicked in.

There was the cliff edge, almost under her left foot – just an elder bush and a couple of dwarf hazels between Anna and the sea hissing and foaming against the rocks far below. She gripped the branch above her and carefully, *carefully* climbed upwards until she wasn't quite so perilously close to the drop.

But where was Freddie?

She couldn't see him.

She'd have to abandon the unrealistic hope of ambushing

him. No way could she catch him up. But maybe she didn't
need to.

She inched back down the slope towards the cliff edge
and crouched there.

'Freddie? Freddie? *Help!*'

She went on shouting. Maybe he was out of earshot. Or
maybe he'd heard her but couldn't care less what sort of
trouble she was in. But then his little pale face appeared
amongst the trees, glaring down at her.

'Oh, Freddie, thank goodness! I think I've twisted my
ankle! Can you help me?' She reached out a hand towards
him.

She thought he might refuse, or just disappear again back
into the trees. But, like a wary forest sprite, he edged forward.
And then he was down the slope, and his little white hand
was reaching for hers.

The moment seemed to expand until Anna was conscious
of each separate sound around her: the mournful cry of a
herring gull, the *ow ow ow* of a kittiwake, a wave shushing
against the rocks far below. The wind in the fresh new leaves
of the trees. A chaffinch piping its repetitive call: *eep, eep,
eep, eep*.

Under her knees, she couldn't feel the ground. She
couldn't feel her own legs. And the arm and hand stretched
out in front of her looked like an arm and hand from
someone else's body.

The boy's hand moved towards hers as if through a solid
or a liquid rather than air.

She touched the ends of his fingers.

Soft, smooth skin.

Pink fingernails, so small.

At her back, she could feel the air beneath her, the noth-
ingness of it, and her brain reeled, suddenly, at the thought of
the drop, the one, two, three seconds of free fall in which

you'd have time to think, to know that these were your last few seconds of life.

And then the rocks.

Would you lose consciousness at once?

Or would there be a moment of unimaginable pain?

'Freddie!' boomed Rod's bass voice. 'Freddie?'

Freddie drew back his hand and turned. 'Here, Dad! Anna's hurt her ankle! I'm helping her!'

'Oh, okay, buddy! Good job! Just wait there, and I'll come down. Don't move, either of you. Looks like there's quite a drop over the cliff. No, you stay on the path, Alfie.'

Anna put a smile on her face as Rod appeared behind Freddie, hooked an arm around his chest and swung him up behind a tree. 'Put your arms right round the trunk, Freddie, and don't move.'

'I heard Anna shouting for help.'

'Freddie, mate, *get your arms round the tree*. Good. That's great. Now keep them there.' Rod's attention turned to Anna. 'You're quite near the edge, aren't you? Stay *completely* still. Okay. Now ... take my hand.'

'Actually, I'm fine,' said Anna, crawling away from the edge on her hands and knees and ignoring his hand. 'False alarm – sorry. Just cramp, I think. Thank you, Freddie, for being such a hero and coming to help me.'

Freddie shrugged. 'Women have weak muscles. You can't help it.' And with that, he let go of the tree and was off, scrambling back up the mossy slope towards Alfie's querulous voice, now raised in strident complaint.

6

PENNY

'Would you like a glass of wine?' said Anna. 'Surely it's time for a break from your work?'

Penny felt like falling to her knees in gratitude. 'Please. That would be lovely. I'm not a big whisky drinker.'

Unlike some. Rod was slumped in one of the wing armchairs, nursing a big glass of the stuff from the decanter that sat on the sideboard. They had already fallen into their usual pattern for the evenings once the kids were in bed – Penny sitting with whatever paperwork she was concentrating on that day; Rod devoting equal care and attention to getting pissed.

Anna was over by the glass doors, looking out at the sunset. 'The Hoodlums seem to have gone off to their roost.'

At this, Rod roused himself to grunt, ''Kay.'

Those bloody crows. Normal people had a dog or a cat or a hamster, not three sinister crows that were there every time you wanted to look at the view, usually just standing on the decking staring at you and thinking their evil thoughts behind those beady eyes.

Why would you encourage that?

Before dinner, Anna had brought through what Penny had hoped was a tray of *amuse-bouches*, but which turned out to be Brazil nuts and peanuts and scraps of bread and oatcake for the bloody birds. She opened the doors and scattered the food on the table between two of the plantation chairs, which was probably contravening all kinds of hygiene regulations for guest houses. Then she came back inside and told them to wait.

The big bastard Penny found particularly disturbing soon jumped up on the table and began going at the food, cramming it into his mouth. Then he marched over to the water dish on the side of the decking and dropped everything from his beak into the water, before picking it all back up.

Eeuuw.

'He's dunking it!' shouted Alfie.

'He is!' said Anna. 'That's what they do.'

'What's his name?'

'Norman. He's the biggest bird, the dad crow. Now, he's going to fly off in a minute and take some of that food to the mum, Daphne – she'll be sitting on the nest.'

After Norman had flown off with the damp scraps, the smaller birds approached the table warily, but before they had a chance to get up on it, Norman was back, picking up food from the table and dumping it into the water again, then starting to eat it. You could see his neck expanding as it travelled down his gullet. *Gross.* Then he got a Brazil nut from the table and hopped down to strut across the decking to the mown grass immediately beyond it.

'Now watch,' said Anna.

The boys, unusually, were cooperating, seemingly fascinated, standing side by side looking at the crow. He spat out the nut, strings of saliva joining it to his beak and making Penny feel sick. Then he began pecking at the grass.

'He's eating *dirt*?' said Freddie.

'No.' Anna smiled. 'Keep watching.'

'The little guy's going to steal it off him!' shrieked Alfie, provoking both Rod and Freddie to shush him. Penny smiled and put her hands on Alfie's shoulders. He had an endearing tendency to get completely caught up in any drama happening around him, whether on a screen or in real life.

'Nope,' said Anna.

One of the other crows was standing a few feet away watching the big one, who had picked up the nut and was placing it in the hole he'd made in the earth. Then he started plucking blades of grass and putting them over the hole.

'You see, he's hiding the Brazil nut,' said Anna. 'It's called *caching*. Quite a few species cache food, but crows take it a step further.'

The other crow jumped forward, for all the world like an eager child, and tossed aside the blades of grass so carefully placed by the big bird.

'He *is* stealing it!' Alfie yelled as the smaller bird snaffled the food.

'Shhhhh!' from Freddie.

'No. Norman wants him to have it,' Anna explained. 'It's a lesson, crow style. Norman is teaching his son how to cache food.'

'Cool,' Freddie admitted.

'That's one of the reasons why crow kids stick around with their parents longer than most little birds. There's a lot to learn.'

'Dad, you could take a photo of them and send it to Auntie Ursula,' Freddie had suggested, and Rod had got out his phone and spent the next ten minutes lining up the perfect shot. Ursula, she was sure, was going to be just thrilled.

Now, when Anna brought through two glasses and a

bottle, Penny said, 'Oh, Rod will stick to the whisky,' as if Rod weren't there or couldn't speak for himself – both of which were close to being true at this point.

'I thought I'd join you, if that's okay.' Anna set the two glasses and the bottle down on the coffee table by the windows.

Great.

Surely it wasn't normal for the B&B owner to spend so much time with her guests? Although Penny supposed they weren't normal guests. They weren't paying, for a start. And Anna and Rod were sort of friends, in a nerdy birder way – which didn't bother Penny in the slightest. When she'd told Mum about this trip, Mum had looked at her and said, 'That's a bit odd, isn't it, that she'd offer you a free holiday when she hasn't even met you?' And when Penny had explained about Rod and Anna being in the Facebook birders' group, Mum had pursed her lips.

Maybe Penny *would* have been jealous ten years ago.

Now, she couldn't summon the energy. If Rod wanted to bonk Anna, he could go ahead for all she cared. A snort of laughter escaped as she contemplated her husband, who was now slumped snoring in the chair. It was hard to imagine anyone less capable of carrying on an affair, even with a woman on tap right here in the same house.

'Are you okay?' said Anna quietly.

Penny ran her hands across her face. 'Fine. Just, you know – tired.'

Without asking again if it was acceptable to join her, Anna sat down and poured the wine, a fruity-smelling red.

Yum. Penny chugged down half her glass before coming up for air. 'That hit the spot.'

Anna hadn't even touched her own glass yet – she was too busy smiling at Penny in her creepy, intense way, like she fancied her or something.

Finally, she spoke. 'Doesn't Rod help with the paperwork and so on?'

Penny went for a hollow laugh, which came out as more of a yelp of pain. 'No. Rod's main function in the business seems to be to create chaos out of order. What little order I've managed to achieve lately, that is.'

'Ah.'

'And when he isn't doing that, he's –' She waved a hand at the comatose Rod. His specs had come slightly adrift from one ear, giving him a lopsided look. 'As you see. But, contrary to appearances, that isn't wallowing in self-pity. That, according to his GP, is *depression*. So who am I to complain? I'm not *depressed*, so I just have to get on with it.'

Anna made a face.

Two years, she wanted to yell at the woman. It had been two years since the accident, but it might as well have been yesterday for all the recovery Rod had managed. *Two fucking years* Penny had been living this nightmare, trying to salvage their family and their livelihood while Rod concentrated all his energy on being 'depressed'. And there was no light at the end of the tunnel. More like a gaping black hole.

'And it's affecting Freddie and Alfie too, presumably?'

Was it? Penny hadn't the first clue what was going on in their little heads half the time. 'Oh, probably.' She sighed. 'Freddie's been threatened with expulsion from his school. Once for knocking another boy's tooth out, once for running onto the stage at assembly and squirting the headmistress with a water pistol.'

Anna, for once, was obviously trying *not* to smile.

'Oh yes, Freddie's antics are often very amusing, unless you're his mother.' She took another gulp of wine. 'Sorry.' She set the glass down on the coffee table.

Anna immediately topped it up. 'He's a lovely boy, but I'm sure he can be ... challenging.'

Penny made a face and picked the glass up again. 'I don't suppose Broc has ever given you any sleepless nights. He sounds quite the paragon.' She hadn't meant that to come out so bitter.

'Oh, I wouldn't say that. Sleepless nights aplenty, I can assure you!'

'I'll swap you.'

Anna smiled and leant slightly towards Penny, a strange, almost eager expression on her face. 'I can see you love them to pieces.'

'Somebody has to!' On the pretext of admiring the sunset, Penny turned away from that intense, unsettling gaze.

'Ha!' said Anna. 'You're not fooling anyone, Penny! You must be proud as punch of the two of them, and rightly so.'

Here was where Penny was meant to wax lyrical about her wonderful children. Other people seemed to find it easy to boast about their kids, even if the kids in question were no-hopers and it was obvious to everyone except their parents that they would never be premier league footballers or nuclear physicists or even average-level worthwhile human beings. Penny always found it really hard to think of anything positive to say about Freddie, in particular, other than the worst boast of all.

Which, let's face it, she was going to have to resort to now.

'Freddie does have an extremely high IQ,' she muttered. 'A hundred and fifty-four. They test them at school, so ...'

'Well then, that probably explains the difficult behaviour. Broc's clever enough, but not exceptionally so. Just an ordinary boy, really. But I'm sure Freddie and Alfie will grow up to be pillars of the community.' Anna leant back in her chair. 'You know, our whole conversation has been about your family. What about you? What do you do in your downtime?'

Penny indicated the glass of wine. 'I know, I know. But I'm

not like Rod. I don't have any hobbies or interests. I'm not an *interesting* person, full stop.'

It could – should – have been so different.

This wasn't the life she'd been meant to have.

From the age of five, running with all the other little girls in leotards into that big drafty room in the community hall, Penny had known that she wanted to be a dancer. She'd loved everything about those lessons. The softness of the ballet shoes on her feet, the slipperiness of the pretty ribbons that tied them to her ankles, the neatness of her hair scraped back into a tight bun. The scuffed wooden floor. The tinny notes of the piano that heralded the start of the dance. The rhythm of the music as it claimed her, the feeling in her tummy as she twirled and leapt and reached and strived to maintain her balance. Mrs Ellis shouting instructions. Even the smell of cigarettes off Mrs Ellis's clothes and hair as she bore down on Penny with her stick, tapping at her back or her stomach to correct her posture.

But most of all, knowing *I'm good at this.*

Penny's exceptional ability had become clearer and clearer as they'd got older, and only the more talented girls had persevered with the classes. It had been obvious that Penny was miles better than any of them, better than Sophie Mistry and Rebecca Zhang, two of the girls in Penny's class at school who always excluded her from their games and their playground huddles. She delighted in watching Sophie and Rebecca struggle to *temps levé* or *ballonné* or even to achieve a decent posture in the *plié*, knowing what Mrs Ellis was about to say.

'Watch how Penny does it.'

When she was fourteen and had passed all her Royal Academy of Dance exams with distinctions, Mrs Ellis had spoken to her parents about auditioning for one of the London ballet schools. Penny remembered every detail of the little office at the community hall in which Mrs Ellis had had her 'chat' with Mum and Dad. Mrs Ellis had sat behind the desk, and Mum and Dad in front of it on those metal-framed chairs with green canvas seats and backs, Mum clutching her bag, Dad with arms folded, feet planted far apart, his rather pug-like face set belligerently. Penny had stood, almost forgotten, at the back of the room with her hands flat against the wall behind her.

'Penny was born to dance,' Mrs Ellis had summed up her case.

Dad had snorted. 'It's a nice hobby for a girl, but you're surely not suggesting that *Penny* could actually make a career *ballet dancing*?' He said the words like he might say *turning water into wine.*

And in a heartbeat, her dream had died.

She'd known there would be no further discussion, no debate. She'd known better than to try to persuade Dad to change his mind.

She'd been sleepwalking through her life ever since, she often thought, and would wake up one day to find herself flying across a stage in New York or Moscow or Paris. Perhaps coming to the end of her career now, but plenty of prima ballerinas continued to dance into their late thirties or forties. Margot Fonteyn had still been dancing in her sixties.

'There's really nothing about me worth knowing,' Penny said. 'I do a Pilates class and some salsa dancing.' It was almost worse than no dancing at all, those Tuesday and Thursday evenings in the back room of a pub, strutting her stuff with her dance partner Jim, a gay accountant from Leicester.

Anna smiled her creepy smile. 'It sounds like your whole life revolves around other people, which makes you very much worth knowing, in my book.' She took a very small sip of wine. 'What's your background? Is your business a family one?'

'No.'

Anna kept smiling at her expectantly.

Penny really didn't want to get into this, but she didn't want to alienate Anna with six days of the holiday still to be endured. So she explained, 'I grew up on a council estate in Manchester. My dad drove – still drives – minibuses in the Peak District, ferrying tourists about, and in my holidays from uni I got myself a minibus licence and joined him, driving for the same outfit. Then after uni, the guy who owned the business was retiring, and Rod and I had just got married, and we thought, why not? We bought him out with an inheritance of Rod's and a business loan. Five years ago, we expanded into the intercity arena, and now we're playing with the big boys, so to speak.'

'Your dad must be very proud of your success.'

Penny flashed on Dad's face, beetroot with anger.

'Uh –'

'Although I'm guessing he's of the generation that don't exactly go overboard praising their kids. Heaven forbid that we get big-headed!'

'Dad's certainly old school.' Penny hadn't talked to him now for over a year. 'Good behaviour was always his thing. He didn't mind how badly you did at school, wasn't really interested in grades – his big thing was that you had to behave yourself and not disgrace the family.'

Penny had always been a daddy's girl. She used to love helping him in the garden – weeding had been her speciality. 'Save my old back,' as Dad used to say. And sometimes he'd let her help in the glasshouse, dividing bulbs and dropping seeds into trays and pricking out tiny plants to grow on in pots. Finally, she would help to arrange them in the brightly coloured borders around the lawn: dahlias and begonias and chrysanthemums and fuchsias. If she said 'greenhouse' by mistake, he'd always correct her: it was a 'glasshouse', as if it weren't a five-by-twelve effort from the local DIY warehouse but a grand construction at Kew Gardens – Dad's Mecca, to which he disappeared for day trips about once a month. If Penny had been good, sometimes he would take her with him.

She sighed. 'I sometimes think our generation has the worst of both worlds. We had to toe the line when we were kids, or else. And now we get it in the neck from our own precious little snowflakes.'

'Although that's maybe a problem of our own making ...'

Rod stirred in his sleep and suddenly shouted out: '*No no no!*'

Penny grimaced at Anna and crossed the room to him. Apparently there'd been some sort of drama in the wood when Anna had gone over her ankle close to the cliff edge. To hear Freddie tell the story, he'd been instrumental in rescuing her, although Penny suspected it had been the other way round. Rod had probably lost the kids, and Anna had had to go looking for them and found Freddie messing about in the most dangerous place he could find.

'Come on, Rod, wake up.' And as he finally cracked open an eye: 'You were having a nightmare. What was it – were you spending some more "quality time" with the kids?'

7

ANNA

The air was perfectly still, as if the whole world were holding its breath in wonder at the return of the light. Anna never tired of watching the dawn, of feeling the magic of it, this transition from night to day when slowly, slowly, the landscape around her regained the form it had lost.

She was sitting on one of the plantation chairs, doing nothing, just watching.

And now here was the machair, the pale ends of its grasses appearing first out of the dark, and then its primroses, tiny pinpricks of yellow, the petals of the flowers still furled tightly together. And then at last the sun was up and the land felt its power. At the south end of the Singing Sands, the rocky headland of Creag an Sgoiltein glowed like a beacon, and long boulder-shadows stretched down the beach as if trying to catch the retreating tide.

The perfect white sand was scribbled over with seaweed at the strandline, dulse and carageen and kelp. The usual group of grey seals were hauled out on the rocks to the north, their mottled humps camouflaged amongst the boulders.

Anna felt like she was the only person in the world, as if she'd been transported back centuries, millennia, aeons, back to a time before humans existed. If you ignored the track through the machair, this view was that rare thing in modern Britain: a panorama without any trace of people whatsoever.

Which made any human presence all the more obvious. She'd been standing just about here, almost exactly twenty years ago, when she'd first seen the smoke from Tam's drift-wood fire.

Anna and her sister Fiona had been spending the long summer holiday from university on the farm with Uncle Henry. Faida had always been farmed non-intensively, with a small herd of Highland cattle and some sheep, but the family had decided to go the whole hog and turn the island into a nature reserve: get rid of the sheep, convert the steading by the harbour into a shop and café, run the cottages as holiday lets and concentrate on tourist income. The first step in that plan had been to commission a survey of the island by an ecological consultant, who had hired some locals with knowledge of the native flora and fauna to help out.

One of whom had been Tam.

Anna had walked down the track to the beach and been horrified to find that he was collecting whelks or something from the rocks, dropping them into a carrier bag. And there was an iron pot of water boiling on the fire.

'You're not going to put them into that water?' She'd strode across the sand to him.

He'd straightened, regarding her with a slight, patronising smile. 'Buckies fresh from the sea. Nothing better.'

'But –' She didn't know where to start. 'This is a nature reserve! You can't just come here and – and *eat* the nature!'

He chuckled. 'I really don't think the loss of a handful of buckies is going to disturb the ecological equilibrium of

Faida.' He had the lilting but precise Highland accent that Anna loved.

'Putting them *alive* into *boiling water* is cruel!'

'Ach, it's a quick death for them. What quicker?' He put his head on one side, as if actually expecting her to come up with an alternative way of cooking the native fauna. He had the Viking look of many of the inhabitants of the Hebrides – sharp cheekbones, very pale blue eyes, a shock of blond hair. And a gorgeous, fit, well-muscled body into the bargain.

'Barbaric!' And with that, Anna turned on her heel and marched off.

It was excruciating, having to help with the survey and finding herself side by side with Tam as they set out their quadrat squares in the machair to record the plant species to be found there. She expected him to refer to their previous encounter, but he didn't. He was faultlessly polite. He even came to her rescue when she was peering in despair at a plant book, and told her what each plant was – common name and, to her surprise, Latin one.

'I'm doing ecology at uni,' he murmured as, no doubt, her eyebrows shot up towards her hairline.

At lunchtime, they all sat with their sandwiches in the lee of a rocky outcrop, Tam and the other local lads talking amongst themselves in Gaelic. 'So rude,' Fiona muttered to Anna. The sisters pointedly turned their backs to take in the view.

The lads started to laugh, and Anna was sure they were talking about her and Fiona. No doubt Tam was contributing the story of Anna and the buckies. She was sure of this when, in the way your own name snagged your attention, she heard it: '... *an Anna àlainn*.'

That evening, she'd told Uncle Henry that the local lads had been rudely talking in Gaelic and she'd heard her own name. What did *an Anna àlainn* mean?

Uncle Henry had put down the book he'd been reading and roared with laughter.

'What?' Anna had snapped.

'It means *the lovely Anna*. Looks like you have an admirer.'

And as Fiona had joined in the laughter, Anna had felt herself blushing, but couldn't stop the huge smile that had lifted her mouth. And it had occurred to her, even then, that Tam had probably *meant* her to overhear those words.

She was smiling again now.

It had been a real whirlwind romance. They'd married straight out of uni and taken over the running of Faida from Uncle Henry, who'd been happy enough to settle into retirement in Glasgow near Mum and Dad. It had been a perfect mix for Tam – using his ecology degree on the nature reserve, but at the same time carrying on the fishing tradition that meant so much to him.

The family trawler would take him and his brothers north to the Faroes and the coast of Greenland, to Spitzbergen and Bear Island and the Barents Sea; east down the coast of Norway to the Skagerrak and the Kattegat; south to Great Sole Bank and the Azores; west to Rockall and beyond, away out into the far Atlantic.

When he was away from home, Tam, like most Highlanders, had a tendency to become maudlin, reading long, sad Gaelic poems and repeating English verses by Highland poets to anyone who'd listen. His favourite was the Neil Munro poem 'To Exiles.' From hearing him recite it so often, Anna knew the last two verses by heart:

Let torrents pour then, let the great winds rally,
Snow-silence fall, or lightning blast the pine;
That light of Home shines warmly in the valley,
And, exiled son of Scotland, it is thine.
Far have you wandered over seas of longing,

And now you drowse, and now you well may weep,
When all the recollections come a-thronging
Of this rude country where your fathers sleep.

They sleep, but still the hearth is warmly glowing,
While the wild Winter blusters round their land:
That light of Home, the wind so bitter blowing –
Do they not haunt your dreams on alien strand?
Love, strength, and tempest – oh, come back and share
them!
Here's the old cottage, here the open door;
Fond are our hearts although we do not bare them –
They're yours, and you are ours for ever more.

'Are all Highland poems about loss?' Anna had once asked Tam. 'Lost battles, lost homes, lost loves?'

Tam had smiled. 'Aye, we're a melancholy race. Nothing we enjoy better than a good tragedy.'

She smiled at the memory.

With the sun had come a brisk west wind, on which Norman Hoodlum swooped down. He stood on the short grass in front of the patio, head into the wind. Anna got up and fetched the mealworm box, at which point Norman started cawing, raising and lowering his head, as if to say, *She's here, she's here, come and get it!*

Anna put the box down on the grass.

When she'd home-schooled Broc, they had often had their lessons out here, textbooks spread on the table between their chairs, both of them frequently looking up to watch the seals or the Hoodlums or a pair of cormorants flying low over the water. Often, the pull would be too strong and they'd find themselves walking, down the track to the beach or through the fields or across the machair, all their senses alive to the natural world around them. There would be a frog, perhaps, to watch hop into cover in the grass, or a moss carder bee on a pompom of purple clover, or a lark, climbing almost vertically into the sky above them, its song tumbling down.

One of the Hoodlum offspring was tentatively approaching the box of mealworms when the doors behind Anna crashed open and Alfie exploded onto the decking. '*Hi, Anna!*' he screamed.

The Hoodlums took off, cawing indignantly, and Anna had to stop herself snapping at the child as anger rushed through her. And now here was Freddie, standing with hands on hips, surveying the scene critically.

She made herself smile. 'Good morning, boys. You're up early! Are your mum and dad still asleep?'

But Alfie had already taken off, running awkwardly down the track to the beach, constantly half-tripping, his trainers flapping on his feet.

Freddie nodded and ran after him.

'Try not to disturb the seals,' Anna called.

'Stop,' said Freddie, grabbing Alfie. At first she thought he was taking her request on board and was about to tell Alfie not to spook the seals, but then she saw he was crouching down, tying the smaller boy's laces. And then he was up and running again, jumping onto the line of rocks at the end of which the seals were hauled out. This caused an immediate stampede as the poor animals made frantically for the safety of the sea.

Freddie shouted with glee.

Anna watched the two of them plonk themselves down on the sand and start to rake at it with their hands, mounding it up into a crude sandcastle. But Freddie soon seemed to get bored of this, running along the beach to scramble up the grassy slope towards the headland of Creag an Sgoiltein, which separated the Singing Sands from Traigh Bheag to the south.

Traigh Bheag, meaning 'the small beach', was not visible from here. It was where *Merry Dancer*, their sailing boat, lay at anchor.

This was her chance.

She wrote a hurried note for Rod and Penny, telling them she'd had to go out but to help themselves to food and use the facilities in her kitchen. She added, after a little thought, that the machair at the north end of the island was the most likely stopping-off point for the Richard's pipit, and drew a rough map indicating how to get there from the harbour.

She took *Merry Dancer*'s keys from their hook in the kitchen and slipped them into her pocket. Then she changed into the soft-soled shoes she wore on the boat and flung on a jacket.

There was a warmth, now, in the sun. It promised to be a beautiful day of blue skies and breezes. Perfect for sailing. From the house, she headed south straight across the machair, keeping out of sight of the beach where Alfie was playing. The bulk of the old stone farmhouse was between her and the guest extension, so even if Penny and/or Rod was up and about, they wouldn't see her.

There was a small stand of stunted hazels above Traigh Bheag, which she skirted around before coming down onto the beach. Freddie was standing right at the edge of the water, jumping back whenever a wave inched up the sand. As she watched him, he suddenly turned and ran up past the strandline to the little stone boathouse where they kept the two inflatable tenders.

He opened the door and looked inside.

'Hello, there, Freddie!' Anna called as she jogged along the sand. 'Are you exploring?'

Freddie jumped back from the door, looking at Anna as if expecting a telling-off for *doing a Freddie*. But Anna kept smiling. 'You know the other beach, the one by the house, is called the Singing Sands? Do you know why?'

Freddie shrugged. 'That's stupid. Sand can't *sing*.'

'Oh, but it can, you know! The sand on this beach does it as well. A strong wind makes it sing, but we can do it too. Would you like to try?'

Another shrug. 'Suppose.'

'There aren't many beaches in the UK, or anywhere, in fact, that sing. You need quartz sand with no impurities, no pollution that might cause friction. And the grains have to be very round and the same size, so they all slip over the ones underneath in unison, like a bow on a violin string.'

He was looking at her with more interest now. That hundred-and-fifty-four-IQ brain clicking into gear, no doubt.

She went on, 'We need sand that's dry, but not too dry. This stuff is ideal, above the high tide mark, before the heat of the sun has taken too much of the moisture from it. Now, you have to scuff your feet along. Like this.' Anna demonstrated. 'Hear that?'

'It's just squeaking.'

'Maybe you can do better.'

Freddie scuffed along the sand, skinny little stick legs scissoring like some kind of wading bird, and the sand started to make an almost bird-like sound under his feet, piping and squealing and, yes, almost singing. Freddie looked back at her, his face alight in triumph.

'Oh, very good, Freddie! That's excellent!'

'It *is* singing!' he crowed, scuffing along the beach away from her. 'I'm making it *sing*!'

'You really are!'

Suddenly, he stopped dead, peering ahead to the north. Damn. Was someone coming? Alfie, maybe? But Anna couldn't see anyone appearing over the headland that sheltered the cove.

'Is that Norman Hoodlum?' said Freddie.

'Oh. Yes, I think it is.'

Norman had taken off from a rock with something in his beak and was flying up almost vertically.

'That's a mussel he's got,' said Anna.

Norman let the mussel go and it fell onto the rocks below, ricocheting off a couple of boulders before plopping into a shallow pool. Norman swooped down, retrieved it, and strutted off to a more distant rock, where he held it down with one claw and started pecking.

'It's his way of opening the shells. He drops them onto the rocks. Pretty clever, eh?'

'I suppose. For a crow.'

Eventually, Norman flew away, possibly to feed the soft body of the mussel he'd extracted to Daphne on the nest. And now Freddie was turning, looking along the beach, looking across the machair ... Looking out to sea.

'Whose boat is that?'

Good.

It was so much better if it came from him.

'That's our boat. She's called *Merry Dancer*.'

'Is it a sailing boat?'

'Bit of a waste of a mast if it wasn't.'

Freddie narrowed his eyes at her. 'Do you use those boats to get to it?' He pointed at the boathouse.

'That's right. We row out in an inflatable tender and then either tow it behind us or leave it moored to the buoy for when we get back from a sail.'

'Can you take *me* for a sail?'

'Oh. Well. You mean right now?'

He nodded earnestly. 'Just a *liiiiittle* sail? *Pleeeease?*'

'Hmm. I don't know. I have to make breakfast soon.'

'Just a *tiny, tiny liiiittle one*?'

Anna smiled. 'Okay, just a *little* one, Freddie.'

'Yesss!' Freddie contorted his body in a sort of victory seizure, punching the air and then running with arms stretched out, down to the sea and back again, as if the joy was too much for one small body to contain and required a physical release.

Anna used the pump to top up the air in the red tender, which was newer than the blue one and had an outboard motor – not that she'd be using the motor to get to *Merry Dancer* now. That would risk attracting the attention of the other Clarkes.

When she'd finished with the pump, she started to pull the tender down the sand to the water, asking Freddie to carry the oars, which he did with a swagger. When the tender was afloat, Freddie stepped in, giggling as it moved under him, and Anna pushed off and jumped aboard.

'Can I row?'

'Maybe on the way back.'

Freddie trailed his hands in the water and then crawled from one side of the tender to the other 'looking for fish'.

'Can we fish from the sailing boat?'

'We'll see.'

Anna, her back to the sea, was scanning the shore, checking that Alfie hadn't decided to follow his brother, and that Penny or Rod hadn't come in search of the boys. But all was still. It wasn't even six o'clock yet. Penny and Rod were probably still asleep.

'Here we are, then,' said Anna as the tender bumped against *Merry Dancer*'s stern. She shipped the oars and threaded a painter through the tender's D-rings. Freddie had grabbed the little ladder, eager to get aboard.

'Okay, up you pop and into the cockpit – that's the bit of the deck that's sunk down, with the benches all round it.' *Merry Dancer* was a fifty-foot boat with a larger than usual cockpit. 'Take a seat on one of the benches while I tie up the tender.'

Anna took the keys from her pocket and unlocked the lazarette hatch aft of the cockpit. Here, in the cargo hold, was where they stowed all the gear – lines, sails, blocks and tools. First, she retrieved the oars from the tender, dismantled them and shoved the four sections into the hold. Then she got out the tow rope, which was kept on hooks just inside the hatch for ease of access, along with the extra line she needed to make a bridle.

As she tied one end of the tow line to the central stern cleat, she was conscious of Freddie watching intently. She found the other end of the line and held it up.

'This knot is called a bowline.' She tied it slowly. 'Now, to make what we call a bridle for the tender, I use this other line.'

'A bridle, like on a horse?'

'A bit like on a horse. See, I thread the bridle rope through the loop in the bowline.' She showed him how she tied the bridle ends to the port and starboard bow D-rings of the tender, and another section of line to its central bow D-ring. 'And now we're ready to let the tender go.'

She released it, and Freddie chuckled as it bobbed away to the end of the tow rope. 'It's like it's trying to escape!'

It was always a challenge sailing single-handed, especially when getting underway. Usually, Anna would use the engine before switching to sail power, but it was important to slip away noiselessly.

'I want to go inside!' yelled Freddie.

This was a great idea.

Anna unlocked the hatch at the front of the cockpit, and Freddie scrambled down the steep steps into the cabin, which consisted of a compact galley just in front of the steps, a seating area with benches that converted into berths and, beyond that, a shower room with a toilet and the berths proper.

Kids always loved the miniature accommodation, and Freddie was no exception, opening cupboards and doors and disappearing forward to the V-berth. While he was occupied below, Anna prepared to sail off anchor. First she raised the mainsail, then the jib. She chose her tack, beating as close to the wind as possible. As *Merry Dancer* sailed away from the chain, the tension slowly pulled her round into the wind, and Anna tacked, then scrambled into the bows to pull in some chain. After repeating this manoeuvre a few times, she was able to break out the anchor and hoist the remaining chain.

There wasn't a whole lot of sea room now to starboard, and she didn't wait too long before turning the wheel hard alee. *Merry Dancer* answered the helm, coming slowly around onto the other tack, and then they were safely away to the south.

8

PENNY

Penny was cosy and comfy and didn't want to wake up. But someone was shaking her shoulder.

'Wha' ...?'

'I'm off out,' said Rod's voice.

Penny cracked open her eyes. The room was too bright. 'Wha' time's it?'

'Almost seven.' He sounded far too cheery. 'Anna's not around, so you'll have to make the boys' breakfasts. I'm going to have a butcher's up at the north end of the island – apparently that's where the Richard's pipit is most likely to make landfall.'

And to that, Penny could think of not a single thing to say.

She showered and dressed in the so-attractive walking trousers and a white fleece and descended the stairs to the big living area. Sure enough, there was a note from Anna on the table saying they should help themselves to breakfast.

Okay, so they weren't paying for this holiday, but it was a bit much to expect Penny to poke around Anna's kitchen in search of the cornflakes. Actually, though, until the boys were up, this meant that Penny would have the place to herself.

She could make herself a cup of tea and have half an hour of blessed peace. As she was boiling the kettle, she noticed a loaf of the homemade bread on the worktop. She would have a slice of toast too. With lots of butter.

Tea made and bread toasted, she took her simple breakfast to what had become *her* tub chair by the window. The house was very quiet. The boys must still be asleep.

Being here, away from the office and the daily grind, was giving not just Rod but Penny a chance to gain some perspective, to take a long hard look at her life.

And she didn't like what she saw.

She took out her phone, intending to check her emails, but instead found herself clicking on YouTube and bringing up a video of Margot Fonteyn and Rudolf Nureyev in *Swan Lake*. It was hard to believe that Margot Fonteyn had been forty-eight at the time.

When Penny watched a ballet, sometimes she played a game in which she pretended she was that ballerina: her body that not of a wine-chugging mum with a sedentary job and no time for proper exercise, but of a ruthlessly trained and focused dancer who could hold an audience in the palm of one graceful hand.

It wasn't fair, she knew, to blame Dad entirely for the way her life had veered off course. His idea that Penny could never make it as a professional dancer had partly been formed by Penny herself. Whenever he was in the audience at a performance, she found her feet wouldn't obey her and her mind went blank. On one terrible occasion, when she'd been dancing a solo from *Giselle* for the finale of the little show Mrs Ellis's ballet school staged each year at Christmas, she suddenly couldn't think of the next step, and the music had raced on without her. No matter how hard she danced, she couldn't catch up. She would remember a sequence, but by the time her feet were performing it, the music had already moved on, and she was left stumbling and floundering in its wake, arms flapping ridiculously.

People had started to snigger.

It had been the most humiliating experience of her life.

Of course Dad had thought she didn't have what it took.

She turned off the video and sat with her tea, looking out at but not really seeing the view.

Until there was movement.

Alfie, running up the track from the beach.

What the hell? The kids were already up and about?

Oh no.

But surely there was limited scope for mischief out there on a virtually uninhabited island? And it wasn't as if Freddie could get on a bus to Devon.

Alfie charged in through the open doors.

'*Hi, Mum!*'

He was filthy. There was wet sand on his sweatshirt and all down his trousers.

'Hello, darling! What on earth have you been doing? Where's Freddie?'

'We've been making a sandcastle!'

It could, she supposed, have been worse. 'I bet that was a lot of fun! Now, go back outside and take off those dirty clothes. Then you can come upstairs and have a shower and put on clean things, and have some breakfast. Are you hungry?'

By the time Alfie was cleaned up and sitting at the table eating cornflakes, Freddie still hadn't put in an appearance. Penny went to the door and shouted in the direction of the beach: 'Freddie! Come and get your breakfast!'

Nothing.

She walked down the track to the beach.

The 'sandcastle' was just a lumpy mess with some shells

and pebbles pressed into it. No doubt it had been the scene of a battle or two.

'Freddie!'

She squinted against the sun. He could be anywhere. Hiding, probably, behind a rock.

'Get out here now, Freddie, or there'll be trouble.'

Nothing but the cries of what she presumed were seabirds – long, sad, wailing cries that gave her the shivers. She returned to the guest house, where Alfie was scraping his bowl.

'Can I go back out to play?'

'No, you certainly cannot! Having one of you go AWOL is bad enough. Brush your teeth and then you can play a game. Where was Freddie the last time you saw him?'

A shrug. 'We were making a sandcastle.'

Give her strength! 'Yes, I know. But when you came back to the house, where did Freddie go? Did he stay making the sandcastle?'

'No. He went off while I was still making it.'

'Off where?'

A shrug. 'He ran off down the beach.'

'Right, Alfie. Teeth, and then you can play on the iPad for half an hour – no more – while I try to find that brother of yours.'

She had the Zoom call with Wayne in half an hour. Trust Freddie to pull one of his disappearing acts at the most inconvenient time possible. She put on her new walking boots, which were already giving her a blister, and tramped off to the beach, cursing Rod.

Freddie took after Rod in so many ways. If she was being honest, she could see nothing of herself in him – apart, perhaps, from his intelligence and a certain amount of stoicism. But he was completely selfish, acting without a thought for anyone else.

'Freddieee!'

She followed a sandy path through the rocks and over a dune onto a grassy knoll, then down the other side to another beach, this one more rocky. There was a little stone shed on a flat area at the top of the sandy part. She trudged towards it, her feet sinking into the fine sand annoyingly with every step, irritating the blister.

'Freddie! If you're in there, get out here *now*!'

She reached the shed and pushed open the door. It had a dank earth floor and contained nothing but a blue inflatable boat and some oars. Thank goodness Freddie hadn't come in here and decided to take the boat onto the water. Maybe he'd tried, but his scrawny ten-year-old muscles hadn't been equal to shifting it.

Could he have headed inland? There was another path of sorts through the grass, possibly made by the herd of alarming shaggy cattle with the big horns. Penny didn't fancy meeting those. She hoped Freddie hadn't managed to do so, and got himself either trampled or impaled. What on earth would happen, away out here, in a medical emergency?

She stopped, hands on hips, and surveyed the land around her: the hummocky grass, a clump of trees, some rocky hillocks in the distance.

He could be bloody anywhere.

But on the walk back to the guest house, it was Rod who dominated her thoughts rather than Freddie. This place was so not suitable for a child like their elder son – a whole, virtually uninhabited island to hide on – and Rod should have known that. She should have checked it out herself, of course. It was her own fault, really, for leaving Rod to arrange it. She should know by now that he couldn't be trusted to buy a pint of milk without cocking it up.

These days, whenever he was out of the office for any

length of time, she got the same uneasy feeling as she had now about Freddie.

Where is he and what the hell is he doing?

Back at the guest house, she sent Alfie up to the boys' room with the iPad and told him to be quiet.

'I've got an important Zoom meeting, and I can't be interrupting it to come and sort you out, okay?'

She set up her laptop with a neutral backdrop of a wall – Wayne was easily distracted – and switched it on.

Freddie would turn up when he was hungry. Probably at lunchtime. She supposed she'd need to punish him somehow for this very bad behaviour, but the prospect of that made her feel bone-tired.

Coffee.

She needed a coffee before she got into the spreadsheets and forecasts and gloom and doom with Wayne. At least Anna had a proper coffee machine.

9

ANNA

Out here in the Sound, the wind was fresher, whistling through the rigging. Freddie scurried over the roof of the cabin to the foredeck, where he clutched the rails to lean over and watch *Merry Dancer*'s bows cleave the water. He hadn't even asked about a life jacket, so Anna hadn't had to trot out the lie that there were none on board and he would just have to be careful.

The water was probably no more than eight degrees. If an adult went into it, they'd be lucky to survive an hour, and a child would die much more quickly. Freddie was so thin that he must have no natural insulation at all.

You'd probably be talking minutes, if not seconds.

Anna knew from extensive googling that sudden immersion in a body of water such as the Atlantic triggered something called the cold shock response. First, the receptors in the skin would go haywire, telling the blood vessels to narrow to prevent inundation of the brain with cold blood. A knock-on effect was that less blood flowed to the lungs to pick up oxygen, so the body compensated by taking huge gulps of air.

With children, in particular, the danger was that they'd

inhale the ocean. If that happened, the child's lungs would fill with water, and he would sink and drown instantly.

But if he survived those first few involuntary gasps, the continued hyperventilating would compromise his ability to swim and cause a reduction in the concentration of carbon dioxide in the blood. This would lead to cramping, disorientation, dizziness, possibly loss of consciousness ... Warmth would leach from his little limbs and torso, and he'd become hypothermic. He would shiver more and more violently as his body desperately attempted to generate heat but his temperature continued to drop.

And then the shivering would stop.

And he would be dead.

'Where the *hell* are those *bloody* dolphins?' Freddie shouted as he jumped back into the cockpit. This was a theme he'd been harping on for the last ten minutes.

'They've probably heard you cursing and decided to make themselves scarce.'

Freddie grabbed the guard rail wire and shouted over the side: 'Sorry, dolphins! Lovely *dollllphiiiins*! Where *arrrre youuuu*?' He turned back to Anna. 'If they come, can I swim with them? I'm a really good swimmer! I'm the best in the school. When we swam against this team from another school who have boys who are, like, twelve or thirteen or something, I came second in the breaststroke and first in the backstroke!'

Damn.

She would have to make sure they were far enough out that there was absolutely no possibility of his making it to shore. He was unlikely to be able to keep swimming for more than a couple of minutes before the cold got to him, but you did hear about miraculous feats of endurance. And perhaps the Clarkes were in the habit of 'wild swimming'.

She adjusted the mainsail as the wind shifted a couple of degrees. 'Have you swum much in the sea?'

'Yeah, loads!'

Damn.

They were now running wing and wing before the wind, with the mainsail on one side and the jib on the other, and the tide in the Sound was with them. Anna always used to find it exhilarating to race along like this, with the wind full astern and the mainsail let right out to give *Merry Dancer* her head. The boat moved with the sea, rocked by it, almost a part of it. They had passed Gigha to port and were now running down the Sound of Jura, equidistant between the Kintyre Peninsula and Islay.

They had sailed in the opposite direction on their honeymoon, she and Tam. They'd made a holiday of fetching *Merry Dancer*, her parents' very generous wedding present, from the marina on the Clyde where she'd been berthed, sailing down the coast of Scotland into the Solway and then across the Irish Sea to the Isle of Man, before heading back north round the Mull of Kintyre and into the Sound of Jura.

Here, Tam had produced a tattered old book of Gaelic poetry and recited to her 'A Song to His Wife, Newly Wedded' by Duncan Ban MacIntyre, Duncan of the Songs, in its English translation. She remembered the lovely first lines:

Mairi Ban Og, thou girl ever thought of,
Still where I am may thou be ...

And the savage last verse, in which the poet listed all the things he'd do for her:

I'd kill for thee swans, seals, and wild geese,
And birds on the bough that rest,
Nor e'er shalt thou want while a forest

Lies near with one antler'd crest.

But she wasn't going to think about Tam now.

She glanced off to port and then starboard. Ten miles, roughly, to either landfall. Surely that was far enough out, even for the most proficient ten-year-old swimmer?

Afterwards, she would return to Bàgh an Ear, the bay on the east of Faida where they moored *Merry Dancer* if westerly gales were forecast. She would make out that the boat had been there all along, that she'd walked across the island and gone off for a sail from there – well away from where Freddie went missing – and then returned to the same mooring.

She fixed the steering brake in place on the wheel, her fingers fumbling with it. Like before on the cliff, she had a weird numb sensation in her limbs, the feeling that her own hands didn't belong to her, that she was watching someone else's body, over which she had little control.

Freddie was heading forward to the steps down to the cabin. As he crossed the cockpit in front of her, she left the wheel and reached out those disembodied hands to grab him from behind.

His upper arms were so skinny that her fingers closed right the way round them. With part of her brain she noted this, although the part that picked up sensation from her fingers still seemed not to be working. But she managed to haul him across the cockpit and lift him bodily over the bench, his trainers scrabbling for a purchase that she wasn't going to let him get as he squirmed, as he cried out, as he shouted something, as he twisted to look at her but she wasn't going to look at him, not at his face.

She pulled him to the guard rail and hoisted him up and over.

He was clinging to her arms.

To the sleeves of her jacket.

Little fingers, clamping on.

But he wasn't fighting her, or begging her not to do it.

And now she found herself looking straight into his eyes. They were very blue. Very wide. There was fear in them, and shock, but no outrage, no blame, no *Why?*

Fear. Shock.

Resignation?

She yanked him back and flung him from her, down into the cockpit, and he scrambled into the corner and pressed himself into it, his back turned to her, his limbs folded into the foetal position, knees to his chest, hands to his face as he started to whimper.

10

PENNY

Where the hell was Freddie?

Six hours, now, he'd been missing. Penny really could do without this. The Zoom session had not gone well – Wayne's ideas for boosting the bottom line by increasing ticket sales all seemed to revolve around discounted fares, which would be sending out completely the wrong message – *Peaks Transit, we're crap, but look, we're soooo cheap!* – and would be a disaster long term, creating an expectation of perma-low fares and leaving them with hardly any profit margin at all, if not running at a loss on most routes.

And no matter how many times Penny had reiterated why this strategy was a non-starter, Wayne had kept coming back to it. She was beginning to think it was maybe time for more redundancies, starting with Wayne himself.

She was sitting at the big table, crunching numbers, while Anna set the places around her and plonked a big plate of sandwiches in the centre of the table.

'Tomato soup, sandwiches and sausage rolls.' Anna looked slightly frazzled, her hair up in a messy bun.

Penny smiled perfunctorily.

Alfie, who had been sitting playing with a wooden puzzle, suddenly leapt up from the sofa and ran out of the open doors, shouting: 'It's tomato soup!' One of the boys' favourites.

So Freddie was back.

This really would require a proper punishment.

But when Alfie ran back into the room, it was Rod who followed him. 'Tomato soup, eh? Smells delicious, I must say! So what have you lot been up to, then?'

'Freddie's done a Freddie,' snapped Penny.

Rod grimaced. 'What happened?'

'I've no idea! He was already gone when I got up. He was probably gone when *you* got up, but you wouldn't have noticed, would you? Not with a Richard's pipit to be ticked off the list.'

'You mean he's been gone since early this morning?'

'Apparently so. He and Alfie were making a sandcastle on the beach, and then Freddie took off.'

'But my God, Penny! Anything could have happened! And you're sitting in here on your arse?'

She sighed. 'I've looked for him, I've shouted myself hoarse, but it seems he's not ready to be found. You know what he's like.'

'But he could have had an accident! He could have got into difficulties in the sea –'

'He didn't take his swimming costume. And in any case, he's a strong swimmer. There's no need to panic, Rod.'

Twice in the last year, Freddie had disappeared overnight, necessitating the police being called and full-scale searches launched. Once he had turned up in Devon at Ursula and Will's house. On the other occasion, he was gone two whole days and was only located after being caught shoplifting a loaf of bread, a pack of cheese and a two-litre bottle of Fanta from the Tesco superstore in Glossop, a good twelve miles away from where they lived in Didsbury. He'd been sleeping, apparently, in someone's summerhouse.

'I'm going out to look for him,' announced Rod.

'You're just reinforcing the bad behaviour if you play his games.'

'And what if he's lying hurt somewhere?'

Rod wasn't so desperate to get out there searching, though, that he didn't have time to grab an egg mayonnaise sandwich and a sausage roll.

As PENNY and Alfie were finishing their lunch, Rod reappeared, breathless, stomping in without removing his boots and demanding to know, 'Is he back?'

Penny shook her head.

'We all need to get out there looking for him *now*. And if we don't find him in the next hour or so, I'm calling the police and reporting him missing. I'm wondering if he might have gone to the abandoned village. The ghost village, as he called it.' He crossed the room to rap on the door through to Anna's accommodation. 'Anna! *Anna!*'

The door came open, and Anna stood there blinking at him, for once without the Cheshire Cat smile.

'We need your help finding Freddie,' Rod said briskly. 'We could cover more ground in one of your vehicles. We need to check out the abandoned village and the hill forts, maybe the harbour, and if he's not there, we're going to have to call the police.'

Penny sighed. 'He's probably holed up in one of the holiday cottages, watching TV and stuffing his face with any food he can find.'

'We could check the cottages first,' Anna suggested.

'Good idea,' said Rod. 'Come on, Penny. We all need to get out there. Alfie, you'll have to come too.'

'Is Freddie going to be in trouble?' asked Alfie.

'Oh yes,' said Penny grimly.

The track to the first holiday cottage was bumpy and potholed, making for a very uncomfortable ride in the old Land Rover. Alfie was loving it, of course, whooping and giggling whenever he bounced up from his seat. If Freddie had been with them, he'd no doubt have spoilt this simple pleasure for Alfie somehow, telling him he sounded retarded or jumping on top of him.

'Here we are,' said Anna unnecessarily as she stopped on a patch of dirty gravel in front of a long, low stone cottage.

The cottage was cold and smelt of damp, but it was as neat as a pin – proof in itself that Freddie had not been here. Penny stood in the little kitchen with its ancient units and red Formica-topped table as Rod went round opening cupboards, as if Freddie could be crammed into one of them.

'He's not here, Rod.'

'No, well, let's have a look at the abandoned village. It's just up the track a bit, Anna said.'

The so-called 'abandoned village' turned out to be just a random collection of tumble-down walls poking out of the bracken, some of them in a rough rectangle with a doorway. Freddie would soon have got fed up here.

'We should try the other cottages,' she said after five minutes of stumbling about trying not to twist her ankle on all the bits of stone hidden in the long grass under their feet.

'And if he's not there, I'm calling the police,' said Rod.

The search of the other two cottages, both situated near the harbour, was just as fruitless. They were also very neat and tidy.

'I thought you said the cottages were being refurbished?' she said as Anna locked the door of the last one, called, very originally, Harbour Cottage.

Anna stared at her for a moment. 'The tradesmen are

starting at the end of the week, or so they say. You know what they're like – all promises.'

Rod took out his phone.

'You won't get mobile reception,' said Anna. 'We'll have to go back to the house.'

'Where can he be? It's –' Rod looked at his watch. 'Nearly four o'clock! I'll never forgive myself if something's happened to him!'

Penny kept a lid on her temper with an effort. 'Nothing will have happened to him. It's just Freddie being Freddie. He'll probably be back at the house waiting for us and complaining that he's starving.'

She fumed silently all the way back to the guest house. Freddie's pattern was to do a runner when Penny was particularly stressed with the business and not, she supposed, paying him enough attention. And no doubt he wasn't happy about Rod spending all his time chasing after wildlife rather than fussing round the boys.

'Freddie!' Rod called as soon as Anna had the back door open. 'Freddie?'

He ran upstairs but was soon back in the big room. 'He's not here!' His lips trembled. 'Anna, we need to call the police! There aren't many hours of daylight left, are there? I know it stays light for longer up here, but ... And the coastguard! Should we get them involved? And are there locals who might help us search?'

Penny bit her tongue. This was a huge overreaction, but she knew better than to try to talk Rod down. That would only send him over the edge, make him turn on her, accuse her of 'not caring'. When he was like this, you just had to go with the flow and hope he saw sense before the situation escalated too badly.

At least they were hundreds of miles from anyone they knew.

Felicity Phillips, who lived next door to the Clarkes in Didsbury, would hopefully never get to hear of it unless Rod or one of the boys let something slip. Felicity was one of those people who lapped up other people's troubles. After the accident, she'd always been 'popping over' to 'offer support' and see how Penny was 'coping'. Wanting to know all the gory details, more like, clever little eyes darting around the lounge as if there might be photographs of the crash scene left lying out on the coffee table. Penny had taken great delight in pretending to be too traumatised to talk about it.

Whenever Freddie did a runner, Felicity seemed to know it, using some sixth sense, and would be straight round to wallow in the crisis. Penny always played a game with herself – how long would it be before the words 'Baggely Heath' left Felicity's lips? Baggely Heath was a private residential school for children with emotional and behavioural difficulties, and Felicity had once even gone so far as to bring Penny the prospectus.

Felicity, of course, hated the boys with a passion because they were always climbing the wall into her garden and causing havoc. On one all-too-memorable occasion, Freddie had somehow managed to collect about thirty gnomes from goodness knew where – there weren't many gnomes to the square mile in the leafy streets of Didsbury – and arrange them, under cover of darkness, in a semicircle facing Felicity's patio doors.

Now Rod was staring at her. 'You're not even slightly concerned, are you?'

She made her voice calm. 'I am concerned. But we've been here before, haven't we? He always turns up safe and sound.'

'Freddie's not used to this terrain! This is *wilderness* we're talking about! Cliffs, bogs ...'

Well you made us come here! she wanted to yell.

She put her hand on his arm. 'Freddie's a tough cookie. And nothing if not resourceful. All right, let's report him missing, but let's not get ourselves worked up into a lather. That's not going to help Freddie, is it?'

Rod didn't reply. He was like a child in a huff, glaring at her as if this was somehow all Penny's fault.

As per usual.

11

ANNA

The guest living room seemed to be full of people in hi-vis jackets. The local grapevine had been busy, and there were about twenty volunteer searchers from the neighbouring islands and the mainland to help cover the ground. Anna knew most of them. Some were Tam's relatives.

John Stewart, the police sergeant coordinating the search, had two maps of Faida open on the table and was assigning search areas to the 'foot soldiers' as he called them. He was small and dark-haired and quick in his movements. She had the impression of a quick mind to match, which hopefully wasn't going to be a problem.

Penny and Rod were sitting in the midst of this on one of the sofas. Alfie had been packed off upstairs to bed, much to his dismay. He seemed to be enjoying the whole drama. Penny looked very tired but was contained, controlled. Rod, in stark contrast, was a mess. His hair was on end, his expression wild, and he was sitting right on the edge of his seat. He seemed to be ranting at Penny, although he wasn't looking at her – he was staring off through the wall of glass.

Anna drank it all in, every expression, every grimace of distress, every agitated gesture as she thought of the images that, despite themselves, would be flashing across their minds.

Freddie lying at the foot of a cliff, in terrible pain, his little stick limbs bent at impossible angles. Freddie up to his neck in a bog, trying desperately to keep his nose above the mud. Freddie in the sea, his foot stuck in a crevice in the rocks as the sea rose up his chest, up his neck, into his mouth ... Or perhaps simply their dead child, drifting out into the Sound.

Although it would be daylight for hours yet, it had clouded over a little, giving Anna an excuse to switch on all the lights in the room, sending a subliminal message that night was on its way.

Sergeant Stewart's radio kept crackling, and he kept breaking off what he was saying to speak into it. She overheard the words 'ebb tide', so guessed it was the coastguard or one of the fishermen who were helping with the search.

Anna moved to his side and raised her voice so it would carry to Rod and Penny. 'My worry is that Freddie might have come to grief somewhere on the shore. It's very rocky and treacherous.'

Come to grief. She was quite pleased with that turn of phrase.

Out of the corner of her eye, she saw Rod flinch.

But the policeman's neutral expression didn't change.

'I probably know the waters around the island better than anyone,' Anna went on. 'I was thinking that, while there's still some light left, I could take my boat out to search the shore from the water. I know Davie McDonald and Neil Nicholson are doing that on their boats too, but I can get in closer – I know the currents and the reefs, where it's possible to get right up to the shore ...' She raised her voice again slightly to say, 'I suppose the RNLI lifeboat is searching further out, where the ebb tide's running, in case he's in the water?'

The policeman nodded and continued to look at her, giving nothing away. Was she sending out some sort of signal; was she talking too quickly or too eagerly or –

'Yes,' he said at last. 'That sounds like a plan. Can I ask you to liaise with the fisher boys and the coastguard?'

Anna nodded.

'Presumably you have a VHF radio on your boat?'

She nodded again. 'I'll get going, then, and –'

Rod was suddenly at her side. 'You think he could have fallen into the sea? Or gone in swimming and –'

'No no.' She made her tone overly reassuring, as if she were trying not to upset him with what she really thought. 'But we have to cover every possibility, no matter how remote.'

'We're wasting time,' Rod rapped out. 'We need to get out there.' He frowned at the map. 'Where do you want me? I guess Penny will have to stay here with Alfie.'

'Well, as you're unfamiliar with the island, Mr Clarke, I thought you could take the area around here, the stores and the outbuildings and the wood behind them, in case he's hidden himself away near at hand. Anna can give you the keys to the other buildings.'

'Good. Right. Yes.' He turned to Anna impatiently. 'And I guess you can take the people who'll be covering the north end of the island in one of the Land Rovers? Your boat's at the harbour?'

'No, I'm moored at Bàgh an Ear, over on the east. I'll take one of the Land Rovers and drop off the searchers who are doing the south-east area. And maybe you, Sergeant Stewart, or whoever's coordinating the search to the north, could take the other vehicle to the harbour.'

She and Penny had each driven one of the Land Rovers to

collect police and locals from the harbour and bring them to the house.

The policeman was folding up one of the maps. 'Right, let's get to it, then.'

Anna raised her voice. 'Everyone, please feel free to use the kitchen to make hot drinks and snacks. I'd like to leave in, say, ten minutes, if the group covering the south-east of the island could be ready by then?'

Rod watched with evident relief as people started to organise themselves into two groups. *Finally*, he would be thinking, *something's happening.* He sort of slumped as some of the tension left his body. His muscles, she knew, would be aching in a few hours with the constant flood of adrenaline telling them to prepare for battle.

But he would never get to fight that battle, other than in his own shattered mind.

'We'll find him,' she said, patting his arm, and watched a tentative smile play about his lips. Time to fan that cruel little flame of false hope. 'Try not to worry too much. I'm sure Penny's right, and he's hiding out somewhere laughing at us all.'

'Thanks, Anna. Thanks so much for all you're doing.'

As SHE DROVE the Land Rover full of searchers up the track that traversed the island, Anna joined in the speculation as to where a small boy might have got to in such a place of tussocky bogs and moorland, woods and rocky outcrops. 'He'll have hunkered down somewhere sheltered, I hope.'

'The woods would be my bet,' came Mhairi Morison's sharp voice from the back. Anna had known Mhairi all her life – they were of an age, and her dad, who farmed on the mainland, was an old crony of Uncle Henry's. Mhairi had one of those piping farmer's daughter's voices, pitched to carry above the sound of the wind.

'Here might be a good place to start,' suggested Anna as they came to the edge of Plantation Wood.

She pulled up, and they all piled out, Mhairi with a big rucksack over her shoulder containing thermoses and sandwiches, which she dumped on a tree stump.

'We should stay in sight or sound of at least one other person while we're searching,' she called out. Staying within earshot of Mhairi wasn't going to be a problem for any of them.

She leant into the driver's window as Anna wound it down. 'You take care of yourself, Anna. Don't try any mad manoeuvres to get too close in.' She frowned. 'Do you want someone to crew for you? You could have Ross. He's a sailor –'

'No, no, I'll be fine, thanks. I'm just going to use the motor. And I'm used to being single-handed. The more feet on the ground, the better.'

She carried on down the track, which wound its way downhill round the edge of the wood. The wind had got up a little, and the swooping branches of the spruce trees swayed above the Land Rover. This wood had been planted about sixty years ago, before ecology had been invented, as Tam joked. They had thinned it rather than clear-felling, as the trees at least provided cover for wildlife, and were using it as a shelter belt for the newly planted native species to the south – oak, Scots pine, birch, ash and hazel. All the species that should be here.

When Broc was little, he used to beg for Tam's scary bedtime story about the dreaded introduced species Sitka spruce – or 'Sssssitka ssssssrpuce!' as Tam used to say, making Broc wriggle in delighted horror. What was it about the human brain that made it want to be scared by stories?

This one was about a small boy left all on his own in a big house at night.

'Then there came a knock on the door. But it wasn't really a *knock* Jimmy heard, it was more of a *jjjzzzhhhhhh ... jjjzzzhhhhhh ... jjjzzzhhhhhh ...!* And somehow Jimmy knew it wasn't their neighbour Mrs Muggins or his Uncle John. It wasn't ...'

'Anything human at all!' Broc would shudder.

'Jimmy wondered: *Should I open the door?*'

'*Nooo!!*'

'No. He decided not to. He made sure it was locked and bolted and drew the curtains closed in the sitting room. He switched on the TV and tried not to think about ... *whatever* was out there. But then –'

Broc would be screwing his eyes almost closed by this point, as if he could hardly bear to imagine it.

'*Jjjzzzhhhhhh ... jjjzzzhhhhhh ... jjjzzzhhhhhh!* At the window! And now there was a new noise. *Eeek, eeek, eeek!* on the glass, like a skeleton's fingernail scraping down it. A fingernail ...'

'Or a twig!' Broc would groan.

The Sitka spruce never did get inside, was never even seen by Jimmy, but somehow the not knowing made it even worse. Would it come back tomorrow night? It was Tam's stories Broc would always request, but Anna he'd want at the end of them for a reassuring 'Mummy hug'.

Whenever they walked on this track, Broc would make the sign of the cross with his fingers and brandish it at the Sitkas, only half-joking as he looked up at the branches moving and creaking above him.

'Sitkas aren't really evil,' Anna would say. 'They can't help that they've been planted in the wrong place.'

And now the track was heading down to the small gravelled parking area behind the rocky shore at Bàgh an Ear. The beach was pebbly, with just a tiny area of sand in the centre. *Merry Dancer* rode at anchor at the sheltered south end of the bay, and she did really seem to dance as the wind whipped at the water under her.

Anna had left the tender pulled high up on the pebbles, with a couple of big rounded stones inside to weigh it down. These she lifted out before hauling the boat down to the sand and into the water.

There was no need, this time, for subterfuge, as everyone knew she was taking *Merry Dancer* out to help with the search, so she used the tender's outboard motor. After she'd tied it to *Merry Dancer*'s stern, she unlocked the cabin hatch and switched on the radio to initiate a voice call on the channel the coastguard had selected for the search.

She depressed the button on the push-to-talk mike. '*Ocean Rose, Ocean Rose, Ocean Rose, Osprey, Osprey, Osprey,* this is *Merry Dancer, Merry Dancer, Merry Dancer.* Over.' She stared stupidly at the mike, the repeated boat names going round and round in her head like a chant.

After a bit of crackling, a disembodied voice said, '*Merry Dancer,* this is *Osprey.* We're just off Mullach Head proceeding north-north-west. No sign as yet. What's your location? Over.' She knew that was Davie MacDonald, but somehow he didn't sound like himself.

Now she had to respond, but her brain was sluggish, and she couldn't think.

Then: 'Bàgh an Ear,' was coming out of her mouth, her lips and tongue struggling with the Gaelic words. 'I'm going to … I'll head out. I mean, I'll head north. Over.'

'*Merry Dancer,*' came a deeper voice a few seconds later. 'This is *Ocean Rose, Ocean Rose.* We're over on the west, heading south off Dubh Sgeir. Likewise no sign. We're thinking we'll keep going until the light fails – how about we rendezvous at the harbour at 22:30 hours? Over.'

For a long moment, radio silence filled the cabin, and

then she found fluency from somewhere and was speaking quite normally again. 'Let's do that. Thanks, Neil. Keep in contact on this channel, but for now – out.'

'Right, Anna. Out.'

'Good luck to you both,' said Davie. 'Out.'

She climbed back up the cabin steps. *Ocean Rose* and *Osprey* were on the other side of the island and would be proceeding very slowly indeed as the experienced fishermen combed the coastline, scanning the shore with binoculars. So she had time to motor far enough out from the shore to do what she had to do. She hauled in the anchor and started *Merry Dancer*'s engine. As they headed out of the bay, the full force of the wind hit them, whining in the rigging and sending spray over the bows. Anna shivered, wishing she'd put on an extra sweater.

When they were, she judged, far enough out from the shore, she cut the engine and turned to unlock the lazarette behind her. She pulled open the hatch and looked down into the depths of the hold.

From the dark, two wide blue eyes looked back up at her.

Penny folded Alfie's little grey fleece and put it into a drawer of the dresser in the boys' room. The house was quiet now. All the searchers had left quarter of an hour ago, with sympathetic smiles and reassurances that 'We'll find him, Penny, don't you worry.'

She hadn't known what to say in response to that. *I'm not worried, I'm hopping mad*? Fortunately, they hadn't seemed to expect her to say anything.

Alfie was lying in bed kicking up at the duvet.

'Where do *you* think Freddie is, Mum?'

'I've no idea.'

'I bet he's found a tunnel that leads to a castle. With big turrets and a moat and a drawbridge. And those toilets where you sit inside the wall of the castle with your bum hanging over a hole and the poo just goes *pllloopppp* down onto the ground!'

Penny shoved socks and pants into the laundry bag at the bottom of the wardrobe. 'There's no castle on this island.'

'It might be a tunnel that leads under the sea to a castle on *another* island!'

She closed the wardrobe door and crossed the landing to her and Rod's room. Rod, of course, had left all his clothes lying on the bed when he was rummaging through his case for his warmer jacket. It wouldn't have occurred to him to put them back in the case, let alone fold them and arrange them properly in the drawers and wardrobe provided.

Rod proudly told all their female friends that he was a feminist, as if saying it made it true. It never ceased to amaze Penny how he could delude himself that he respected women, when he expected his wife to do the housework, the cooking, the laundry and the child care as well as shouldering most of the burden of the business.

The only time Rod did anything remotely domestic was when they had people round for dinner, when he'd spend all morning trawling round delis for expensive ingredients and all afternoon frowning at recipes on his iPad. He'd present the results triumphantly, to admiring exclamations, and Penny was always torn. On the one hand, there was a certain amount of basking in reflected glory. On the other, she would have to fix a smile to her face when their friends made envious comments along the lines of 'I wish Jack could cook like this!' She always wanted to scream: *He only cooks to show off at bloody dinner parties! At least Jack cooks his own breakfast, at least Jack takes the kids to football, at least Jack knows how to turn on the bloody washing machine!*

Rod did literally nothing.

And so, because everything was Penny's responsibility, anything that went wrong was her fault. As Rod had been leaving with the searchers, he'd hissed at her: 'This is down to you!' Penny, apparently, was wholly responsible for Freddie's absence. While Rod was out enjoying himself staring at birds, presumably the little woman should have tethered herself to the kids so this kind of thing couldn't happen.

Of course, most of the women she knew had similar

issues with their male partners not pulling their weight, but at least most of those men were very driven and ultra-successful. Jack Evans had a property portfolio that brought in an annual net profit in excess of a million pounds. The Evans had an *au pair* and holidayed in Meribel and the fucking Seychelles.

And Jack made his own breakfast.

She swept the clothes off the bed and onto the floor.

'Oops!' said Alfie behind her.

'What are you doing up?'

'I want a drink of water.'

'You've got a glass on the bedside table.'

'It's got fluff in it. Mum, where has Freddie *really* gone?' Alfie pushed out his lower lip.

'Don't do that with your mouth. It makes you look like a guppy.'

Alfie sucked the lip back in. 'But Mum, where *is* Freddie?'

'I've no idea.' Penny marched back into the boys' room, snatched up the glass, and emptied the contents into the sink in the en suite.

As she turned on the tap to refill it, Alfie whined from the doorway, 'I want *kitchen* water. Toilet water is *eewww*.'

'The water from this tap comes from the mains, just like the water from the kitchen tap.' Although there wouldn't be mains water here, actually. It probably came from a grotty well.

She handed the glass to Alfie, who held it as if she'd just handed him an actual turd.

'Drink the bloody water, Alfie! I've *had* it with you boys today, I really have!'

Alfie sulkily put the glass to his lips and drank.

'Right. Now put the glass on your bedside table and get to bed.'

Alfie trotted back into the bedroom, holding the glass,

which he set down on the coaster on the bedside table with a jolt that made the water slop over the sides onto the wood.

'Alfie!'

'Sorry, Mum.' Alfie started to use his sleeve to slowly, slowly mop at the water, pushing it around in swirly patterns on the top of the cabinet. This, of course, was a delaying tactic to put off the moment of getting into bed.

'For God's sake! Now you've got a wet sleeve! Well, you'll just have to *have* a wet sleeve. You've only got one other set of pyjamas with you, and I'm not going to spend all week bent double over laundry! Let *me* do it.'

Penny pushed him away from the cabinet and mopped up the water with a tissue. When she turned round, Alfie was standing, hands on hips, staring at her.

'It's not fair that Freddie's still outside and I have to go to bed.'

Oh, for crying out loud!

She made her voice level. 'Freddie's going to be in big, *big* trouble when he gets back, don't you worry. Do you want to get in trouble too?'

Alfie mutely shook his head.

'Then *get to bed*! And I don't want to hear another *peep* out of you, Alfie. *Do I make myself clear?*'

Alfie nodded and dived under the covers, pulling the duvet up over his head so he was completely concealed by it.

Penny sighed and touched the mound of duvet. 'I'm sorry Mummy shouted, darling. Don't I get my goodnight kiss?'

Alfie's tousled head appeared, but he didn't move towards her or even raise his face to be kissed. As with everything else in this bloody family, it was left to Penny to do the necessary, to lean over and plant a kiss on his guppy mouth.

'Goodnight, Alfie.'

But he was already back under the duvet.

13

ANNA

For a long moment, Anna stared into those unblinking blue eyes. The sea slapped against *Merry Dancer*'s hull and the wind tugged at her hair, as if the elements themselves were telling her to hurry up, get a move on, get the little bastard out of there and *just do it.*

She had no other option. She'd come too far to turn back now. All her planning, her meticulous planning, had been leading to this moment. She'd chickened out once, but she couldn't do so again.

Freddie Clarke was a nasty little brat, and the world would be a better place without him in it. Just a quick *heave-ho* over the side and it would be goodbye Freddie.

She thought of Penny and Rod, weeping over his sea-raddled body. Or maybe the body would never be found, and they'd never know for certain what had happened. That might be better.

Just do it.

Freddie stared up at her. Just his face and hands were visible poking out of the sleeping bag he was wrapped in, very pale in the gloom. His hands were gripping the dark blue material as if ready to pull it up over his head.

She'd always known that this would be the most difficult part. But she'd made her decision, and the longer she delayed, the harder it was going to be.

'I had to wee,' he said. 'I'm sorry. I did it on the rope.' One small hand detached itself from the sleeping bag to point into the shadows of the hold.

He spoke quietly, but it was as if he had screamed at her, his words drumming on her ears, battering their way into her brain. She stared down at him. He had some pale freckles across his nose and a tiny white scar on the round part of his chin. He had an IQ of one hundred and fifty-four, but, like most boys, he seemed to place more importance on physical prowess than academic achievement. She remembered his artless boasting about his success in the swimming competition, and how pleased he'd been when he'd made the Singing Sands sing so much better than Anna had. She remembered his small smile as he'd watched Norman Hoodlum drop the mussel onto the rocks.

His name was Freddie Clarke and he was ten years old.

This wasn't some little monster from a cautionary tale, this wasn't some caricature of a revolting little boy who perfectly suited her purpose, this was *a real, actual child*.

'Okay,' she got out. 'Okay. That's okay.'

Her hands were shaking as she reached into the lazarette and took hold of the sleeping bag. 'It's okay. It's okay,' she repeated, over and over. 'I'm sorry. I'm so sorry. It's all right, I'm not going to hurt you. Out you come. You must be so cold. Out you come, Freddie, and let's get you warmed up in the cabin.'

Slowly, the boy sat up, his head poking out through the hatch opening. He eased himself out of the sleeping bag, out of the lazarette, like a creature emerging from a chrysalis.

And then he was crawling over the bench and crouching in the cockpit, looking at her with the intense focus of a cornered animal.

'I'm so sorry I did that to you,' was all she could think to say. 'I'm not going to hurt you. Are you all right?'

His eyes were huge, his lips slightly parted as if there was something he wanted to say. She waited, but still he was silent.

'Come down into the cabin and I'll get the heater on, and the stove, and we'll have some soup. How about that?'

After a long moment, he nodded.

Why wasn't he crying and screaming?

He must be in shock. He climbed down the steps into the cabin and stood passively as she wrapped a red woolly blanket around him. As she pressed the softness of it to his shoulders, she could feel how thin he was, how fragile a little human being ... The blanket was very soft, like thistledown under her fingers. She pulled it over his chest, but he stepped back.

She turned away to switch on the heater.

'There's a hot air vent on the wall there. If you sit at the table, you'll get nice and warm.'

'I don't want soup,' he said as he shuffled along the bench seat away from her.

She opened a can of tomato soup anyway and put it on to heat. It seemed to be a particularly strong-smelling soup, very tomatoey, savoury but sweet. Maybe when he smelt it, he'd change his mind. He was sitting staring at the surface of the table, hugging the blanket around himself. As if feeling her gaze on him, he looked up. She had expected the blank face of shock, but his expression was sharp, watchful.

'I said,' he enunciated slowly, as if to an idiot, 'I don't – want – soup.'

How could he be so composed, after what he'd just been through?

What Anna had put him through?

An innocent child.

She had tried to kill an innocent child.

Only she hadn't. She had never really been going to kill him.

Had she?

And suddenly it was Anna who was shaking and crying, staggering back to sit on the steps, sobs heaving up from deep in her chest. 'Freddie, I'm sorry,' she got out. 'I don't know what I was thinking.'

The boy just stared at her.

She took a long breath. 'I had this crazy idea ... I think I have been a bit crazy, lately. It was nothing – nothing personal, nothing to do with you ...' She was babbling. How could trying to push someone overboard and then locking them in the lazarette all afternoon not be *personal*? 'I'm so sorry. I'm really not going to hurt you or do anything to you.'

His only reaction to that was to raise his eyebrows slightly.

'It must have been horrible, locked in the hold.'

He shrugged. 'It wasn't too bad. Stank a bit of fish and oil and stuff, but the sleeping bag was warm.' Another shrug. 'I was okay.'

The soup in the pan was bubbling.

If he could hold it together, surely so could she?

She wiped at her face with a tissue and gave the soup a stir. 'If you're worried I might have put something dodgy in it, I'll have some myself. And you can watch what I'm doing. You can choose which mug we each have.'

Warily: 'Okay.'

Freddie got up from the table and inched towards the stove, where Anna was stirring the soup. 'Is there any bread?'

'No, but I think there are savoury biscuits and peanut butter in that cupboard. And I'm going to heat some water to fill you a hot water bottle.'

Five minutes later, she and Freddie were sitting opposite each other at the veneer table, drinking hot soup and eating crackers and peanut butter. At least, Freddie was eating, a hot water bottle tucked against his side, although he'd let the blanket fall from his shoulders. Anna had to resist the urge to reach across and pull it back up around him. She didn't want to freak him out by touching him again.

She could hardly swallow even the soup – it tasted too strong, like tomato puree – but forced some into her stomach to demonstrate to Freddie that it wasn't doctored in any way.

'Do I have to go back in there?' Freddie said at last, glancing up briefly from his plate of biscuits.

'No! No, of course not.'

'What's going to happen now?'

What indeed.

She should take him back to Engster and, she supposed, tell Sergeant Stewart what she'd done. Tell Penny and Rod Clarke. Confess to attempted murder, although it hadn't really been that, had it? Or was she kidding herself? Was there an offence of I-thought-I-could-kill-him-but-I-couldn't?

A hysterical bubble of laughter became trapped in her throat, and she coughed to disguise it. His abductor cackling maniacally was hardly going to set Freddie's mind at rest.

She held his wide blue gaze.

'Nothing bad,' she said at last.

Not for Freddie, anyway. Maybe she couldn't kill him, but she could still get something from this situation.

'I'm going up on deck for a bit. I'm going to lock you in here, but don't worry. You're quite safe.'

Anna locked the cabin hatch and started the engine to get *Merry Dancer* underway. She opened the throttle wide, and the boat started to pitch against the ebb tide. The wind had veered a few points to the north. She swayed with the movement of the boat, conscious of the shifting of her centre of gravity as she never normally was.

She needed to get back closer inshore if she was to keep up the pretence of assisting in the search for Freddie. *Osprey* and *Ocean Rose* should be rounding Sgeir Fhada and off the Singing Sands, respectively, if she was right about their speed of travel. If she anchored at the north end of the island, that would give her long enough to settle Freddie before returning to Bàgh an Ear – having, like the other two boats, apparently circumnavigated Faida.

She'd never had a plan B, but that didn't mean she couldn't formulate one now. She might not be able to kill Freddie, but she could keep him on the boat for a couple of days at least. Let Penny and Rod think he was dead. Make them suffer a little longer.

When *Merry Dancer* was riding at anchor off the north shore of the island, she returned to the cabin to find Freddie eating more crackers and peanut butter at the table.

'I'm not going to put you back in the hold, but I need you to stay on the boat for a short while. I'm sorry.'

'Why?'

What could she say?

'I'll explain later. For now, I'll bring you more food, and I'll show you how to turn the heater off and on. There are games and jigsaws stored under the bench you're sitting on, and some of Broc's books.'

'Is there an Xbox?'

'No.'

'Or a TV?'

Really? His only concern was a lack of entertainment?

'No, sorry, Freddie. No TV.'

Anna rummaged in the food cupboards and came up

with some chocolate and cereal bars, which Freddie ripped open and started to devour.

Freddie Clarke was a very intelligent boy. Presumably he realised that Anna's horror, her shock at what she had almost done was genuine. But did that explain why he was so strangely relaxed around her? Surely he should be more on his guard? How could he know that she wouldn't flip back to psycho mode at any moment?

'I'm going to lock you in here.' And she'd have to disable the radio. 'I'll make up one of the beds. You'll be perfectly cosy. And you'll soon be back with your mum and dad.'

Freddie crumpled the wrapper of the cereal bar he'd just demolished and ripped open another. 'Is Mum pissed off that I've gone AWOL?'

'No, of course not! She's very worried, yes, but I'll explain to your parents what happened. They won't blame *you*.'

Through a mouthful of cereal, he said, 'They call it doing a Freddie.'

'What?'

'Running away. I do it all the time.'

'Oh. Well. This time, you're not going to be blamed.'

He grimaced. 'I went off and left Alfie on the beach. I'll be blamed for *that*. And for going off with you on your boat.'

'I'm the adult here, Freddie. I'm the one who'll get the blame, and rightly so.'

For a little while, there was no conversation. Anna forced a mouthful of cracker and peanut butter down into her stomach.

'Would you like something to drink?' she asked him. 'We have cans of Coke or lemonade, or maybe you'd prefer water?'

He scowled. 'Not *water*. I want Coke.'

She fetched two cans from the cupboard. 'They won't be

very cold, but I don't want to turn on the fridge. The heater's already draining the battery.'

'We could put seawater in a bucket and put the cans in that.'

Was this a ruse? When she made for the steps, was he intending to pounce, hit her over the head with something? Make a bid for freedom? Surely he wouldn't attempt to swim for shore in the gathering dusk, in a choppy sea? But she wasn't taking any chances.

'I'll fill a bowl with cold water from the tap,' she said. 'You can put the cans in that.'

'Okay.'

While the cans cooled in the bowl, Freddie looked around him. 'Is the boat called *Merry Dancer* because it kind of dances on the waves?'

Now he wanted to talk about the boat? Anna was beginning to think Freddie wasn't normal. He didn't seem to have the usual range of emotions of a ten-year-old boy. Surely any normal boy would be too terrified, too traumatised to even begin to wonder about the name of the boat he'd almost been shoved off? Broc, she knew, would have been hysterical if some madwoman had just done to him what Anna had done to Freddie.

He was looking at her, now, with an expression of polite interest.

Was he trying to lull her into a false sense of security before jumping her?

She got up from the table and backed to the steps. But she made herself smile at him. 'The Merry Dancers is the name we give the Northern Lights, the *aurora borealis*. Do you know what they are?'

He shook his head.

'There's a sort of a wind that comes from the Sun – a stream of charged particles. It's called the solar wind. These particles slam into the Earth's atmosphere at millions of miles an hour, bombarding us with energy that could be deadly if it reached us on the surface. But the magnetic field that goes right round the Earth protects us by deflecting the particles, which stream towards the North and South Poles and become light: all different colours, red and green and yellow and orange and pink, rippling across the sky, almost as if they're dancing. So up here, that's what they're called: the Merry Dancers.'

'But really it's a fight? A fight between the Sun's wind and the Earth's magnetic field?'

'I suppose it is.'

'Might I see the Merry Dancers? When it's dark?'

'No. It's the wrong time of year, I'm afraid.'

This was only partly true. The winter months were best for the Northern Lights because the skies were dark, but it was possible to see them at any time of year. Somehow, though, she didn't want to think of Freddie, all alone under a wide night sky swept by that awe-inspiring display of violent colour.

'I'm going to take us back round the island,' she said. 'And then I'll leave you here in the cabin while I get some more food.'

She ascended the steps to the cockpit backwards, watching him the whole time, but he seemed less interested in jumping her than in the cans of Coke, lifting one out to test its coolness.

She locked the hatch on him and started the procedure of weighing anchor.

When she used the engine to move the boat forward, the vibrations from the motor seemed to thrum through her, firing the nerves all up her body and jangling in her head, ricocheting inside her skull. And the soles of her trainers, as she edged up the side-deck to the bows, seemed thinner than usual, so she felt every lump and bump.

Her body felt strange.

She stopped, and breathed in the cool air of dusk, but the air itself seemed to rip into her, to burn her lungs, making her cough and gag and fall to her knees in the bows. It was as if all her senses, all her nerve endings had been stripped down, left exposed and raw.

As she unwound the line that took the strain from the anchor to a cleat, she found herself staring at the rope, at the way the fibres were twisted, as if she'd never seen it before. And the feel of the windlass in her hand – it seemed to dig in, to bruise her, her skin and flesh to offer no resistance.

But she managed to weigh the anchor, and to motor slowly up the west coast of the island, past Engster, where figures could be seen moving about in the dusk. The heightening of her senses brought them close, as if she could have reached out and touched them.

She anchored once more at Bàgh an Ear and, without returning to the cabin and Freddie – she was sure he would rather she left him alone – she untied the inflatable tender and used the outboard motor to get to shore. She wouldn't have been confident about rowing it. But when the bows of the tender bumped onto the sand, and she jumped out to pull it up onto the pebbly part of the beach, she found it was easy. The muscles in her legs and arms and back felt strong, eager to respond to what she was asking of them.

You needed to take care when walking on a beach like this, with all the layers of rounded stones moving under your feet, making you lurch and slip about – but she almost relished the feeling of instability, the challenge as the surface under her constantly threatened to tip her over. Sometimes one of her feet would become submerged in the stones and flick one out to skitter over the others with a hollow clonking sound.

She stopped and looked back at the sea.

In the low light, the froth of white where the waves broke on the dark, outermost rocks contrasted with the glassy calm of the pools they sheltered. She took a deep breath of the fresh, salty sharpness underlain with a whiff of decay, of slimy seaweed and algae and a thousand dead creatures stranded by the tide.

The way the sea was constantly moving almost made it seem alive, a malevolent thing forever prowling round the land, waiting for its chance to get you. She looked out at *Merry Dancer* riding at anchor, and thought of Freddie, locked in the cabin, and what would have happened to him if she had pushed him into the sea. He would have struggled against it, but very soon the sea would have flooded into his nose and mouth, into his heaving lungs –

Her hands, her legs began to tremble again, their newfound strength leaching away.

What must be going through his little head?

And it occurred to her, for the first time, that he hadn't even asked her *why*.

He hadn't asked her *why* she had done this to him.

Not once.

14

PENNY

Just as Penny was lifting the wine glass to her lips, the back door opened, and she heard boots clomping in the hall. She set the glass back down on the coffee table with a sigh and stood as two policemen in bulky uniforms and yellow fluorescent jackets strode into the room.

'Have you found him?' she rapped out.

The men both grimaced, and the taller of the two, a big-boned sandy-haired man, said, 'I'm sorry, Mrs Clarke, but we have not. There has been no sign of him as yet.' He had the silly sing-songy voice of the Highlander. He looked about the room uneasily, like a peasant who suddenly found himself in a mansion. She could imagine this man hunched over one of those fires without a chimney in the blackhouses Rod had gone on about.

'We've spoken to your husband,' said the smaller, more nondescript man. 'He tells us Freddie has a bit of a habit of running away.'

'And that being the case,' said the sandy one, 'we felt it

could be profitable to have another word with you about where you think he might have headed.'

'Would you like a coffee, Mrs Clarke?' asked the other. 'We're going to take the opportunity to refuel before getting back out there.'

'Oh. No, thanks.' She glanced at her glass. Would it look bad for the mother of the missing kid to be knocking back the pinot grigio? Well, too late now if it was. They must already have seen the glass. She sat back down and took a slug of wine.

'The search and rescue helicopter from Prestwick is on its way,' said the sandy one, sitting down opposite her. 'They have a spotlight, which is going to be a great help as the light fails.'

A *helicopter*? This was a first, even for Freddie.

'Good. That's good to know,' she said, when it became clear that some sort of response to this information was expected.

'Everybody is doing their very best to find your son.' The sandy cop's gaze was full of sympathy. 'I can only imagine how worrying a time this must be, particularly as you are having to stay here with your other boy and let others do the searching. It must be very difficult for you.'

She nodded, a little warm glow going through her. It felt good to be the object of someone's concern for once. He was right – it *was* very difficult being the mother of a boy like Freddie, constantly having her world turned upside down by his thoughtlessness, but hardly anyone seemed to realise that or, if they did, to care.

PC Nondescript went off through the door to the kitchen, and PC Sandy opened a notebook. 'Now ... On previous occasions, I understand from your husband that Frederick has boarded public transport and spent many hours riding on buses and trains. Twice he travelled to the home of your husband's sister in Devon. He has frequented malls and shops and taken shelter in garden sheds and outbuildings.' Even for a cop, the man spoke with a weird formality.

She nodded. 'Freddie likes his comforts. He wouldn't sleep rough.'

The PC nodded and made a note. 'So on an island like this ...' He pronounced the word *ayyye-land*.

'Freddie's not used to this sort of place. He's a city boy. I imagine he'll have made himself comfortable in a building. I've already told one of your colleagues all this.'

'Yes, but now, you see, we've searched all the buildings on the *ayyye*-land.'

It was making Penny want to laugh, but she made her face serious. 'Right. Okay.'

'So where else do you think Freddie might have gone?'

PC Nondescript was back. 'There you go, Bill.'

He set a mug of coffee and a plate of chocolate digestives on the coffee table next to 'Bill' and stood nursing his own mug.

Penny had no idea where Freddie could have gone. If she had, she'd have found him, wouldn't she? These men were obviously thinking the kid's mother should have some useful insights into his mental processes, but that couldn't be further from the truth. Freddie had been a mystery to Penny from the moment the midwife had plomped him on her chest, that strange little purple alien who'd supposedly come from inside her but to which, in her exhausted, aching, disorientated state, she had felt no connection whatsoever. 'Take it away,' she remembered saying. '*Please* take it away!'

It was as if she had known, immediately on setting eyes on him, that Freddie was not a normal child.

Freddie, she wanted to say now to the cops, *is an unpredictable nightmare, and I have no clue where he's gone. Your guess is as good as mine.*

She took another gulp of wine.

She needed to give them something.

'Anna was telling us about the Iron Age forts on the island. Freddie's into military history.' Was he? He enjoyed fighting, anyway. 'He could have tried to find the forts.'

PC Bill nodded. 'It is possible that a ten-year-old child might expect a fort to be a building he could hide in, rather than merely earthworks.'

'Possibly, although Anna did tell us there's nothing much left except mounds of earth.'

'I will check that the forts on the *ayyye*-land have been searched.'

PC Nondescript sat down next to his colleague on the sofa. 'Anywhere else you can think of that might attract him?'

On this bloody ayyye-land?

'Not really.'

'Bill' leant forward slightly. 'And Anna ... Um. How is she holding up? Is she okay?' Suddenly, the formality had dropped away.

Penny couldn't believe what she was hearing. 'Is *Anna* okay? *Anna?* My son's missing – *my* son! And you're asking me if the owner of the guest house where we happen to be staying is okay?'

'No, no, I'm sorry. I didn't mean –'

'I'm going out of my mind with worry here, Freddie's out there somewhere, a ten-year-old boy, and it's getting dark. And you're worried about *Anna?*'

Bloody yokels. They were probably all inbred. Anna was probably related to them all.

'Is she your cousin or something?'

'Uh.' PC Bill was blushing. 'I am her husband Tam's cousin.'

'Yes, of course you are.'

'It's just that we have all been a little concerned about

Anna.' His slight smile was apologetic. 'She has become something of a hermit, you see. She hardly leaves the island now.'

'There are mental health concerns,' added the other guy.

'Oh yes! Let's all worry about how my son's disappearance might affect *Anna's mental health!*' The anger, the righteous anger that flooded through her felt good. She got to her feet.

'Can I suggest that you spend a little less time worrying about your cousin's wife's ...' She struggled for the right word. '... *psyche!*' Yes, that was good. 'And a little more *trying to find my son!* Sorry, I don't mean to hurry you. Why not sit on your arses for another fifteen minutes and see how many more chocolate digestives you can get through?'

Both of them were now standing.

'Mrs Clarke – I'm sorry,' said PC Bill. 'That was most insensitive of me. As I say, we're doing our very best to find Frederick. If you think of anywhere else he might be ...'

'Fossils,' Penny snapped. 'There are fossils ... I forget where. Somewhere on the island. Freddie might have gone looking for them.'

Both cops were nodding encouragingly.

'Very good. It's the north of the *ayyye*-land that has the fossil beds,' PC Bill said to his colleague. 'We'll comb that area too, Mrs Clarke, be assured of that.'

The two of them slunk sheepishly from the room, and Penny sat back down and poured herself more wine.

It was going to be a long night.

15

ANNA

The shaking was back as Anna stopped the Land Rover on the apron of tarmac at the harbour and got out. Gulls wheeled and mewed above her head, crying like babies, and the sound went straight through her to whatever primitive place in a woman's brain responded to that wordless appeal. She had to lean back against the Land Rover and shut her eyes for a moment. She wanted to shut down her whole body, to squat here with her hands over her ears and block it all out.

It was as if she'd been existing at a remove from everything, insulated by a carapace of indifference, but now she had slammed back into the world, and she had no defences against it. The air itself on her skin seemed abrasive, making her flinch from it.

Voices assaulted her.

But she needed to hold it together.

Just for a couple more days. She would give the Clarkes two more days of hell, and then it would all be over.

She opened her eyes and took a long breath and started to walk across the tarmac. She could see *Ocean Rose* and

Osprey tied up at the quay, and Neil Nicholson and Davie Macfarlane standing together looking down at them. Fishermen seemed never to get tired of just standing staring at their own boats, checking them over, automatically, for damage, for any slight deviation from the norm. They were noticing people, trained to use their eyes and ears constantly when out on the hunt on the unpredictable, deadly ocean.

Would they take one look at Anna and know something was up?

Was she going to take one look at Neil Nicholson, at that kind, wise face, and break down completely?

Before she was halfway down the quay, the two men were coming towards her. They'd probably expected her to bring *Merry Dancer* to the harbour for their twilight rendezvous rather than rolling up in the Land Rover.

'I'm anchored back at Bàgh an Ear,' she babbled, when they were still not quite in comfortable talking range. She should say something about Freddie, about the search, but what? Her mind was suddenly blank as she stared at Neil, as he looked back at her, and she half expected him to shake his head and say, *Anna, what have you done?*

But he just nodded and turned to look out at the Sound.

Ridiculously, she *wanted* to break down, to have Neil take her in his arms and comfort her, as Dad would have done. Neil Nicholson was in his late sixties, she guessed, short and stocky with big reddened hands and reddened cheeks. He was one of those modest people who seemed completely content with their lot in life, with no ambition to be more than what his grandfather and father had been before him.

You only had to look at him to know you could depend on him in a crisis, that he would know what to do and what *you* should do.

She had a sudden urge to tell him everything.

'Just had the coastguard on,' he said. 'The helicopter from

Prestwick will be here in a while, and the lifeboat will stay out a few more hours yet before calling it a night. There's been no luck on land, he was saying. No sign at all.' He turned to her, his eyes gentle. 'It's a bad lookout, Anna.'

She needed to say something. She couldn't just stand here gaping at him.

But all she could manage was to shake her head.

'The poor parents must be going demented,' added Davie, and Anna wheeled round to face him. Davie was in his thirties, and she had known him since he was a child, but now it was as if she were looking at a stranger. Had he always had that unruly tuft at the end of his left eyebrow? As if self-conscious under her gaze, he took off his beanie hat, rubbed a hand over his crew cut, and replaced it again.

'Here's the gang,' said Neil.

No. Anna couldn't cope with more people. But a group of searchers were coming towards them, Mhairi Morison, as usual, front and centre.

'Ach, Anna,' she said, pulling her into a hug. 'A ten-year-old kiddie.'

And suddenly this was just what she wanted, what she needed, someone to hold her, to hold her up, almost, as her senses reeled. Anna clutched her friend, feeling the toned muscle of a woman who was on the go from dawn till dusk, breathing in the mix of deodorant and farm and rather sweaty human. She wanted to close her eyes, unwilling to let it end.

Mhairi seemed to sense this and prolonged the hug for a few beats before letting Anna go and, as Neil had, looking out at the Sound. 'I'm just going to come out and say what we're all thinking.' She took a breath. 'He's in the water.'

Gavin Murray, a retired postman with a sharp little nose and a stubbly beard, nodded. 'Faida's tiny. If he was on the island, we'd have found him.' He stuck his hands in his pockets. 'Mind that tourist laddie on Islay last year disappeared just the same way? Out playing on a beach on his own. Eight years old. Body found washed up on the sand in Machrihanish Bay two weeks later. He must have decided to go for a swim or fallen off the rocks into the water.' He pursed his lips. 'Folk come here thinking it's safe to let their wee ones go off playing on their own, which, aye, local kids who are savvy, it's safe enough, but these kids from down south who've never had that kind of freedom before, who aren't used to thinking about dangers ...'

'Are you ready to head off?' Neil interrupted, turning away from Gavin to roll his eyes at Mhairi. Gavin was somewhat notorious for his peevish monologues. 'Davie and me'll be back at first light,' he told Anna.

'The cops are staying on,' said Mhairi. 'Kipping in one of the cottages, I think they said?'

Anna nodded. She'd given Bill, Tam's cousin, the keys to Creel Cottage earlier.

'But it's an exercise in futility to keep searching the island, eh?' added Gavin. 'Like Mhairi says – he's in the water.' But even Gavin didn't actually say the words: that they were looking not for a living child but for a body.

If Freddie had been found washed up on a beach, Anna could imagine Gavin nodding to himself, sorry for the lad, yes, but grimly satisfied to have been proved right. The confused jumble of emotions that surged up inside her at this thought took her by the throat and made her want to scream, to tear at her hair, to shout at them all: *It was me, it was me, it was me! I took him!*

But she just hugged her arms around herself and looked down, at her wet shoes, at the stones of the quay, as voices jabbered around her, receding and coming closer and receding again.

They thought they knew her, but they didn't.

She couldn't do this.

She couldn't stand here with them all and try to act normal.

'I – I just have to ...' And then she was fleeing back up the quay, across the tarmac to the low slate-roofed building that housed the café and shop.

Mhairi's piping voice called after her: '*Anna!*'

And then Neil's: 'Leave her be, lass. Just leave her be.'

She ran round the side of the building until she was out of sight of everyone at the harbour, and then she just stood, staring across the scrubby foreshore to the sea.

How had she got here?

How had Anna MacLean, a girl afforded every privilege in life, every advantage, every kindness, ended up here?

She'd grown up in Glasgow, in the palatial red-sandstone house on Langside Drive where her parents still lived. It had been a childhood of Victorian grandeur, of sweeping driveways and high hedges and big drafty dining rooms, of fern-filled conservatories and sunny playrooms, of her mother reading on the lawn in the shade of the limes and copper beeches while Anna and her two older sisters rampaged down the laburnum walk, convinced they were being chased by the villain from whatever book they were reading at the time.

A childhood not much changed since the 1950s. Generations had taken that same walk home from school, kicking through the leaves with other children in private school uniforms, the boys swinging instrument cases at each other; home to a roaring fire, cocoa and hot teacakes, Great-Aunt Muriel sitting talking to Mum about anything from the disgrace of her friend's MP husband to which pictures Mum might hang in her exhibition.

There were lots of artists in the family. Musicians. Architects. Anna's great-grandfather had been a friend of Charles

Rennie Macintosh. She had grown up with a sense of being at the heart of the cultural life of the city. Of Scotland. Of the wider world. A sense of being at the centre of things.

And now here she was, at the edge.

Slowly, she walked back round to the front of the building, to the front door of the shop, and put both her palms flat against it. There were little rough areas of paint where it was starting to lift from the wood beneath.

Keys.

She needed the keys.

They were in the zipped inner pocket of her jacket. She fumbled with them, looking at them stupidly before selecting the long bronze-coloured one and setting it in the lock. She opened the door and flicked on the lights. Belatedly, she wondered what she would say if Mhairi did decide to come after her.

That she was picking up supplies for the guest house?

For a moment she just stood, staring stupidly at the silent aisles.

She and Tam had deliberately designed the layout of the place so that, to get to the café, people had to come in and out through the shop. The aisle on the left, on the café side, contained the tourist fare, cards and fridge magnets, scarves and woolly hats, tweed purses and cotton bags with a map of Faida on them or a Highland cow. The other aisles, now half empty, were devoted to food – snacks for the day trippers and things like tins of soup and vegetables and packets of rice for the holiday let folk and the campers. In the summer season, the empty shelves would be filled with bread and rolls and pastries from the bakery on the mainland, and the chiller cabinet would be stocked with milk and butter and pies and meat and ready meals, and the sandwiches they made up in the café each morning.

She grabbed one of the Highland cow bags and started to

fill it with crisps, biscuits, sweets, cereal bars, chocolate, cans of Coke, and tins of soup, curry and baked beans – and a couple of Pot Noodles.

Not exactly healthy eating, but she imagined that getting his five-a-day was the least of Freddie's concerns.

Freddie.

She stood in the harsh fluorescent light of the shop, the bag hanging from her hand. What was she doing? She thought she could make everything all right for him by stuffing him full of rubbish?

But he needed to eat. He needed to be fed and warm. She thought of Broc, of what she would give him if he had been in the same situation, and added to the bag a jar of hot chocolate powder and a packet of Jaffa cakes.

Outside, the harbour was quiet again. *Ocean Rose* and *Osprey* were puttering out beyond the quay, taking the searchers home. She raised a hand, in case any of them were looking back her way, and hurried to the Land Rover.

FREDDIE MUST HAVE BEEN asleep on the V-berth in the bows of the boat, although she'd forgotten to make it up for him. He stood, curly hair on end, little white feet bare and horribly vulnerable looking, in the doorway that separated the main cabin from the V-berth and the tiny shower room and toilet.

'I've brought you some supplies,' she said. 'Sorry, did I wake you?'

As she came down the steps with the bag, he backed off a little, gripping the edge of the door as if ready to slam it in her face if she came too near.

'I was awake,' he asserted.

'I'm afraid none of it's very healthy!' Her tone was too bright and breezy. She set the bag down on the table and took a moment to breathe, to try to slow her thumping heart. Then she started unpacking the food, naming each item, like in the stories she used to tell Broc when he was very little and couldn't sleep at night, stories with long, soporific lists of nice things.

'Salt and vinegar crisps, and ready salted, and lentil curls. More tomato soup. More biscuits – oatcakes and cheesy crackers and multiseed things ... Hot chocolate. Would you like some hot chocolate?'

He shrugged.

'And there's a choice of chocolate biscuits, look, and Jaffa cakes.'

Freddie slipped onto the bench seat behind the table and accepted a plate of Jaffa cakes and a mug of hot chocolate. Again, Anna made two mugfuls and let him choose which he wanted, and took the other herself.

He was soon wolfing down the Jaffa cakes, just as Broc used to, finishing each one in two bites.

'Did you see Mum and Dad?'

'No. I'll see them later.'

He tipped up his mug and drank up the last of the sweet drink. 'Can I have another?'

'Of course you can!'

Anna hurried to put the kettle back on and spoon more powder into the mug.

'Are the police here?' was his next question.

'Yes. They've been searching the island for you, with some local people.'

'So there's been a fuss.'

'Well, naturally everyone's very worried. But you'll soon be back, as I said, with your family.'

'Is Alfie okay?'

He thought she might have tried to hurt Alfie? Well, how was he to know she wouldn't? Only yesterday, she *had* been contemplating not just hurting Alfie but *killing him*.

'He's fine,' she got out.

'Where is he?'

'Tucked up in bed fast asleep, I should imagine.'

She poured boiling water into the mug and stirred until the powder dissolved, her mind jumping from one image to the next as she stared into the swirling pinkish-brown liquid: Freddie and Alfie arriving at the harbour. Alfie making a sand castle. Freddie curled up in the cockpit after she'd almost pushed him overboard.

'You must be very tired too,' she said briskly. 'Why don't you drink this while I make up the V-berth with a pillow and duvet so you'll be more comfortable?'

On the shelf above the sleeping platform in the V-berth, Anna noticed one of Broc's books: *Under Their Skin* by Margaret Peterson Haddix, one of Broc's favourites. Freddie must have found it in the storage area under the bench.

She got a duvet, a pillow, sheets and a pillowcase from the locker under the berth and made it cosy for him. She would refill his hot water bottle, too. And there were spare toothbrushes in the cabinet in the shower room. If she didn't think too hard, she could almost kid herself that this was a normal situation, that she'd taken Freddie out on *Merry Dancer* for an adventure, and the two of them were having fun.

'What did Mum say after I went missing?' Freddie said when she returned to the main cabin.

'Well, just the things you'd expect. She's worried about you.' But, now that Anna thought about it, that wasn't exactly true. Penny had seemed more annoyed than anything. 'I think she's hoping you've just run away, like you've done before.'

He nodded, grimacing down into his mug.

'But she's going to be so glad to see you back safe and sound!'

The grimace became a weary, unchildlike smile. 'No she's not. She's going to be really, really angry.'

'Oh, no, I'm sure she won't be.'

'I think I maybe know her a bit better than you.' He fixed Anna with that unsettling blue gaze. 'She's pretty much permanently in angry mode these days.'

Anna thought of that sour expression, the discontented set of the thin mouth.

'Your parents have money worries, and the business isn't doing so well, is it?'

'Peaks Transit is going down the toilet. Mum thinks that's all Dad's fault. She wants a divorce. I've heard her on the phone to her lawyer. Problem is, they'd have to sell our house, and she'd have to buy Dad out of the business, but she's hoping her lawyer might get her a deal where she doesn't have to pay Dad very much because the business is basically not worth shit and Mum's been the one keeping it going anyway. But then she's worried that Dad will play the depression card.'

Anna reached out a hand to him, but he snatched his arm away before she could make contact.

'I'm sorry. That must be hard for you and Alfie. But maybe they'll work things out. Often people do. All marriages have their rocky patches.'

'If they do get a divorce, the judge will probably not let me and Alfie stay with Dad because usually the kids stay with the mum, and Mum's lawyer is going to say Dad isn't a fit parent. Because of his depression and stuff.'

What a choice for those poor kids: Penny or Rod.

'But you'd rather be with your dad?'

He nodded. 'Dad's really soft with us.'

For a while, Freddie drank in silence.

'I see you're reading *Under Their Skin*,' Anna said at last.

'Yeah, I like sci-fi.'

As he spoke, the unreality of the situation hit her afresh. How could the two of them be sitting here, quite calmly discussing children's literature? What must this poor little boy have been thinking when she grabbed him? When she pulled him up over the guard rail? When she locked him in the lazarette?

He must have been absolutely terrified. He must have thought he was going to die.

But it all seemed to have happened in another world, to two completely different people.

For a moment, she couldn't think what to say next.

If this was Broc, what would she say?

'Is it good so far?'

A shrug. 'It's pretty good. I think Broc and me probably like the same kind of stuff. He's got all *The Boy from Planet Doom* series. I've read all of those.'

'Broc loves science fiction. And all that dreadful dystopian stuff about people surviving after a nuclear war or a pandemic or –'

'Alien invasion!' Freddie grinned. 'Or, like, everyone's zombies apart from maybe three people, and they're trying to get out of the city and see if there are any other normal people left in the world.'

Anna smiled. 'Yes, terrible stuff like that. Broc can't get enough of it.' She pointed to the corkboard attached to one of the galley cupboards. 'That's Broc trying to be an alien.'

In the photograph, four-year-old Broc wore miniature green overalls and a mask that featured one huge, staring eye in the middle of the face and antennae sticking up on top. He used to insist on going to the mainland dressed like that, and all round the shops. It had been entertaining watching the adults he met trying not to smile, pretending to be scared.

'He was just little then, of course. Younger than Alfie.'

Freddie nodded.

'You can keep any of the books you like – Broc's read everything on the boat.'

'Would Broc be cool with that?'

'Oh yes.'

He took another Jaffa cake. 'I guess when you take me back, we'll just leave Faida, and I won't get to meet Broc. But he would probably think I was a brat anyway.'

'Well, he might think that at first, but once he got to know the real Freddie, I'm sure you would be friends.'

Through a mouthful of Jaffa cake, Freddie said, almost proudly, 'I'm a psycho.'

Anna couldn't help smiling. 'I don't think so, Freddie. You're just a bit naughty sometimes, like all boys.'

'Nope. I'm a psycho. Although I've never actually tried to kill anyone.' He took another Jaffa cake. 'Yet.'

Anna's heart started to hammer. 'When I grabbed you, before ... I would never actually have done it. But don't you want to know why I ... Why I *thought* I wanted to?'

Freddie shrugged. 'I was being a brat.'

What?

'No no! And even if you were, that would be no reason to ...' She had to say it. 'To push you over the side. Like I said, I went a bit mad. I've been a bit mad for quite a long time, but I'm not any more. Nothing like that is going to happen again. I'm not going to hurt you.'

Freddie looked at her. 'Yeah. You said.'

16

PENNY

Rod, for once, was not hitting the booze, but Penny wished he would. He kept pacing from one side of the bedroom to the other, ranting about how the local searchers and even the policemen had been looking at him with 'tea and sympathy' faces and tearing up.

'It's like they've already given up on Freddie!'

'Well, that's pretty ungrateful. Those people are putting a lot of time and effort into looking for him.' Penny got into bed and picked up her iPad.

'And you're just going to sit there looking at YouTube?'

'Oh, okay. My bad.' She unscrewed her tube of cream. 'Why don't I get up and start stomping round the room with you, and we can both be two-year-olds throwing our toys out of the pram?'

Rod glared at her, for all the world as if he really were two years old. In fact, being married to Rod was a bit like having a third child.

She felt like weeping.

How had it come to this? How had her life veered so spectacularly off course? Looking back, there were two, or maybe three, defining moments when she'd taken the wrong path. The first had been that afternoon in the community hall office with Mrs Ellis and her parents, when her dreams of being a dancer had died. The second had been that day in the Peak District when she'd first met Rod.

She blamed Lechy Leo, this guy who used to get on the minibus Penny drove around the Peak District during her university holidays. The minibus was meant to be a service for tourists, doing a scenic circuit from Alton Towers to Leek to Dovedale several times a day, to allow people to get out and walk and then get picked up again. But Leo was a local. He'd get on at Ilam, where he lived, and do the whole circuit, sitting in the seat behind Penny with his onion breath and pawing her under cover of praising her driving. 'Nicely negotiated, Penny!' Excuse to rub her back. 'Watch out, child alert!' Excuse to squeeze her shoulder. When he'd put a hand on her hair, Penny had stopped the minibus at the side of the road and announced to the other passengers that they were going nowhere until Leo got off. Even then, his smile hadn't wavered. He'd hopped off the bus, grinning and chuckling and insisting he was 'just being friendly' when Penny had informed him he was banned.

The next day, there had been Leo as usual waiting outside the pub in Ilam, ginger sideburns twitching as he leered up at her. There had been passengers wanting off there, so Penny couldn't just drive on past. When the people had got off, she'd stepped down onto the pavement for a private word. But when she'd told Leo that he wasn't coming aboard, he had started to protest, trying to put a hand on Penny's shoulder.

That had been when Rod had intervened.

'Mate, if the driver says you're banned, you're banned,' he'd said, unfolding his lanky frame from the back of the bus and jumping down to stand between Penny and Leo.

As they'd resumed their journey, Rod had taken Leo's

usual seat behind the driver, and Penny had filled him in on the situation. Rod had got off at Dovedale to do the circular walk to Hall Dale, and Penny had picked him up again at the end of the afternoon. In the course of conversation, he'd revealed that he worked in a London bank, and Penny, naïvely, had assumed this meant he was an investment banker in the City of London, making million-pound deals before breakfast and snorting cocaine in exclusive nightclubs. By the time she'd discovered that Rod was a humble assistant manager in the TSB in Ludgate Hill, it was a lunch and a dinner later, and she'd obtained the much more promising information that his dad had just died and left him and his sister Ursula almost seven hundred thousand pounds each, which Rod was at a loss to know what to do with.

Penny had just been turned down for a business loan. Too young, apparently.

And she'd liked Rod Clarke. He'd been attractive enough, and his *I'll protect you* response to the Leo situation had given her the false impression that he was a forceful alpha-male type. The fact that he'd not bothered to go to university should have been a red flag, as should his airy assertion that learning to drive wasn't something he planned on doing any time soon – there were too many cars on the roads as it was. And he enjoyed travelling by train and by bus – look at the interesting people you met!

And here they were, fifteen years later, and he still couldn't bloody drive. Why bother, when he had Penny to chauffeur him anywhere he wanted to go?

He stopped pacing and turned, flinging out an arm towards the window, where there was no longer a view, only the room reflected back at them. 'Our son is out there some-where *in the dark*! And you're just carrying on as if nothing's happened! How can you just *sit there* looking at your iPad and putting on bloody hand cream?'

Penny sighed. 'You know as well as I do that he's probably lying low somewhere, laughing at us all. The chances are that Freddie is perfectly fine.'

Rod came bounding across the room to the bed, and Penny shrank back, but he didn't touch her, he just stared into her face, as if looking for something. 'How can you ...? *The chances are* – that's acknowledging that there *is* a chance he's *not* okay!'

'Calm down, Rod.'

'Calm down? I can't *calm down*, and my God, there'd be something wrong with me if I could!' He snatched up the jacket he'd discarded on the chair by the bed. 'I'm going back out there. It's possible he's been dodging the search groups and made his way back somewhere we've already searched.'

Penny laughed mirthlessly. 'And there we have it. Now *you're* "acknowledging" that, deep down, you know Freddie's just run off as usual. And off you go, trotting after him, just like he wants.' She turned on the iPad.

Rod went so still that she thought, at first, that he'd gone. But when she looked up, he was there, leaning back against the door frame.

'That's not what he *wants*. If Freddie has "just" run away again, there's a good reason for that, and I'm looking right at it!'

'Oh yes, of course. I wondered when we'd come to this. It's all my fault, isn't it? Everything bad Freddie and Alfie do is my fault, because in your eyes it's the woman's job to look after the kids. Along with, it seems, everything else. By Rod logic, that means the business failing is down to me too, I suppose.'

'No.' Suddenly, he sounded bone tired, leaning all his weight on the door frame. 'I bear equal responsibility for that.'

'Well, that's big of you! *Equal* responsibility? So you think

I'm equally to blame for the cash we're haemorrhaging? New tyres for all the intercities, drivers limited to two-hour stints before taking a break, services for the whole fleet every five minutes – I'm to hold my hands up to all that, am I, for letting you get away with it, I suppose?'

'I'm rearranging the deckchairs on the *Titanic*, Penny. That's all I'm doing. You're right. We're finished. And I'm so tired of playing the blame game. I'm going to look for our son.'

G ood.

As she drove towards the house, Anna could see there were still lights on in the guest living room, and Rod was stretched out on one of the plantation chairs on the decking. And just off the reefs of Creag an Sgoiltein, a cone of illumination moved slowly over the water as the search and rescue helicopter quartered the inshore waters.

Anna let herself into the extension and went straight through the hall and the living area and out onto the decking. Her heart was pounding. This must be how an actor felt once they had walked on stage. Up for it. Ready to do what they had to do.

'Oh, Rod,' she sighed, plomping herself down on one of the other chairs. 'Still no sign?'

'No.' He barely looked round at her. The only light was from the windows behind them, but it was enough to be able to tell he looked wrecked – hair on end, face pasty. He had taken off his glasses, and without them he looked different, more boyish, more vulnerable.

'I'm so sorry.' She made her voice treacly with sympathy.

'I've been back to the cottages – the two the policemen aren't in, anyway. And I've looked in the farm buildings, and the outbuildings here, and the sheds at the harbour. Even that little boat hut thing.' He sat up and put his glasses back on and looked at her. 'Where else is there? What other buildings are there on the island?'

'There's another boathouse at Bàgh an Ear,' said Anna. She left just enough of a pause to raise his hopes before adding, 'But I've just come from there.'

He slumped forward, his head in his hands. 'Oh God.'

Chug-chug-chug went the helicopter, coming nearer.

Perfect timing.

Anna looked up at it. 'They're certainly going all out trying to find him.'

Rod looked up too. 'They're looking in the *sea*. Not on the land.'

'No, well, but the island is tiny, Rod.' She lowered her voice. 'And we've already searched it from side to side and top to bottom. The shoreline too. That was possibly the most likely place – if he'd twisted an ankle on the rocks or something – but I've been all round it in my boat, as have two very experienced fishermen. And the searchers have walked the shore too.'

'And he's nowhere to be found,' Rod finished, his voice breaking.

'I'm so sorry.'

And now Rod started to weep in earnest.

She watched him. She drank him in, every heave of his shoulders, every snottery intake of breath, every swipe at his face. He wasn't even bothering with a tissue.

After a while, she went inside to get a box from the kitchen and brought it out to him.

'Thanks, Anna,' he choked, pulling out a handful of

tissues and rubbing his face hard, as if it were possible to rub away the pain.

'This is karma,' he said at last.

She left a beat. 'Karma?'

He stared at her, his eyes behind his spectacles wide.

'What do you mean?' she said gently. 'Karma for what?'

He shook his head.

'Rod.' Her voice dripped with compassion. 'It's not *karma*. For God's sake! There's nothing you could possibly have done to deserve this.'

He laughed suddenly, the harsh sound making her flinch. 'Oh, I think there is.'

'It's not –'

'You don't understand!' he rapped out. 'We killed seven people, Anna. *Seven people*.' His eyes now were wild, staring at her almost desperately, as if he couldn't quite believe what he was saying himself, as if maybe he was hoping she would tell him it wasn't true.

'What on earth do you mean?'

'One of our intercity buses – there was an accident, and five of the passengers, plus the driver and the driver of the other vehicle, were killed. Four more people were left with what they call "life-changing" injuries. Organs removed, faces scarred, limbs amputated.' He took in a shuddering breath. 'It happened two years ago. Late at night, on the A69 between Carlisle and Newcastle. The driver failed to negotiate a corner, and the bus slid sideways into the path of an articulated lorry.'

'Oh *no!*'

'The Crown Prosecution Service brought a case against us for gross negligence manslaughter, and there was a trial, but we got off. Insufficient evidence to convict.'

'So it wasn't your fault.'

His face contorted in an approximation of a smile. 'It was our fault, all right.'

'But it sounds like it was just an accident. If the driver lost control –'

'*Why* did he lose control, though? That was the question.' He gazed off into the dark. 'The driver, Merv Taylor, had been on the road for twenty hours. *Twenty hours* with just a few short breaks for a cup of coffee and a sandwich. Do you know what the legal limit is in the UK for driving time in any one working day?'

'No.'

'Ten hours. Merv had been driving the bus for *twice* that long! We're not just talking a few hours here or there. The accident happened around midnight, and he'd been on the go since *four o'clock that morning.*'

Anna kept her voice level. 'He was covering someone's shift? If it was a one-off –'

'Oh no.' He gave another harsh laugh. 'The drivers were regularly rostered on to do twenty-hour days, because that way we could employ fewer people and keep the wages bill down. We pay those guys a pittance anyway, so they were all too willing to do the extra hours.'

'But surely the buses have those things that record when they're moving and when they're stationary, to make sure drivers stick to the legal driving time limits?'

'Tachographs. Yes, we had them fitted to all our buses. It's a legal requirement.'

'Okay ... So –'

'We also issued each driver with a magnet. Nothing fancy, just an ordinary magnet you can pick up for a couple of quid in any hardware shop. Stick it on the tachograph sensor – which is easily accessible, mounted on the gear box – and that will stop it picking up movement. The magnet basically disables the tachograph. So the drivers could keep driving for as long as they wanted. Or I should say, as long as *we* wanted.'

She stared at him. 'That's –'

'Unconscionable. Yes. Oh, yes.'

'But didn't the crash investigators find the magnet?'

His face contorted again. 'We got lucky, as Penny put it. The accident happened during one of Merv's "legit" driving periods. He'd used the magnet earlier in the day, on a different route. The practice was that, when not in use, the magnet would be kept well away from the tachograph in the luggage area. The crash investigators never found it. It would have been disrespectful, I suppose, an invasion of privacy, for them to poke through people's luggage, and there was no reason to do so, as far as they knew.'

'But wouldn't there be some other evidence that he'd been driving for way too long? Duty rosters, or –'

'Nope. As soon as she found out about the accident, at one-thirty in the morning, Penny was on the computer creating a brand new duty roster and replacing the old file with a new one. And when she'd done that, she printed off a paper copy and took it to the office and put it in an orange folder just like the real one, and creased some of the pages and spilt tea on them and rumpled them a bit to make out like they weren't fresh from the printer. She took the real roster home and chucked it in the recycling.'

'Oh my God.'

For a while, they sat in silence.

Anna said slowly, 'If *all* your drivers were regularly sleep-deprived, hadn't there been other incidents before that one?'

'There had been, yes. None of them serious, thank God – and all swept under the carpet. A bus went off the road just outside Leeds. But it had been raining heavily, the roads were slick ... Nothing was made of it. Another went into the back of a car at traffic lights. That was dismissed as momentary loss of concentration. Then we had one of our drivers, Herik Patel, refuse to complete his journey – made all the passengers get off at a service station and find their own onward transport while he had a kip. Penny sacked the guy. Herik testified at the trial, said Penny was making all the drivers cut corners, stay on the road for way longer than was legal, use magnets to tamper with the tachograph, but our lead defence lawyer tore him apart on the witness stand. No magnet had been found, of course, at the crash scene. And the lawyer made much of the fact that Herik had had a bit of a breakdown after he was sacked from Peaks Transit. Lost his driving licence after he was caught drunk at the wheel of his car. And there was CCTV footage that showed him ranting outside the office, making threats against Penny. Our lawyers managed to discredit him completely, made out that he was just a disgruntled former employee who unfairly blamed us for all his problems. They even tried to turn round what Herik had done to get himself sacked, said he had continued driving when he was rostered to stop ten hours previously – and of course, the doctored duty roster backed up that version of events. His blatant disregard for health and safety was what got him the sack, the lawyers claimed.'

'When in fact it sounds like the opposite was true,' she said tightly. 'Herik Patel was sacked because he'd refused to endanger his passengers by following the roster you'd made him work to. But when you say your lawyers claimed this or that – you mean they knew the truth?'

'No, no. Penny and I – we spun the lawyers the party line.'

'Weren't there other witnesses to what had been going on? Your employees?'

'The police questioned the other drivers, of course, and other people in the company, but they all kept quiet because they didn't want to lose their jobs – plus, if it came out that they'd all been going along with bending the rules, who else would employ them? A couple of passengers on the bus testified for the prosecution, said the driver seemed "tired and grumpy", but our defence lawyer argued, successfully, that Merv Taylor was naturally taciturn and had a "tired" face. They put a big photo of him at his daughter's wedding up on the screen in the court room. Miserable bugger, he looked.'

'So how did the defence explain the accident?'

'Momentary loss of concentration. The driver had no points on his licence, was very experienced ... Possibly a passenger distracted him. Two of the passengers who died were a sixty-nine-year-old woman called Theresa Fernsby and her thirty-two-year-old son Roger – they were sitting right behind the driver. Roger Fernsby had autism. Penny had this idea ... that he could have made a sudden noise or lunged forward or something, and distracted the driver. This theory was brought out in cross-examination of the passengers testifying for the prosecution. They all denied it had happened, but the damage was done. The idea was planted in the jury's minds.'

'Clever.'

'Oh, Penny had the whole thing worked out basically within a few hours of the accident. How we could wriggle out of it. Make out that it was all down to bad luck, and there was nothing we could have done to prevent it.' He swept his arms around him, encompassing himself, the house, the island. Dead Freddie. 'And here we are, scot free.'

Anna left a long silence.

Rod eventually filled it with, 'Making the drivers work long hours was just one of many, many corners we were cutting in pursuit of profits. *The bottom line.* That's all Penny cared about. That's still all she cares about. She doesn't care that all those people died because of what she did. And I'm – what's the term? – I'm her enabler. I've turned a blind eye. Gone along with it. As Penny says, I was quite happy to let her cut corners with safety as long as the school fees were being paid and I had enough disposable income to go on all my twitching holidays. Even though I knew, deep down, that it was only a matter of time before something dreadful happened ... And she's still doing it. Our profits have fallen through the floor after all the bad publicity – no one wants to travel with Peaks Transit any more, so she's still trying to cut corners.'

Anna studied him – the tousled, boyish hair, the polo shirt collar that needed straightening, the muddy boots he hadn't bothered to remove. Pathetic. He was a weak, pathetic man, but not, she thought, fundamentally evil.

'Penny is dangerous,' she said, clearly and slowly.

His head snapped up. 'What do you mean?'

'You just said she's still trying to cut corners. That needs to stop.'

He closed his eyes briefly, as if in pain. 'I'm *trying* to stop her. But now she's blaming me for the business failing, saying my new fixation with OTT health and safety is costing us money we can't afford.'

'Well, but can't you –'

'To be honest, Anna, I don't care any more about the business. Maybe I've been subconsciously trying to sabotage it ever since the accident. I've even thought about coming clean, going back to the police and telling the truth, telling them what we did. Penny always argues that we can't do that because we'd both go to prison, and what would become of Freddie and Alfie then? But they'd be fine with my sister for a few years. They might even be better off, to be honest.' His face altered. 'Oh God, *Freddie*! I'm never going to see Freddie again, am I? Freddie's *gone*!'

'No,' Anna said forcefully, reaching forward and taking his hands in hers. They were like blocks of ice. 'We'll find

Freddie. I'm sure Penny's right, and he's just playing a game with us, dodging the searchers.'

The look of hope he turned on her was heart-wrenching. 'Do you think so?'

Anna tightened her grip on his hands. 'And when you get home, you need to go to the police and tell them everything you've told me about the accident – which wasn't an accident at all, was it?'

He shook his head in shame, like a schoolboy she was chastising.

'As I see it, the only way you're going to be able to live with yourself is if you make a clean breast of it.'

'I will!' He gripped her hands. 'I've got evidence! I retrieved the original duty roster from the recycling. I've got it in my locker at the bird sanctuary where I volunteer.'

'Why did you do that?'

He blinked at her. 'I don't know. I guess I ... I guess I knew I'd not be able to live with it, as you say. I knew I'd have to come clean at some stage, only, like the bloody coward I am, I kept telling myself *not yet, not yet* ... For the boys' sake, which is a load of crap, Anna. If you want the truth, I'm afraid of her. Of Penny.' His voice shook on the name. 'Of what she'll do if I finally stand up to her.'

18

Penny couldn't sleep. Thoughts of Freddie kept going round and round in her head. She kept seeing his grinning face, hearing his mocking laughter. Oh yes, Freddie would be loving this. He'd no doubt heard the helicopter, wherever he was hiding.

This holiday was meant to be for Rod, to get him back on an even keel. All Freddie had to do was let that happen, but oh no. As per usual, he had to ruin everything. Far from bucking up, Rod was losing it again.

Penny needed to find bloody Freddie.

She dressed quickly and went downstairs. She'd start with the outbuildings behind this house. It would be just the kind of stunt he'd pull, hiding metres away from them in some inaccessible place adults couldn't get to, but Penny knew his tricks. If he was there, she'd find him. If he wasn't, she'd try the holiday cottages.

There were lights on in the big living area, and she could hear voices drifting in from the decking. Rod. And Anna. Rod's voice was whimpery, whiny, rising and falling peevishly.

Typical. He claimed to be worried to death about Freddie, but instead of looking for him, he was whining about it to anyone who'd listen, leaving Penny to pick up the pieces.

She opened the extension's back door and stood in the cool of the cobbled yard, considering the options. Could he have sneaked into the Land Rover? It would be a nice, relatively comfortable place to sleep. She opened the driver's door and peered inside.

No Freddie.

Next, the garage. It was a relatively new building beside an old stone barn. There were two big roll-up doors and a normal one to the side, which she found wasn't locked. Inside, though, there were no vehicles for Freddie to be sleeping in. She supposed the police must be using the other Land Rover. There were some piles of tarpaulins and things, which she systematically poked and kicked and flung about.

No Freddie.

The stone barn was next. It wasn't locked either. She flicked on the lights, illuminating old metal oil drums and farm equipment and tools. There were shelves along one wall and a workbench along the other, which seemed to be for woodworking. Bits of wood were scattered about, some in the shapes of birds. The smells of oil and sawdust and old paper had her suddenly flashing on Dad's shed at home, the neat rack of tools, the workbench, the hook on the back of the door from which the broom had always hung.

There was nowhere here to hide, but an old wooden ladder led upwards, presumably to a loft area, which was exactly the kind of place Freddie would choose to bed down.

Hopefully, if he was here, he might be asleep.

She climbed stealthily up the ladder and eased herself onto the dusty wooden floor above. Straightening, she stood perfectly still, only her eyes moving as she scanned the space. There were boxes and piles of newspapers. A stack of paint cans. A purple surfboard with a logo so faded you couldn't see what it was any more. Some clear plastic storage boxes with what looked like clothes inside, and books and papers.

No sign of a small boy.

She walked between the stacks of boxes to make sure.

No.

There was no one here.

So why were the hairs suddenly standing up on the back of her neck?

She wheeled round.

No one.

But something had spooked her. Something she had seen ... She slowly retraced her steps, trailing her fingers across the dusty tops of the cardboard boxes. Near the ladder, there was another stack of the clear plastic boxes, the one on top full of paper.

She stared through the lid.

And then she was yanking it off, throwing it aside, snatching up the envelope she must subconsciously have noticed as she walked past.

The envelope addressed to Thomas Gillies, Engster, Isle of Faida, PA30 9WT.

Thomas Gillies was one of the people who had died on the bus. Thomas. Tom. Tam, maybe, was the Scottish equivalent. But he had lived in *Glasgow*! Penny was sure of it. Anna's family were wealthy, though. They probably owned property all over the place.

Everything slotted into place with a thunk.

Of course.

Thomas Gillies was Anna's husband, or more likely partner, as they had different surnames – or maybe she hadn't changed her name when she married. Whatever. The point was that he wasn't away on a fishing trawler, he was dead, killed in that fucking accident! And there must have been *two* sons, because Thomas Gillies's son Calum had also died, two days after the crash, in the Royal Victoria Infirmary in Newcastle.

She thought suddenly about the Buckaroo toy and how Anna's reaction to Alfie breaking it had been a bit extreme. Had that been because the Buckaroo had belonged not to Broc but to dead Calum?

She was sure she was right.

Anna had lured the Clarkes here. She had befriended Rod on the internet, pretending to be another bird nut, and dangled a free birding holiday in front of him, which he'd jumped at, of course, without a second thought. *It'll be good for us. It's just what we need.*

That *idiot*!

Trust Rod to get catfished by a bloody psychopath!

Had Anna done something to Freddie?

Yes. Of course she had. She must have killed Freddie in an act of twisted revenge, to give the Clarkes a taste of their own medicine, to make them suffer through losing a child just as Anna had done, because presumably Anna must blame them, despite the acquittal, despite Penny and Rod having been cleared of all responsibility *in a court of law*!

That bitch.

Why wasn't she going after the driver's family? He was the one to blame for those people dying. He was the one who'd lost control of the vehicle. Penny and Rod had been asleep in bed a hundred miles away. It had been ridiculous that the police and the CPS had ever come after them in the first place.

Oh fuck!

She could just imagine how Rod was going to react to this. He was going to fall apart completely. Go total fruit loop. And that would be goodbye to any chance of salvaging life as she knew it.

Penny would be devastated too, naturally, to have lost Freddie.

Freddie. Her firstborn.

She conjured up an image of him, but all that came into her head was the Freddie she'd been thinking about earlier, Freddie laughing at her, sneering, mocking ... All she felt, still, was annoyance. Bloody typical Freddie, getting himself killed by this mad bitch.

No doubt the grief would hit her soon.

This was the denial phase, presumably. Only Penny wasn't in denial. She knew she was right. This explained everything, from the free holiday to why Freddie hadn't been found. Presumably Anna had already buried the body. It wouldn't take long. Freddie was average height for his age but very scrawny. She could bundle him up into just a small hole in the ground. Or maybe she'd tossed the body overboard from her yacht.

Penny pushed the envelope into her pocket and slowly descended the ladder. Down in the workshop area, she found herself still scanning the shadows. Her brain obviously hadn't accepted its own deductions yet. That Freddie wasn't just hiding somewhere. That Freddie was dead.

She stood still, waiting for the hit of emotion.

She imagined telling Mum and Dad all about it. She imagined Mum taking Penny in her arms, and maybe Dad would go all gruff and pat her back and tell her he was sorry. There was nothing worse, after all, than losing a child. He would be, if not on Penny's side, at least sympathetic. Kind, even. Wasn't everyone duty bound to be kind to a grieving mother?

She imagined herself crying.

But still, she could feel nothing but anger.

She needed to confront Anna and demand to know what she'd done with Freddie. Her son. Her child. And if Anna denied everything, Penny would wave the envelope in front of her face. *How do you explain this, then?*

She strode across the farmyard and in at the back door of the extension.

Rod was in the hall, sitting on one of the benches there, his head in his hands. Penny fumbled the envelope out of her pocket and was about to show him the name on the front when he looked up at her with a pathetic tear-stained face and whimpered, 'I've told her everything.'

'What? Who? Who have you told what?' But she had an awful sinking feeling.

'I've told Anna that we covered up our culpability in the deaths of all those people. The negligence. The wilful negligence. The cover-up. Everything.'

No. No no *no*!

'I'm going to the police in the morning. I can't live with it any more, Pen. I just can't.'

She bit back what she wanted to say, what she wanted to scream at him. Her mind racing, she kept her voice level. 'Oh, right. That's the most urgent thing on your agenda, is it? That's what's been occupying your mind? Have you forgotten that *our son is missing*? You want to distract the people looking for him with all that nonsense?'

'It's not *nonsense*.' But she could tell that what she'd said had hit home. 'Of course we have to prioritise the search for Freddie, but once we've found him, we have to come clean.'

'We'll go to jail. And we might never find Freddie – not alive, anyway. Is that what you want for Alfie? His brother dead and his mum and dad banged up for gross negligence manslaughter?'

He was staring at her like she had two heads. 'I'll never forgive myself for going along with all the horrendous things you've done, Pen. And don't you dare talk to me about the kids! They'd be better off *away from you!* Away from both of us!'

That bitch Anna had been in his ear.

Chipping away.

Manipulating him into this sudden decision to confess everything.

Of all the people in the world for her idiot husband to spill his guts to, he had to choose Anna, wife and mother of two of the victims? A woman bent on revenge? The woman who'd just *fucking murdered Freddie*?

What had Penny ever done to deserve being shackled to Rod Clarke? It was like being one of those Siamese twins whose sibling had died – you knew it was only a matter of time before the dead tissue you were joined to poisoned your bloodstream and killed you too.

Being married to Rod was like being conjoined to a rotting corpse.

He was still whinging on. And on and on, about the accident. He didn't even know any of those people, yet for the last two years he'd been drooping about the place like they'd been seven of his closest family members.

As he put his hands back over his snivelling face, she looked down at the envelope she was still holding.

Was it possible she could turn this around?

Freddie was probably dead. She couldn't do anything for him now, but maybe this cloud had a silver lining.

She pushed the envelope back into her pocket.

19

ANNA

It was going to be one of those days of sunshine and showers, the rain sweeping across the Sound in veil after veil. Anna stood at the bedroom window watching the next one race towards Faida but fizzle out to almost nothing, already backlit by the sun, a short rainbow arcing up from the sea. She always used to love standing here in the morning, Tam behind her with his arms around her waist, watching the weather come at them.

But now she was reminded of the spotlight from the rescue helicopter, shining on the water last night.

If Tam could be here now, what would he say?

Probably not much. He'd just look at her in that way he had, eyebrows slightly raised. Like Broc, Tam had always been so sure of what was right and what was wrong. Her moral compass, she used to joke, although it hadn't really been a joke at all.

Her sister Fiona had this theory that, in any relationship, one person was the minder and one the loonie. When they were teenagers, Fiona would groan, having met Anna's latest bad-boy date, 'Not *another* loonie!'

After a week of getting to know Tam that summer on Faida, Fiona had pronounced one night, in the bedroom they'd shared across the hall, 'It's about time you had a minder.'

'Thanks a lot!' Anna had snorted into her pillow, and the two of them had dissolved in giggles.

But Fiona had been right.

Before Tam, Anna had been the sensible Sally in her relationships, the one doing the reining in, and it had been an exhilarating experience to be kicking against the traces for a change. When Tam had come to stay with the MacLeans in Glasgow that autumn, Anna had made him sneak out one night and go to a dodgy casino and lose all the money in his wallet. On the way home, she'd decided it would be fun to get to the house through other people's gardens rather than walking along the pavement like boring people, and they'd skinned their hands and knees climbing walls and tripping over flowerpots. At one point they'd been caught in a security light, and a window had opened, and someone had shouted at them.

Back at the house, Anna had collapsed on the sofa in the dimly lit drawing room, but Tam had perched on the chair opposite, and frowned at her, and said, 'I'm not really comfortable with trespassing, Anna.' As if he'd been anticipating a whole week of sneaking into other people's properties.

When she'd repeated this to her sisters, of course, it had become a catchphrase. 'Do you think Tam would be *comfortable* with that, Anna?' *Ha ha ha.*

She turned away from the view.

Downstairs, she found Rod already up – or maybe he hadn't been to bed. He was wearing the same clothes he'd been in last night, sitting at the table staring at the map of Faida.

'Where might he have bedded down overnight?' was the first thing he said to her. 'If you were a small boy ...'

Anna joined him at the map. It was on the tip of her tongue to tell him that Freddie was on her boat, that he was fine, that she could take Rod to him now and then the Clarkes could leave and Rod could go to the police back in Manchester and tell them everything about the accident. Anna herself, of course, would be arrested too – for kidnap. For attempted murder. But she couldn't care less about that.

The important thing was that Penny suffered for what she'd done.

For killing seven people.

The grief, the crippling grief, hit Anna afresh as it did every few minutes, still, two years later. She wanted to double up with her arms around herself, as if it were a physical pain she could alleviate in a physical way. She wanted to scream. To run through the house ripping down curtains and hurling breakables to the floor. To pummel Rod's shoulders as he sat there hunched at the map.

She wasn't going to tell him about Freddie.

It wasn't just Penny who deserved to suffer.

'I can't think of anywhere,' she said bleakly. 'The search was really thorough, Rod.'

Tap tap tap.

Norman Hoodlum was perched on the door handle, looking in at her through the glass doors. Anna sighed. 'All right, all right, I'm coming.'

Rod looked up at her in puzzlement.

'Sorry, I was talking to the crows.'

She returned to the kitchen for the mealworms and some bread, and then, instead of going back into the extension, she opened the front door of the farmhouse. Norman flapped onto the drystone wall that separated the outside space of the extension from the traditional farmhouse garden. Like most farmhouses, the front door was hardly ever used for coming in and out of the house, and had a similar purpose to the glass doors in the extension: a means of accessing the garden.

Daphne and the little ones joined Norman on the lawn, and soon all four crows were pecking about for mealworms.

Broc used to squat with them on the grass, seeing how near they would come. Once, Norman had actually taken a piece of bread from his hand, early one snowy morning when he must have been really hungry. But the feat had never been repeated.

Not for want of trying. She could see Broc now – it must have been early spring, because the daffodils under the study window had been coming into bloom. He'd been leaning back against the wall there, arms folded as he watched his beloved crows, bemoaning the fact that Norman wouldn't feed from his hand again.

'Crows are wary of humans,' Anna had consoled him, 'because of all the ill treatment they've had down the centuries. It's nothing personal.'

'But Norman knows I wouldn't hurt him! He knows we're friends. He brought me that stone!'

One day, Norman had arrived at the open front door of the farmhouse and dropped a wet stone on the step before marching across the lawn and jumping up onto the wall to await his food. Broc had swooped on it. 'Look! He's given me a present!' The stone had been smooth and oval and pure white, like some of the others in Broc's collection. Broc had been sure that Norman must have seen him arranging his stone collection on the picnic table by the front door, and decided that an appropriate gift for Broc would be a nice white one.

The stone incident was open to various interpretations, but Broc was convinced that it was an example of a corvid 'reciprocating' and bringing a gift to their feeder friend.

There were documented cases of this happening. A little girl in Seattle had a whole lot of objects brought to her garden by the crows she and her mum fed – mainly shiny bits of metal or glass. Her favourite was a little pearly heart. Once, her mum had dropped the lens cap of her camera when out in the neighbourhood. A crow had brought it to their bird bath, rinsed it, and left it there.

'Was the stone a present?' Anna said softly now, and Norman glanced up at her, for all the world as if he understood but was keeping his counsel.

Slowly, she went back into the kitchen, and then through to the guest living area.

Rod was still at the table.

'Would you like tea or coffee?' Anna asked. 'And what do you fancy to eat?'

When she returned with his coffee, Penny was also sitting at the table and Sergeant Stewart was standing by the door, as if unwilling to come any further into the room. Rod was haranguing him.

'Where have all the local people gone who were here yesterday?'

'They're on Grulin – there's a small chance he could have been swept there by the current.'

'Where's that?'

'It's a small uninhabited island just to the south of here,' Anna explained, setting down her tray with the cafetiere, milk jug and mugs.

Sergeant Stewart came across to the table, and Anna said, 'Would you like a mug of coffee?'

'That would be great, thanks. The three of us are heading back to Balnaban, the abandoned village, and then we'll do another sweep of the centre of the island and the forts on the coast. The local searchers will be back this afternoon.'

'Why can't some of them search this other island and some search here?' Penny demanded.

'The fishermen who are transporting them are out in the Sound, searching out there this morning. They'll bring the folk back to Faida once –'

'So they're looking for a body,' Penny said briskly. 'That's what you're saying.'

How could she say that so calmly? This was *her own child*.

Anna turned to the policeman. 'There's still hope we'll find him alive and well. Isn't there?'

He nodded. 'There's always hope.'

Rod was in tears again.

'People come here on boats, on their own boats, don't they?' said Penny. 'Sailing boats? What if some psycho rolled up when Freddie was on the beach?'

'*Oh Goddd!*' Rod wailed, pushing back his chair and lurching to his feet.

Penny gave him an impatient glance. 'We have to face the possibility that someone has done him a mischief.' And she looked straight at Anna. 'The searchers should look for disturbed soil. I'm guessing the sandy soil around the beaches is easy to dig in? If someone's murdered him –'

'How can you say that?' Rod groaned, walking to the windows and back. 'How can you sit there calmly suggesting that someone might have *murdered him*?'

'Now then, folks,' the policeman hurried to intervene. 'That's very, very unlikely, in a place like this.'

'You get psychos everywhere,' said Penny grimly.

'I'm a psycho!' trilled Alfie, running into the room and jumping up onto a chair. 'Can I have scrambled eggs, Anna?'

'Of course you can. What would the rest of you like? Sergeant, would you like some breakfast before you go back out there?'

'No, thank you, I've eaten. I'd better get going.'

Anna returned to the kitchen to make the scrambled eggs. She could take some eggs and bread to Freddie and make him scrambled eggs on toast too. And then she'd bring him back. She found she was quite looking forward to Rod's reaction when he saw Freddie, safe and well after all.

She wondered what Freddie was doing now. Maybe he would be reading. He was obviously a very brave boy. But still, he must be frightened. How could he know, really, what Anna's intentions were?

She'd feed the Clarkes their breakfast and then go and get him.

When she served the scrambled eggs, Rod absently pushed his plate to one side untouched, still intent on the map. He was asking Anna about the buildings at the harbour when Alfie whined, 'They're slimy!'

He was poking his fork in the eggs.

Penny snapped at Anna, 'I told you that Alfie needs his scrambled eggs *well cooked!*'

'They're all slimy, Mum!'

'Yes, I can see that, darling.'

'Sorry,' said Anna lightly. 'I'll make you some more, Alfie.'

'*I don't want eggs now!*' Alfie screamed, pushing his plate away and bursting into tears.

'Alfie, mate.' Rod went round the table and picked him up in his arms, rocking him like a baby. 'I know it's a tough time. I know we're all worried about Freddie, but we have to eat to keep our strength up – eh, Mum?'

'Can you get him some cornflakes?' Penny glowered at Anna. 'I'll find you a tissue,' she told Alfie, standing up and flouncing past Anna, trailing the scent of citrus behind her.

'I'm sorry,' Rod muttered. 'We're ...' He looked down at Alfie's head, which was buried in his shoulder. 'We're all completely stressed out.'

'Well, of course you are.' Anna put Alfie's plate back on

the tray. 'I'll get your cornflakes, Alfie, and then I'm going to have another look for Freddie over on the other side of the island.'

Rod, tearing up again, just nodded.

20

PENNY

enny stood at the landing window and watched Anna scuttle from the back door of her accommodation to the Land Rover, a canvas bag in her hand. What was she up to now? Had Penny's hints to that idiot cop about disturbed ground prompted Anna to rethink, to decide to move Freddie's body? Did she have overalls in the bag or something? Maybe a spade already in the Land Rover?

Penny would have liked to have followed her – difficult on foot, but the island was so small she would surely find the vehicle eventually.

However, she had other priorities just now.

Rod was downstairs putting on his boots. He had decided to go and help the cops search the abandoned village again. He had promised he wouldn't say anything yet about the accident, he wouldn't distract them from their task of finding Freddie, but Penny didn't trust him to keep his word. Freddie being missing-presumed-dead was really messing with Rod's head. Once he was with the cops at the ruins, getting all emotional about Freddie, who was to say he wouldn't start shooting his mouth off like he'd done to Anna?

Penny jogged down the stairs. 'I'll go with you. And on the way we could check the café. I know they searched it yesterday, but isn't it quite likely Freddie could have sneaked in there last night and still be there? All that food on offer would be quite a draw for him.'

Rod nodded numbly.

'Come on. We mustn't give up hope! Where's Anna?'

Rod waved a hand at the window. 'Gone off to the other side of the island to look there.'

'Right, well, we need keys to the café. Where would she keep them?'

'We can't leave Alfie on his own.'

'He'll be fine. I'll lock him in.'

'You should stay with him.'

'Okay, okay, I'll stay!' *God!* 'Can I trust you to search the café properly? You know what you're like. You swear blind you don't have any clean pants, and then I find three pairs in your drawer.'

'Of course I'll search it *properly!*' He walked towards the door.

'Aren't you forgetting something?'

He turned, his face blank.

'The keys.' He really was completely hopeless. 'Come and help me look in Anna's accommodation.'

While Rod searched the kitchen, Penny ran upstairs. The first door she tried was a kid's room – Broc's or the dead Calum's, she supposed – and the next was an old-fashioned bathroom with one of those massive enamel baths. The third was what she assumed was the master bedroom, a large corner room with a view out to sea. The furnishings were old-fashioned – a big wooden bed, an antique chest of drawers. On top of this was one of those old mirrors with three small drawers in the base. The first contained mobile phone and Kindle chargers. The second had what she was looking for.

A tangle of necklaces and bracelets.

Good-quality stuff, mostly silver, in an unfussy style that Penny could have predicted Anna would favour, although she hadn't seen her wearing any jewellery. That bangle was probably antique, with what could be garnets set into it. And she seemed to like pendants. There was quite a variety to choose from – polished stones, Celtic designs, an enamel bird, a trio of what looked like real, natural pearls. But the locket would be best.

Penny pulled the sleeve of her fleece down over her hand and picked up its chain, shaking it to free it from the others. Hopefully it would hold photographs of Tam, Calum and Broc, but even if not, it was distinctive, with a design of forget-me-nots inlaid into the polished silver in green and blue enamels.

Penny unzipped her fleece pocket and dropped the locket inside.

In the other pocket, she had the envelope.

She looked around the room and, out of curiosity, opened the panelled doors of the fitted wardrobe, careful still to use her sleeve over her hand. The division wasn't equal – two-thirds of it was devoted to Anna's outfits and only a third to those of her husband. Partner. Whatever. Whose clothes consisted mainly of casual, outdoorsy stuff. There was one solitary suit.

She had a pang of doubt.

Nearly two years after his death, would she really still have all his clothes in the wardrobe, when she could have taken them all to charity and gained full use of the space for her own stuff?

She crossed the room to the en suite.

One toothbrush in the mug on the glass shelf above the sink. But if he was away on a trawler, presumably he'd have taken his toothbrush with him.

Back down in the kitchen, predictably, Rod still hadn't found the keys.

'They're probably somewhere in here,' Penny said. 'Keep looking. I'll check the other rooms.'

She found the study through a door off the kitchen. It was a very small room with just a desk and chair and shelves, on which there was a run of handily labelled boxfiles. Most of them were business-related, with labels like 'Shop: Invoices' and 'Creel Cottage: Repairs etc.'. But there were seven red files at the end of the shelf with the labels 'House', 'Utilities', 'Holidays', 'Insurance', 'Merry Dancer', 'Medical', and 'Important Stuff'.

She took down 'Important Stuff'.

On top was a letter from 'Woods for the Future' thanking Anna for notifying them of her husband Thomas Gillies's death and assuring her that his name would be removed from their membership list. She flicked through the papers underneath. Similar letters from a range of organisations, and then several copies of the same two documents.

Death certificates for Thomas Gillies, aged 41, and Calum Gillies, aged 12. In both cases, the 'Antecedent cause' of death was 'Motor vehicle accident'. For Thomas Gillies, the 'Disease or condition directly leading to death' was 'Traumatic brain injury' and for Calum it was 'Acute internal haemorrhage and organ failure'.

So she was right.

She smiled, and quickly returned the file to the shelf.

In the kitchen, Rod was on his knees, peering into the cupboard under the sink.

'Oh, for crying out loud! She wouldn't keep keys in there!' And then she saw them: a row of hooks on the wall above the old pine dresser with keys dangling from them.

Wordlessly, she pointed.

'Ah.' Rod began poking at the keys, examining their

labels. 'Here we go!' As if the discovery was all his. 'Handily labelled "Café". I'm off, then!'

'There's probably Wi-Fi in the café. Take your phone, and call me if you find him.' There was no mobile reception on the island. 'Well, get going, then!'

While Rod was dithering, looking in his jacket pockets for his phone, Penny raided the pantry. She grabbed two large packets of crisps, a bag of salted peanuts, a family-sized bar of Dairy Milk and a Tupperware container with what looked like homemade millionaire shortbread squares in it. Rod looked at her in puzzlement as she passed him, but she didn't bother trying to make up an excuse to explain what she was doing. She hurried up the stairs in the guest accommodation to the boys' room, where Alfie was playing games on the iPad.

'Have they found Freddie yet?' His small face looked even more pinched than usual.

'No, darling, I'm afraid not. Now, Mummy's busy because of Freddie, so you have to stay in this room. But as a special treat for being a good boy, I'm going to allow you to eat as much as you like of this lovely food! Look, millionaire shortbread!'

Belatedly, it occurred to her that Anna might have put something harmful in the millionaire shortbread squares with the intention of feeding them to the boys. But no, that was very unlikely. And Alfie had seen them now – if she told him she'd changed her mind and he couldn't have them after all, that might well precipitate a tantrum, which could scupper everything.

The homebakes were probably fine.

Alfie's eyes widened when he saw how many were in the box, and widened again when she brandished the huge bar of chocolate.

'But you must stay in this room, okay?'

He nodded vigorously.

'If you do, you can keep all the food. But if you don't, it will be taken away, and you will have to eat *only* healthy food for two months – no crisps or nuts, and nothing with chocolate in it allowed. And I'll know if you move, because Anna has hidden cameras in the corridors so she can check on what the guests are up to.'

'I'll stay *right here*, Mum.'

'Good boy.'

Downstairs, she shrugged on her jacket and changed into her walking boots in the hall. Then she found a pair of rubber gloves in Anna's kitchen, folded them into her jacket pocket, and left the house. She had studied the map of Faida last night, so knew she could make better time to the harbour by cutting across the fields instead of walking along the little single-track road, as Rod would be doing. She didn't want to get to the café before him, but if she overtook him, she could always hide in a bush or something until he appeared.

21

ANNA

'I saw dolphins!' was the first thing Freddie said when Anna opened the cabin hatch. He was kneeling on the bench seat behind the table, looking out of the window. 'There were three big ones and one little one! They were jumping out of the water and everything! Auntie Ursula's going to be well jealous – dolphins are her favourite animal.'

Anna came down the steps and put the bag on the tiny galley worktop. 'Wow, you were lucky.' She could have bitten her tongue, but Freddie smiled round at her.

'Do they not usually come so close in to the shore?'

'Not usually. They must have been putting on a display especially for you.'

Freddie wrinkled his nose, as if to say *I'm not five years old, you know*, and Anna smiled. 'Actually, they do come close in quite often, chasing fish into the shallows.'

Freddie nodded, as if satisfied now with this truthful response, and went back to his observation of the sea. On the little ledge under the window, a tiny plastic figure was standing, turned to face out of the window. One of Broc's? She didn't think so.

'I've brought some eggs and bread and butter and tomatoes. Would you like scrambled eggs on toast? With tomatoes on the side?'

'Yeah, okay then.'

'How did you sleep? I hope you –' She hoped he what?

But Freddie was shrugging. 'Fine. I was nice and warm, and I pigged out on Coke and biscuits.'

'Ah, so maybe you're ready for some proper food, then?'

'Maybe.' He picked up the tiny figure and pushed it into the pocket of his jeans, then bumped down on the bench seat to sit properly at the table.

Anna got a bowl from the cupboard and began cracking the eggs into it.

'After breakfast,' said Freddie, 'can you show me how the boat works? Can we go out for a sail?'

What?

He really wanted to do that? Or was this a ruse of some sort? She didn't think so. She didn't think his enthusiasm was faked.

'Well, no, sorry. After breakfast, I'm going to take you back to your mum and dad.'

Freddie's face fell, and Anna couldn't help staring at him. None of this was normal. He really didn't seem to be traumatised at all. Wanting to go out for a sail, for God's sake!

'How about I show you round the boat, though, before we eat?'

'Yeah!' Freddie crowed, jumping up.

'First of all, you should put on a life jacket. We'll both put one on, in fact.' She retrieved adult's and child's orange life-jackets from the locker opposite the galley. 'Put your arms through here, and then it zips up the front ...'

They started in the cockpit.

'This is where most of the action happens,' explained Anna. 'The wheel, obviously, is for steering the boat.'

Freddie jumped round behind it.

'We're riding at anchor, so I'm afraid we're not going anywhere, Freddie. But if we were going for a sail, the first thing we'd need to know would be the wind direction. We have a gadget for that – you see the little windmill thing on top of the mast? That sends a signal down to the display in the cabin, which tells you the wind speed and direction and other things. But it's a lot easier to just look at the red ribbon tied to the shrouds. You see what direction it's blowing in?'

'Towards us.'

'That's right. When a boat rides at anchor, it always faces into the wind. Today, the wind's coming from the west, so if we were leaving the bay –'

'I want to go for a sail!' Freddie turned the wheel back and forth.

'Not today, Freddie. Your mum and dad will be worried about you.' She gave him a very brief lesson on points of sail and how to tack into the wind, and then she showed him the cunning storage under the cockpit benches.

'What's *that*?' Freddie pointed into the locker she'd just opened. 'Is that a gun?'

'It's just a flare gun. For firing flares up into the sky if we need help.'

'Can I hold it?'

Anna took the little red pistol out of the locker and handed it to him. Freddie grasped it with a grin. 'Cool!' He aimed it up at the sky. 'Can we fire it?'

Anna almost laughed. 'No, I don't think that would be a good idea.'

She took the flare gun from him and returned it to the locker.

Back in the cabin, she cooked the eggs and put a couple of slices of bread into the toaster, while Freddie wandered around opening lockers and peering out of the windows, no doubt in the hope of seeing more dolphins. Anna was stirring the eggs in the pan when she became aware of Freddie standing at her elbow. Of a photograph appearing in her line of vision.

Of a boy smiling up at her from the cockpit of *Merry Dancer*. The wind was tousling his hair, and he was zipped into the same life jacket Freddie was now wearing. It was one of the photos from the little album they kept in the drawer under the table.

'Is this Broc?' Freddie's voice was very small.

The smell of the eggs cooking lodged at the back of her throat, and Anna pushed the pan away, off the heat, and backed into the bulkhead behind her.

'Anna?' Freddie was staring at her. 'Are you something to do with the bus people? Is that why you took me? Is that why you were going to push me over? *Anna?* Is this Broc?' He held the photograph out to her.

'Yes,' she said.

The next thing she knew, she was sitting on a step, gripping the rails on either side, staring at the varnished teak floor. She felt a pressure on her arm and looked up. Freddie had one small hand on her sleeve.

'Is Broc, like, his nickname? Is his real name Calum?'

Anna could only nod.

'He's the boy who died on the bus.'

She finally managed to swallow, to speak. 'We called him Broc because – it means "badger" in Gaelic. When he was very little, when he was just starting to crawl, we thought he moved a bit like a badger.' Low to the ground with a sort of rocking motion. He'd been so pleased with himself to be moving independently at last. He would gurgle and chuckle as he went, and she and Tam would be laughing too, one or other of them kneeling on the floor, arms held out to him.

Freddie was still holding the photo out to her, as if it would bring her comfort.

She took it from him and gazed, properly, into her son's face.

His sun-bleached hair was flopping into his eyes. Surfer-dude hair, as Tam used to tease him.

This photograph had been taken a few days after his twelfth birthday.

Three months later, he was gone.

And now he would always be a twelve-year-old child. There would be no more for him than this. He'd just been beginning to shoot up in height, and Anna had had to buy him new shoes and clothes every few weeks, or so it seemed. Sometimes, when his jaw set in a certain way, or he smiled indulgently at her, or whipped back his arm to send a stone skimming across the surface of the water, she'd had a glimpse of the man he would be.

The man he would never be.

'The boy who died was called Calum *Gillies*,' said Freddie. 'Not MacLean. And he was from Glasgow. But when I saw this photo, I recognised him, from the photographs on the internet of all the people who died on the bus.'

'I kept my maiden name of MacLean when I got married,' Anna said. 'Tam's name was Gillies, and Broc – Calum – took that as his last name. After the accident, after Tam and Broc both died, I ... I couldn't cope with all the people who wanted to talk to me. My sisters took over dealing with the authorities and the police and the journalists. My eldest sister Deirdre and I own her house in Glasgow jointly.' It had been bought for them by their parents, as somewhere for Deirdre to live but for Anna to have a stake in, because, running the family business on Faida with Tam, she was missing out on the chance to own property and build up equity. 'That was the address we gave for Tam and Broc, so people wouldn't come here to Faida bothering me.'

Which meant there had been nothing connecting Anna MacLean of Faida, in the public eye, to the Thomas and Calum Gillies of Glasgow who had died on that bus, although local people, of course, knew what had happened. Anna had not attended the trial. After Penny and Rod had escaped justice, she had realised that she could use this apparent lack of connection to her advantage. She could lure the Clarkes to Faida, and they would have no idea who she was. They would have no idea that Anna's husband and son weren't just away, but had died on that bus two years ago.

Tam had an old school friend in Newcastle with a son of Broc's age. They'd planned to attend a football match with the other father-and-son pair and also to try go-karting. Maybe see a film, do the sights. Broc had really been looking forward to the little holiday, their 'city break' as he kept calling it. They had boarded *Venus* at the harbour, and Anna had hugged them both and told them to call her when they got there, and Broc had squirmed out of her arms, embarrassed to be hugged by his mum in front of the young guys on the boat. She had waved them off, already counting the hours to their return.

When she had spoken to the Clarkes about Tam and Broc, telling them that Tam was away on the trawler and Broc on the mainland, she had allowed herself, just for the few seconds in which she spoke the lies, to pretend that this was true. That one day she would be back at the harbour to meet them off the boat and kiss Tam full on the lips and pull Broc into a proper hug, whether he liked it or not.

'You were going to kill me to get back at Mum and Dad?' Freddie had removed his hand from her sleeve and was staring at her with those big blue eyes.

Anna remembered Penny on TV after the acquittal,

standing straight and tall on the steps of the courtroom in her designer navy blue suit and white silk blouse. Vindicated. Blameless. Grace under pressure. She remembered that little smile she'd given her lawyer before he'd read out their statement.

There had been something in that smile that had prompted Anna to get in touch with Herik Patel, the driver who had testified against the Clarkes at the trial. He'd told her all about Penny making the drivers use magnets to disable the tachographs, and regularly rostering them on for twenty-hour days. He had put her in touch with some of the other drivers, without telling her their names, and they had spoken to her or messaged her anonymously, unwilling to put their heads above the parapet and risk prosecution themselves, or at the very least, the loss of their livelihoods. They had confirmed what Herik had told her, although she hardly needed it. She had believed him.

If Penny walked into the cabin right now, Anna would –

She would what?

She would do nothing.

She'd been living in a fantasy. She had plotted and planned, going through the motions of her life with just one end in view, shutting herself off from everything except that. Nothing had mattered but Tam and Broc and her grief for them, the anger that had raged through her like a cleansing furnace when she thought of the Clarkes and what they had done. What they had got away with.

She saw now that her grief and the need for revenge had been all-consuming – everything else had seemed unreal, including Freddie and Alfie.

Especially Freddie and Alfie.

It had all been a house of cards. Everything she had done had all been for nothing, because she hadn't factored in the one thing that had condemned all her carefully laid plans to failure from the start.

The fact that she could never kill anyone, let alone an innocent child.

In the moment she'd unlocked the lazarette and looked into Freddie's eyes, reality had come roaring back. It had been like waking from a nightmare.

She rubbed her face. 'You know when you play make-believe? When you pretend you're Superman or Dracula or a zombie? I was playing make-believe, only I had somehow convinced myself it was real, that I was actually going to go through with it.'

How could she have done that, though? How could she have hardened her heart, convinced herself that exacting revenge, making the Clarkes pay for what they had done was all that mattered?

How could she?

Freddie nodded. 'You're not a psycho like me. You're a good person. You're just sad.'

'Yes,' she said simply. 'I am sad.'

She looked down at Broc.

There was something cruel about photographs, about the trapping in two dimensions of a person you had loved, a real person who had once breathed and walked about and laughed and cried and lived, someone you could talk to and listen to and touch and love. Here was Broc, frozen in one of the moments of his life, and here was Anna in a moment of hers. They had no way of reaching one another, and never would again.

Broc.

They'd been so self-contained, the three of them, so self-sufficient. Anna had often marvelled at the biology that had created their little family unit, at the way half of what made Anna and half of what made Tam had come together in their little boy. It was more bizarre, when you really thought about it, than anything in Broc's science fiction books. She often used to look at him and try to work out which bits were from her and which from Tam. He had Tam's athletic body shape and shock of blond hair, and Anna's thin-bridged nose. Maybe her smile. He had both Anna and Tam's tendency to laugh at things you shouldn't really laugh at – when Freddie had put the dead crab down Alfie's neck, for example. If Broc had been there, he would have had a hard time concealing his amusement.

They had had so many in-jokes and little bits of catch-phrase only they would pick up on. One had been '*Cheeeeer* up!' It had originated in Anna's story about a building site she had to walk past on her way from her halls of residence to university in Edinburgh. Every morning, a group of men on scaffolding would call down to her, 'Cheer up, love, it might never happen!'

Did they expect her to go around with a grin fixed to her face or what?

The fourth or fifth time it had happened, Anna had stopped and smiled and shouted back, 'Actually, I *am* quite cheery today, because I've reported you to your manager for sexual harassment, and that's him watching you in that car.' Of course it wasn't, but the man's face had been a picture, giving Anna her cue to shout up at him: 'Cheer up, love, it might never happen!'

Broc and Tam had both loved this story, and once when they were in Edinburgh they'd made Anna take them to the place, now a nondescript block of flats, like tourists visiting the scene of some momentous happening in history.

'There should be a plaque here,' Tam had suggested. '*On this spot on 21 April 2000, Anna MacLean kicked ass for the sisterhood.*'

'Even when you smile, you look sad,' said Freddie.

She saw that he was offering her the tiny plastic figure, holding it delicately between his finger and thumb. She recognised it from all the *Star Wars* films she'd watched with Broc.

'Yoda,' she said.

'He's kind of lucky. His ears are nice and spiky if you touch them.'

Anna obliged. 'They are quite spiky, aren't they?' She stood. 'Thank you.'

''S okay.' He pushed Yoda back into his pocket.

'You know, Freddie, you're a very empathetic boy. Do you know what that means?'

'Uh, no.'

'It means you can tell what other people are feeling. And when you saw I was sad, that made you feel a bit sad too, didn't it?'

He nodded warily.

'That means you certainly are *not* a psycho. Psychopaths don't do that. They only care about themselves.'

'Mum says I'm really selfish. I do things like run away, and I'm always rude to people and kicking off and stuff.' He turned away to the galley worktop and poked the spatula into the eggs.

'And why is that? Why do you run away, Freddie?'

A shrug.

Anna waited.

'Mum and Dad argue all the time. Mum covered up making the drivers keep working when they were too tired, and Dad gets upset, but then Mum's all, "You went along with it." At school –' A deep intake of breath. 'There are these boys – in my class – who keep saying Mum and Dad are murderers.' A sob escaped. 'And I can't say anything back because *they are*.'

'Oh, Freddie.' Tentatively, Anna put her hands on his shaking shoulders.

'I'm really sorry they killed your husband and your little boy,' he gulped.

'It's not your fault.' Anna rubbed his back. 'I was so, so wrong to do what I did to you. None of this is anything to do with you. It must have been very scary, when you were locked up in the hold.'

He pulled away from her, dragging his sleeve across his face. 'It was okay.'

'Of course it wasn't *okay*!' Now she was the one who was sobbing.

'No, it was. When I kick off, sometimes Mum locks me in a cupboard. It's really small and I have to crouch over with my legs squashed up. I can't sit up or lie down, and my back gets sore. In a boat, there's a lot more room.'

Had she heard that right?

'Your *mum* locks you in a *cupboard*?'

'Only when I kick off. You won't tell her I told you? If you do, I'll get in trouble.'

Anna made her voice calm. 'But that's not right, Freddie. She shouldn't do that, no matter how much you "kick off".'

'I know ... But Mum says she has to discipline us because Dad can't be bothered.'

'What else does she do to "discipline" you?' asked Anna slowly.

'She hits us. Mostly me.'

He unzipped the life jacket, wriggled out of it and lifted his sweatshirt.

A mass of yellow and purple bruises disfigured the pale, smooth, little-boy skin of his torso, especially across his ribs. Anna couldn't stop the gasp escaping from her mouth.

'That looks very sore,' she managed.

Freddie shrugged. 'They're sore for a while, but then not so much.'

Anna remembered the bruise she'd seen on his arm. She had assumed Alfie had caused it, but she'd been wrong.

It had been Penny.

Freddie, his face going red, pulled his sweatshirt back down and held onto the hem, as if worried she would make him show her again.

She didn't know what to say. She couldn't think what to do, what to say, to this brave child.

'What does she hit you with?'

What kind of question was that? What did it matter?

'The potato masher. Sometimes the big serving spoons.'

Oh God.

She imagined Penny striding across the kitchen. Opening the cutlery drawer. Freddie and Alfie backing away, knowing what was coming ...

'But when she does the discipline, she always gives us a treat the day after, like she takes us out for burgers or buys us a new Xbox game or something. And Mum only gets angry because I'm a psycho. She's at her wits' end with me.' It was Freddie speaking, but it was Penny's voice she was hearing.

'You are not a "psycho", Freddie!'

'I am. When I kick off, it's like there's something inside me that takes over. And it makes me really, really angry, as angry as Mum, and I want to smash up the whole world.' He stared up at her.

'You have every right to be angry.'

'Sometimes I hit Alfie.'

Anna let out a shuddering breath. 'People who are hurt often lash out. I think there's something deep inside us that, when we're hurt, sort of takes over and makes us fight to defend ourselves. So sometimes, when we're very scared or miserable, we can't really control what we do.'

Freddie frowned and stared off, as if thinking this over.

'What about your dad? Does he know that your mum hurts you?'

'If Dad sees the bruises, Mum says I've been fighting again. Or I've fallen down the stairs. Or out of a tree.'

How could Rod possibly be in blissful ignorance of the fact that his wife was abusing their children?

Freddie was staring at Anna, still clutching the hem of his sweatshirt. 'Me and Alfie will probably have to live with Mum if there's a divorce.' His lips wobbled, and he muttered, so quietly that Anna could hardly hear him, 'I don't want Dad to go.'

'Oh, *Freddie!*'

Anna had been wrong in every possible way. She had thought that, by taking their child's life, she would be visiting on the Clarkes the hell that she'd been trapped in for the past two years. But how could they love Freddie and do this to him?

They couldn't.

They couldn't care about him at all. Not really.

All Anna had done was heap abuse on abuse.

Now Freddie had bent to pick up the discarded life jacket. He set it carefully on the table and flicked a look at Anna. 'Can I ... Can I stay here a bit longer? When you take me back, Mum will be *really* angry that I went off with you on your boat.' His little chest was heaving, his eyes were desperate, but he managed to keep his voice almost level to say, '*Please* can I stay here a *little* bit longer? I won't make a mess.' He pressed his sleeve to his face.

'Of course you can.' Anna took two steps forward and, very gently, took him in her arms. She murmured softly, like she would to Broc, and stroked his hair, and after a moment's resistance he hugged her back. She felt his little fists closing tight on the material of her jacket.

And maybe it was something to do with her new, strange state of heightened sensation, but it was as if Broc came back to her, just for a second. For a second, he was here with them in the cabin, and she heard him say, *Mum. You have to help them.*

Anna spoke, clearly and calmly:

'I'm going to sort this out with your parents. For now, you'll stay here. But Freddie, I promise you, this is going to stop. I'll make sure your mum *never* hurts you again.'

As she came to the top of the little grassy hill, a view opened out ahead of her: there was the sea, and the harbour, and the ugly buildings in front of it. From the harbour, the road snaked up past the café and into a little copse of trees.

Halfway between the copse and the café, Rod was striding along, focused straight ahead, on a mission.

Penny lay down flat on her stomach in the grass.

She'd let him get inside first.

The grass was unpleasantly wet, and pungent with the smells of the earth and crushed growing things. She thought of the lawn at her parents' house, that perfect green sward that couldn't have been more different from the tussocky stuff she was lying on now. Dad mowed the lawn not every week or two, like the neighbours, but every single day. 'It's maybe just a council house, but that doesn't mean we shouldn't take a pride in it.'

Rod strode to the door of the café and felt in his pockets.

Oh, for goodness' sake! He hadn't lost the key, had he?

No. He was inserting it in the lock.

And now he was disappearing inside.

Penny stood, and hurried down the slope and across the road. She could see him inside, just standing there like the useless great lump he was. She pushed open the door, and he turned, mouth dropping open.

'Pen! What are you doing here? Where's Alfie?'

'With Anna. I thought I'd come and give you a hand.'

He nodded. 'It doesn't look like anything's been disturbed in here. No sign of him having raided the shelves for food, or stuff to bed down on.' Absently, he reached out and fingered a scarf.

'You've looked through the whole place, have you?'

'No, I just got here.'

'Okay, you look here and in the café, and I'll check out the back premises. Presumably there's a kitchen and storeroom and so on.' She walked down the length of one of the aisles to the counter, which seemed to double as the serving area for the café. There was an empty display stand with glass shelves for cakes and things, and a coffee machine and other gadgets on the worktop against the wall. A door at the end of the worktop presumably led to the behind-the-scenes parts of the operation.

As Penny slipped behind the counter, Rod walked past and into the café area, where he stood staring at the tables and chairs as if expecting Freddie to suddenly spring up from under them. Swiftly, Penny pulled on the rubber gloves from her pocket and opened the rear door. This led to a small hallway. To the left was another door.

The kitchen.

She began opening cupboards and soon found what she was looking for: a good, heavy-bottomed frying pan. She took it back out to the counter area and set it on the worktop. Then she retrieved the envelope from her pocket and placed it on the shelf under the counter. Peeling off the gloves, she chucked them down on the worktop next to the frying pan.

'Rod?' she called. 'Come and look at this!'

He bounded through from the café. 'What?'

She pointed.

He came round behind the counter to stand by her side.

'That envelope. Look at the name on it. Thomas Gillies. Isn't that one of the people who died on the bus?'

Rod stared at the envelope.

Pick it up, pick it up.

'Thomas Gillies?' she repeated. It was like dealing with a not-very-bright child.

'But what ...' Finally, he picked up the envelope. 'Thomas and Calum Gillies lived in Glasgow. The address on here ... This is Anna's address.'

Duh.

'Oh my goodness!' Penny was forced to exclaim. 'Thomas Gillies ... he must be *Tam*!' She stared wide-eyed at Rod.

'No. He can't be.'

'Can you remember the wife's name? Thomas Gillies's wife?' It was the kind of thing he *would* remember.

Rod had gone white. 'Yes. It was Anna. But it's a common enough name ...'

'Her husband isn't really off on a trawler, Rod! He's dead! And Calum Gillies must have been her son!'

'But ... No, no. That makes no sense. If Anna knows it was our bus company, why did she invite us here? Why has she been so nice to us?'

Penny couldn't help laughing. 'She's not being *nice* to us! Don't you get it? She catfished you! She's lured us here intending all along to – to do whatever she's done to Freddie as revenge for her own son dying on that bus!'

'Oh my God.' He looked at the envelope in his hand and then at Penny.

'You *idiot*, Rod! Your little friend Anna has *killed Freddie*! I knew straight away there was something off about her, remember I tried to tell you she was creepy, but oh no, you wouldn't hear a word against her, would you?'

For a long moment, Rod stood staring at her, frozen in place.

'*Freddie!*' she repeated, blinking rapidly and gulping, as if choking back tears.

And suddenly Rod was in her face, he was growling at her, 'You can drop the act, Pen! You don't care about Freddie, and you never have!'

'Of course I do! It's *your* fault if he's dead!'

'So it was me, was it, determined to squeeze all the hours I could out of dog-tired drivers?'

'You went along with it!' Penny yelled right back at him.

'And now it's come back to bite us. Just like I always knew it would.' He laughed wildly, head thrown back as tears streamed down his face, mouth open, eyes scrunched shut. 'I told Anna it was karma. Little did I think it was *her*! *She's* our karma, Penny!'

'Oh, don't be so stupid.' She stepped away from him in disgust. There were strings of saliva between his top and bottom teeth, reminding her, suddenly, of that nasty crow.

And then his mouth snapped shut, and he advanced on her. 'You care *nothing* for Freddie! Alfie, yes, maybe a little, but not Freddie! He isn't "accident-prone"! He doesn't get into fights all the time at school!'

She backed up.

He grabbed the front of her jacket.

Their faces were inches apart.

Penny held his gaze. She knew he wouldn't hurt her. She knew he didn't have the guts. He didn't even have the guts to come out and accuse her of what he must surely have suspected for years, that her disciplining of the kids was sometimes the old-fashioned physical sort, which he would no doubt say was 'child abuse'. The truth was, of course, that she wouldn't have had to resort to extremes if he'd been any use as a father.

Sure enough, he slowly released her, and slowly turned away, and walked stiffly, like an automaton, back into the café area, where he just stood, staring at nothing. And then he suddenly collapsed, dropping to a crouch on the floor, his face in his hands.

Penny put the rubber gloves back on and picked up the frying pan. It was good and heavy. Rod was making so much noise whimpering in his usual disgusting, snotty way that she was pretty sure he wouldn't hear her, but still she slipped off her trainers. Then she tiptoed across the shop and into the café.

She moved quickly up behind Rod where he crouched on the floor and, putting all the weight of her body behind it, whacked the frying pan as hard as she could against the back of his head.

There was a satisfying crack, and he tipped forward and lay still.

Standing there holding the frying pan, Penny felt a bit like a character in one of the boys' cartoons. There should be birds twittering round Rod's head. Silly music in the background. Only Rod wasn't about to come back to life for the next episode.

Was he dead, though, or just unconscious?

She was lucky in that there was no blood. No need for her to clean herself up. She'd planned on immersing herself in the sea, clothes and all, if blood spatter had landed on her, and claiming, if necessary, that she thought she saw Freddie in the water.

But there would be no need for that.

Unless she had to hit him again and this time burst a blood vessel. Head wounds could be messy.

'Rod?' she said experimentally.

No response, but that didn't mean anything.

She needed to be sure he was dead. She squatted at his side and hauled on one of his arms, pulling him over onto his back. His eyes goggled up at her through the lenses of his glasses, which were rather miraculously intact, but she was pretty confident there was no one in there. To make sure, though, she pinched his nose closed with one hand and his mouth with the other, and glanced at her watch. She'd give him ten minutes. If he was still alive, that should be ample time for him to suffocate.

It wasn't very comfortable, squatting on the hard floor, and not at all easy to change position while maintaining her grip on both nose and mouth. She wouldn't have put it past Rod to suddenly open his eyes, suddenly struggle, making her have to hit him again.

But no.

He had been remarkably cooperative throughout. What was the phrase?

Nothing in life became him like the leaving it.

She snorted.

She shouldn't laugh. But really, when she thought of the years and years she'd had to put up with him sucking her dry – she wouldn't have been human if she hadn't been enjoying this just a little.

No more Rod.

Her heart leapt at the thought. Finally, she was free of the millstone round her neck!

Oh dear – she was full of clichés today. But as she stared down at his dead face, she did actually feel physically lighter. Surely it was a dead face now, if it hadn't been seconds after frying pan had met cranium?

She sat back on her haunches.

She could leave him here, but any murderer worth their salt would make some effort to conceal the body of her victim. Fortunately, he was a lightweight in every sense of the word, and Penny might not have had the physique of a professional dancer, but she was reasonably strong and toned from all those years of Pilates and salsa. She had no trouble dragging him across the café, through the shop and into the kitchen.

'Right then,' she said briskly.

Rod looked back at her blankly.

'Right then, Roddie-boy.' She had never called him that in her life. She giggled again as she unzipped the pocket of her fleece and removed the locket. Hmm. The chain would be broken, wouldn't it? She looped it over the catch on the window and pulled to snap it. Then she closed Rod's right hand around the locket and pushed the envelope into his pocket.

Her fingerprints would be on the envelope, of course, so when she returned with the cops, she'd have to 'notice' it and, mad with grief – she could say she thought it could be a suicide note – snatch it from his pocket.

She adjusted it so that the end of the envelope peeped out.

Okay.

Someone who'd just committed a murder would lock the body in, wouldn't they?

'Where did you put those keys?' she demanded of Rod.

He stared back at her glassily.

She supposed it was the shock, making her want to talk to him. To pretend this hadn't happened. Looking down at him, at what she'd had to do, suddenly she wanted to weep. It just wasn't fair that she'd had to do this, to put herself through it, and all because of that bloody woman.

But she had to stay strong.

She pushed her hand into one of his jacket pockets and, through the glove, felt the metallic coldness of the keys. Rod continuing to cooperate. She took one final look at him – even in death, he was wearing his usual expression of bafflement, which gave her the fortifying hit of anger she needed – and shut the kitchen door. One of these keys on the ring must lock it.

Again, first time lucky.

Damn, there *was* blood. Smeared on the terracotta tiles in a snail's trail where, presumably, his head had dragged along the floor. But that was good. That was excellent, in fact. There was just enough for Penny to 'notice' when she returned with the cops, but not so much that a desperate murdering psycho couldn't conceivably have missed it in the blind panic that had overwhelmed her.

In the shop, she left the keys on the counter and took a moment to think.

What had she touched in here with her bare hands?

Nothing, apart from the door handle.

Outside, she scanned the road and what she could see of the harbour before turning and pulling the door closed with her gloved hand. Then she wiped the handle with the edge of her fleece and ran across the road and up the grassy slope on the other side. She'd return to the guest house the way she came, cross-country. But what about the gloves? Could they have left microscopic traces of yellow rubbery stuff behind at the crime scene? Maybe she should throw them in the sea. The salty water, presumably, would wash away her DNA.

Yes, that was a good idea.

After about quarter of a mile, she crossed back over the road and ran down a sandy track into a grassy dip where a couple of those massive shaggy Highland cows were grazing. They lifted their heads to stare at her, and she left the track to give them a wide berth. The track continued through a gap in one of those loose stone walls to a little beach.

She jogged towards it, turning the gloves inside out as she went, pulling the ends of the fingers all the way out. At the beach, she picked her way across some flat rocks to get further out to the deeper water. Then she chucked the gloves as far as she could into the sea.

Done and dusted.

She stood, hands on hips, watching the gloves bob about in the water. Hopefully the current would carry them away, but if they did wash up on a beach on Faida, the chances were that no one would think anything of it. Just two more items of ocean litter.

23

ANNA

Anna parked up in the farmyard next to the other Land Rover. Its presence, she supposed, meant that the policemen using it must be here. Good. She would tell them everything after she'd talked to Rod on his own and made him confront what Penny was doing to the kids. She was sure he must already be aware of it, on some level. He must know that whatever excuses she was coming up with to explain Freddie's injuries were nonsense.

Her hands were still gripping the steering wheel.

She took a long breath and relaxed them, let go the wheel, wiped a sleeve over her face. Like Freddie had.

She had to stop crying.

She'd hardly been able to see to row, to drive, for the unceasing flow of tears. Her throat was raw with them. Her eyes tight-feeling and sore.

Freddie.

Broc.

Tam.

What a terrible, terrible place the world was.

But she'd left Freddie apparently happy enough in the

cosy cabin with more junk food than he could eat in a week and a good supply of reading matter, little Yoda standing on the table at his elbow. He'd been pathetically grateful when she'd told him he could stay on the boat for as long as it took Anna to sort things out with his dad.

Could she sort this out with Rod? Could she persuade him to leave Penny, take the boys with him, tell the police what she'd been doing to them? He was evidently as weak as water where Penny was concerned. If he didn't immediately agree to divorce Penny and make sure she never saw the boys again unsupervised, Anna would tell the police, social services, whoever, that Rod couldn't be trusted to keep the boys safe. She would get the boys taken away from both parents.

The proof of what Penny had done, what Rod had allowed her to do, was all over Freddie's poor little body.

A tap on the window made her jump.

'Anna? You okay?' It was Bill, his gentle face full of concern as he frowned through the glass at her.

Bill had been so kind over the last two years. Unlike most of her friends and family, he hadn't tried to make out that there was an expiry date on grief. There had been no *Don't you think it's time you ...* Or *I think it would be good for you if you could ...*

She made herself smile. She made herself nod.

'Tired,' she said as she got down from the vehicle and, as if to demonstrate the truth of this, stumbled slightly.

He steadied her. 'Come on inside, and we can have a cup of tea. There's still no trace at all of the boy, I'm afraid.'

Anna made no response to that.

'Anna. You're running yourself ragged. The searchers will be back this afternoon, and, it is to be hoped, my fellow police officers not long afterwards. They had to leave for the mainland. There has been some trouble in one of the hotels, a rampaging stag party who seem to have –' He stopped, evidently belated remembering that he wasn't meant to gossip about police matters. He pursed his lips and raised his eyebrows in a tacit admission that he knew what she was thinking and, yes, he was a terrible blether.

Something in that expression, in the self-deprecating good humour, reminded her, fleetingly, of his cousin.

Of Tam.

Good old Bill from the good old Old Bill, as Tam used to call him. He'd been one of Tam's closest friends as well as his cousin.

The thought opened the floodgates again.

And now Bill's long arms were around her, and he was pulling her tight against his chest.

'Sorry,' she choked, pulling away and using her sleeve again. She needed a tissue. 'Bill, I – Is Rod here? Rod Clarke? I need to speak to him. And then I need to speak to you.'

'Rod Clarke is not in the house, no.' He patted her arm. 'Come and have that cup of tea. And I would venture to suggest that you have not been eating properly.' He smiled down at her. 'You may remember that I do a mean fry-up.'

Anna couldn't help smiling. There was something very reassuring about Bill, the measured, considered way he spoke, the old-fashioned courtesy with which he treated people, as if he weren't quite of the present day, as if he should be living in a previous, gentler age. When he lapsed into a modern colloquialism, it always used to make Anna laugh. She suspected he did it deliberately for that reason.

They'd crossed the yard to the back door to Anna's part of the house when the door to the guest accommodation flew open.

Penny.

Anna's heart started to bump.

She wanted to run at her, to push her hard to the ground and stamp on her stomach, on her face –

'Where are the other cops?' Penny rapped out at Bill.

'They had to attend an incident on the mainland,' he said smoothly. 'They will be back as soon as they can manage.'

Penny folded her arms, her sour mouth a long line. 'What "incident" can possibly be more important than a missing child? And where are all the bloody searchers? And how can you –'

'Where's Rod?' Anna interrupted coldly.

Penny blinked at her. 'What?'

'Where – is – *Rod*?'

'I thought I saw him leave with you?'

'Well, he didn't. I need to speak to him urgently.'

'Hmm.' Penny's expression of anger changed. 'Wherever he went off to, it's odd that he isn't back yet.' It was almost as if she was trying not to smile.

When Penny had returned inside, Bill raised his eyebrows at Anna. 'Does it strike you that Mrs Clarke's behaviour is ... somewhat erratic? One moment, she's behaving as if nothing is wrong, surfing the internet, humming away to herself, as if her child being missing is no real cause for concern. The next, she's berating us for not making enough of an effort to find him.'

Aha. This was good.

If the police were already looking at Penny askance, they would be all the more receptive to what Anna had to tell them about the abuse.

'As if she's playing the part of a worried mother for show,' said Anna.

'Aye,' said Bill. 'That's exactly it.'

'I don't think she cares about Freddie at all.'

Bill visibly blanched at that. 'Oh, now, Anna.'

'You just said she's behaving as if nothing's happened. And I don't like the way she is with Alfie.' In fact, she hadn't seen any evidence of Penny abusing her younger son, but

Freddie had said *She hits us.* 'Bill, can I ... This might sound weird, but I don't think she should be left alone with him. I need to talk to Rod, and then I need to talk to you about her.'

'But you are surely not suggesting that Penny Clarke could have something to do with Freddie going missing?'

'Just watch her is all I'm saying.'

Bill frowned, and nodded, and headed after Penny through the door into the extension.

Anna entered her own part of the house, going straight to the Aga in the kitchen and pressing her cold hands to one of the hotplate lids. She could smell citrus, acid in the back of her throat. Penny must have been in here, making herself at home.

She strode across the room and flung open a window, trying not to breathe too deeply.

So where would Rod be? Had he gone to check the holiday cottages again? He had a fixation about Freddie hiding out in one of them.

The keys were kept on a row of little hooks above the dresser. She went over and checked them. All the cottage keys were present and correct, but the spare set of keys for the shop and café was gone.

When she got to the shop, she parked the Land Rover on the forecourt and, scooping up her own set of keys from the well under the dashboard, strode to the door.

But it wasn't locked.

Pocketing the keys, she went inside and called, 'Rod?'

There was always something a little unsettling about a shop that was closed. The aisles of goods waiting to be bought seemed different, somehow, like props on a stage set. Again, she could smell citrus. But if Penny had been here with Rod, why had she not said? Why had she pretended not to know where he was?

It was cold in here in the gloom. Anna zipped up her jacket as she checked the café, but of course he wasn't there – if he had been, he'd have heard her call out. And the place had that indefinable quality she was very used to, by now – a stillness to the air, maybe, that told her there was no one else here.

But the door behind the counter to the back premises was standing open. And there was something on the floor. A long smear of red leading through the doorway, as if someone had dragged a mop through a spill of tomato soup.

She stepped into the little hall. 'Rod?'

Silence.

The red smear disappeared under the door to the kitchen.

She hesitated, her hand on the door handle, and called out again: 'Rod?'

No response. And the door, oddly, was locked. She found the right key on the ring and unlocked it.

From the floor, Rod stared up at her.

There was a strong smell of urine.

'Oh no. Oh no, oh no,' she found herself babbling as she dropped to her knees beside him and did all the things she'd learned to do on the first aid course she and Tam had completed before moving to the island.

First, she watched his chest to see if it was rising and falling.

No. It was completely still. But to make sure, she bent close to his nose and mouth and listened, waited for a puff of air against her cheek.

Nothing.

She was just going through the motions. It was obvious he was dead. But she felt for a pulse on his neck anyway.

Nothing.

Which meant she should attempt CPR. For five minutes, she administered chest compressions, keeping her elbows locked and her shoulders above her hands as she'd been taught. Thirty chest compressions, two rescue breaths into his dead mouth. Thirty chest compressions ... Her hair kept flopping forward onto him. She found a hair tie in her pocket and caught it back in a ponytail.

She needed to call 999. They would send a helicopter. She would have to turn on the router so she could use the Wi-Fi –

As she got up, she saw something familiar.

A chain, dangling from Rod's right hand. It was the antique silver chain from her locket. She recognised the fastening with its tracery of engraving. And inside his hand, she could see the top of her locket.

Why did Rod have that?

And then she saw what was poking out of the pocket of his coat. An envelope with the end of a word visible – 'llies'. She pulled it out.

Tam's name shouted at her from the snowy white paper:

Thomas Gillies

And the pieces started to slip into place.

Had Penny done this?

She had wanted a divorce, but that would have meant financial disaster. And then last night, maybe Rod had told her that he'd had a heart-to-heart with Anna and decided to confess everything to the police.

At some point, maybe just this morning, Penny must have found the envelope and realised who Anna was. She must immediately have suspected that Anna had kidnapped Freddie, or worse, out of a desire for revenge. But instead of confronting Anna and demanding to know what she'd done to Freddie, or going to the police, she'd seen an opportunity to get rid of Rod and pin the blame on Anna?

Was that what had happened?

But would any woman, even Penny, really have been prepared to sacrifice her own child's safety, possibly his life, in order to dispose of an inconvenient spouse?

Yes.

Penny must be capable of that.

How else to explain Anna's locket in his hand? The envelope in his pocket? Penny's strange claim, in front of Bill, that she'd seen Rod leave with Anna?

Penny was setting her up. The perfect scapegoat. For all Penny knew, Freddie was dead. What more credible than that Anna's revenge plan had consisted of taking the life of Penny's husband as well as that of her son, just as Penny had killed Tam and Broc? When Rod's body was discovered in a locked room to which Anna held the keys, together with the envelope, presumably Penny would 'realise' who Anna was, and explain to the police that she and Rod were the owners of Peaks Transit and that Thomas and Calum Gillies had been killed in a terrible accident on one of their buses.

She could just imagine Penny's play-acting.

Oh God! Anna is Thomas Gillies's wife?

And Freddie would tell the police that Anna had tried to kill him.

There was no way they were going to believe Anna over Penny. Anna would go to prison for Rod's murder, and Penny would get off scot-free, just like she'd done before. With no Rod to at least act as some sort of buffer, Freddie and Alfie would be left completely at her mercy. She would probably explain away the bruises on Freddie as 'Anna must have done that', and Freddie might well be too scared of her to tell the truth.

Anna had to outwit her somehow.

And fast.

Penny was presumably waiting until it became obvious that Rod was missing too.

Where can he be? I'm sure he left with Anna, but she's saying he didn't ... They drove off in the direction of the harbour – I think he said something about searching the shop and café. But then Anna came back without him. It's so weird that she's saying he wasn't with her!

Anna had maybe a couple of hours before Penny led the police here. She had to make sure that Rod's body wasn't where Penny left it.

She shoved the envelope into her own pocket and eased the locket on its chain out of Rod's clammy fingers, wincing at their dead touch on her skin. The chain was broken, as if Rod had clutched it as they struggled and snapped it off her neck.

As if Anna wouldn't have noticed! As if she'd have left the body here clutching her own locket! But maybe Penny's plan was to paint Anna as so mentally unstable that she wasn't thinking clearly. In reality, thoughts were flashing through Anna's mind at lightning speed. She hurried out to the storeroom at the back of the building and fetched the red trolley that they used to move bulky deliveries. It had four sturdy wheels and low sides made of a metal mesh that could drop down. She positioned it next to Rod's body. He was skinny. He wouldn't be too heavy.

She undid the pins securing the side and end mesh sections and lowered them flat. Then she pushed her hands under Rod's armpits and heaved.

His head lolled back, his hair brushing her jeans, and she shuddered. She could see, now, where the hair at the back of his head was matted with blood, although there didn't seem to be a huge amount of it. Penny must have hit him with something from behind. Dragged him in here.

She managed to heave him up onto the trolley and

manoeuvre him centrally on the flatbed part. Then she put up the sides and secured them with the pins. The end section, with his legs flopped on top of it, was more of a problem. She had to haul the legs off it one by one and hook them over the side sections, as if he was manspreading, exposing his damp crotch. When she'd secured the end section in place, somehow she couldn't bear to leave him in that undignified pose. She moved his legs back together so they flopped over the end section at the knees. His glasses had been knocked askew. She set them straight on his nose.

There was a pool of urine on the floor. That and the blood would have to be cleaned up. She got a mop and bucket from the cupboard and filled the bucket at the sink. She would just use water for now – the smell of bleach or some other cleaning product would alert the police to something having happened here.

She dipped the mop into the water, squeezed it out on the wringer and swished it over the tiled floor. There was something about the mundane action, which she'd performed in this room a hundred, a thousand times, that threw into terrible contrast the man's body slumped there on the trolley, legs dangling over the end of it, one hand flopping over the side as if pointing out, 'You've missed a bit!'

She gasped.

And now it wasn't Rod's body she was seeing but Broc's, lying so still on the hospital bed, his head swathed in a bandage, his face swollen almost unrecognisably. Fiona holding one of her hands, Mum the other. None of them speaking, as if Broc's silence, his endless silence, now, was something too vast, too terrifying, too completely unimaginable for any of them to touch with words of their own.

She doubled up, sobs heaving, supporting herself on the mop, unable to stand straight, let alone do this. She couldn't. It was –

Mum. You have to. For Freddie and Alfie.

She knew that Broc was not speaking to her.

She knew that it was her own mind summoning his voice.

But it let her take a breath, and stand up straight, and find a tissue in her pocket to wipe her face. It let her keep moving the mop on the floor, rinse it in the bucket, repeat, as she followed the trail of blood to the café. It let her clean the bucket in the sink and hold the mop under the running tap until the water ran clear.

She returned mop and bucket to the cupboard and got an old towel to dry the floor with. After doing that, she chucked the wet towel into the cupboard and shut and locked it.

Fingerprints!

But it would have been strange if her fingerprints *weren't* all over everything here. That was fine. But the mop and bucket being wet ... Might the forensics people notice that?

They wouldn't, if this wasn't a crime scene.

Quickly, Anna checked all over the floor, the walls, the tables and chairs in the café, looking for spatters of blood. But there was nothing that she could see. The wound evidently hadn't bled much. The damage, she supposed, had been mainly internal, as his brain had whacked into his skull with enough force to kill him.

What about the weapon? What had Penny hit him with?

She couldn't waste time on that now.

Later.

Now, she had to get Rod out of here. She went to the front door of the shop and peered out. There was no one in sight. The searchers were due to come back this afternoon at some point, but it wasn't even twelve o'clock yet. And Bill was at the house with Penny and Alfie.

She hurried back into the kitchen and pulled the trolley with its terrible burden through the hall and down the step. There was a small area of tarmac at the back of the building between it and a couple of old stone sheds. Behind the sheds was a wide path that led up along the rocky shore to the cliffs.

Should she bring the Land Rover round?

But would she be able to get Rod up into it? It had been hard enough hauling him onto the much lower trolley. No – best not to waste time attempting something that might not even be possible.

She pulled the trolley across the tarmac and onto the path. The ground was peaty here and easily eroded, so they kept the heather cut back and the grass short to create a path three or four feet wide in order that people's feet weren't continually wearing away the same ground, but in places the grass was eroded down to spongy, peaty mud with wormlike heather roots through it. Soon Anna was sweating with the effort of pulling the trolley through the boggy bits and up the steeper inclines. Rod's body jiggled as the trolley wheels bounced around on the uneven ground, making it seem horribly animated. His long legs jumped and kicked, as if he were trying to help her propel the trolley along.

Overhead, seagulls wheeled and cried. There were more standing absolutely still on the sunlit rocks further out, right at the tip of Laimrig Head, bright white conical shapes against the grey and orange background. The orange was from a lichen that made the rocks seem to glow in the sun.

Ack-ack-ack-ack one bird suddenly called out, as if laughing at the silly humans.

The tang of the sea was in her nostrils, on her lips.

She could hear the waves slapping the rocks, the hiss of spray.

The path climbed gradually until it came to a clifftop bench positioned to afford a view into a wet, dingy V-shaped crevasse in which kittiwakes nested. Not that the cliffs here were particularly high, but they were high enough to give the birds protection from predators. They were making their usual racket, the *kittiwake kittiwake* calls bouncing around off the rockfaces. There was an acrid, salty stench from their droppings.

The rocks on this part of the shore were thick slices stacked one on top of the other and then tipped vertically, millions of years ago, by some primeval geological force. The sea had then eroded the softer rocks to create these clefts that seemed to stab into the land.

There was a steepish slope beyond the bench, but then the ground flattened into a grassy semicircular dip, like a corrie on a mountainside, before plunging into the cleft. Anna and her sisters sometimes used to lie in that grassy dip in late summer, after the young birds had fledged, cloud-watching and listening to the sea. At high tide, the sea came roaring into the cleft, funnelled to the point of the V, where it crashed with tremendous energy, sending spume high into the air.

From the bench or the path, you couldn't see into the point of the V. Even in the grassy dip, you had to crawl right to the edge to look down on the white foam swirling there.

If she could tip Rod down into the cleft, he wouldn't be visible from the land or, probably, from the sea. And the tide might carry him away.

She pulled him off the trolley and, with the help of gravity, dragged him down the grassy slope into the dip quite easily. On the flatter, tussocky ground, she had to roll him, pulling one arm and one leg sharply to flip him over onto his side, onto his front, and then grabbing the other arm and leg to flip him onto his other side and then onto his back.

It was almost like they were children, playing a strange game.

She avoided looking at his face, but she could imagine his voice suddenly booming: *All right, Anna, your turn to be the body!*

His glasses had come off and were lying in the grass. For a moment she stared at them stupidly, the thought flitting through her mind that he wasn't ever going to need those again. She used a tissue from her pocket to pick them up and throw them into the cleft.

At the edge of the dip, the wind funnelled upwards, making her shiver. The birds on their nests screamed at her, and some took fright, taking off and gliding out over the water.

She looked down. In the deepest recesses of the crevasse, the rocks were blackened and dank, perpetually wet even at low tide, the sun never penetrating that far.

'Over you go,' she muttered to Rod. 'Sorry.'

She couldn't use her pulling technique now, unless she wanted to tumble over with him. She had to push him from behind, shoving at his shoulders until his upper body tipped out into space and he was falling –

But he wasn't.

His jacket had caught on a jagged bit of rock, so he just dangled there, suspended over the cleft about four feet down from the edge, long legs and arms swaying out and back, out and back above the drop. She couldn't reach him to free the jacket.

Damn damn damn!

She'd have to go back to the shop for something, a broom handle maybe, something she could use to push him off that bloody rock.

As she trundled the trolley back down the path, her breath sobbed in her throat and the wind tugged at her hair, freeing strands of it from the tie to slap at her face. She was pushing the trolley across the tarmac to the back door when she heard it.

The sound of an engine.

A vehicle was coming down the road, although she

couldn't see it from here. The other Land Rover. Bill and, no doubt, Penny.

She abandoned the trolley and dived in at the open back door, fumbled in her pocket for the keys, unlocked the cupboard door and hauled it open, grabbed the broom, pushed it shut and ran out of the building, pausing only to shut the back door behind her. Then she was flying, across the tarmac and up the path. The shop building and the sheds were between her and the road. They wouldn't have seen her.

But they'd have seen the Land Rover.

They would know she was here. And it was only a matter of time before Penny realised what had happened and they came looking.

24

PENNY

As they drove down the road towards the harbour, Penny saw that Anna's Land Rover was parked on the café forecourt. Excellent. She was very unlikely to have gone into the kitchen – possibly wasn't in the building at all. But the presence of her vehicle here would be another strike against her.

'Anna must be here,' she said unnecessarily as the cop pulled in next to the other vehicle.

Alfie scrambled out of the back seat as soon as they'd come to a halt. 'Can I get an ice cream?'

'The shop's not open, darling. Alfie, come back here!'

Alfie ignored her, running across the forecourt towards the door.

She and the cop got out.

'I'm sure Rod mentioned that he might search the shop – he thought Freddie might have come here looking for food. Which makes sense.' She made her lip tremble. 'First Freddie, and now Rod! Why did we ever come to this godforsaken place? And what's Anna doing here?'

'I imagine that she is searching for your son,' said the policeman coolly, and started across the forecourt.

Alfie was jumping about like a lunatic. Penny grabbed his sleeve, bent over him and hissed, 'Get back in that Land Rover *now* unless you want to get in *big* trouble!'

He scuttled away to the vehicle.

Penny hurried after the cop. 'Anna's been acting very strangely. I definitely saw Rod with her in her Land Rover before – why would she lie about that? There's something off about her.'

'Aye, well, Anna has had a lot to deal with in the past couple of years.'

Haven't we all!

She pushed ahead of the cop to open the door, just in case any of her fingerprints or DNA remained on the handle. 'Rod! Rod, are you in here?'

She walked through the shop to the counter.

'What's ...' *that on the floor*, she had been going to say, but in fact she couldn't see the smears of blood. Maybe they'd dried a similar colour to the terracotta tiles and weren't so visible now? She couldn't very well get down on her hands and knees and peer at the floor.

'Your husband is not here, Mrs Clarke,' said the cop, coming out of the café area and heading back along one of the aisles towards the open door.

'What's through there?' said Penny rather desperately, indicating the closed door behind the counter.

Closed?

Hadn't she left it open?

'The kitchen and so on,' he said.

Penny called out, 'Rod?' and opened the door into the little back hall.

The kitchen door was standing open.

She walked inside and just stood, staring down at where

Rod's body should be, her heart slamming in her chest. Was it possible that he hadn't been dead after all? It wasn't as if Penny was used to this sort of thing. It wasn't as if she'd ever killed anyone before. Maybe she should have held his nose and mouth for longer?

Had he come round and –

No.

Of course not.

'There's no one here,' said the cop behind her.

'I can see that,' she couldn't help snapping.

Anna.

That bitch had been here and moved the body! But she couldn't have taken it far. Her vehicle was still parked out front. Unless she'd put the body in the Land Rover, driven somewhere, concealed it, returned ...? But then why come back to the scene of the crime?

No. The chances were that she was even now trying to hide the body somewhere nearby. Catching her in the act of doing that would be the icing on the cake.

'Can we search out the back? What's out here?' She pushed past the cop, out of the kitchen and into the little hall. At the end of a short corridor was a door with frosted glass, which obviously led outside. She strode to it and tried the handle, expecting it to be locked, but it came open to her hand.

Anna had been this way.

She stepped out onto an area of tarmac with a row of green, blue and brown commercial-sized wheelie bins against the wall of the building and crates stacked against a couple of sheds alongside one of those little pull-along platform trucks with mesh sides.

'Rod?' she called. '*Rod!*'

From behind one of the sheds, Anna appeared with a yard brush just as the cop came out of the building behind

Penny. Casually, as if nothing had happened, Anna propped the brush against a stack of crates and came over to them.

'I've been checking around here again,' she said.

The cop nodded.

Penny strode across the tarmac and flung open the door of the nearest shed. It smelt strongly of oil and contained gas cylinders and more crates and stacked boxes. The shed next to it contained tools and an old sink and wooden pallets, two of which held shrink-wrapped soft drink cans.

No Rod.

She turned on her heel and marched back across the tarmac to where the cop and Anna were standing, Anna staring at her with an inscrutable expression on her face, the cop bent over his radio.

But what could she say to him?

The body was right here! She's hidden it somewhere nearby! You have to look for it!

She could tell him that she'd found out that Anna's husband and son had been killed on the bus, and Anna must have lured the Clarke family here bent on revenge ... That she must have killed first Freddie and now Rod ...

But the cop would ask: *And when did you find out who Anna was?* If Penny said she'd known for a day or so, he would ask why she hadn't come to the police with the information immediately, given that Freddie was presumably in peril. And if she said she had only just found out, he would think it a bit of a strange coincidence that her husband had gone missing at exactly the same time. No, it would be much better if she let the information about the bus crash connection come out organically in the course of the investigation into Freddie's and Rod's disappearances.

Would Anna try to land Penny in it for Rod's murder?

Well, good luck with that! Anna would have to tell the

cops everything, about luring the Clarkes here, about killing Freddie ... No. Anna would keep her mouth shut.

It was stalemate.

For now.

'I don't want you to get your hopes up, Mrs Clarke,' said the cop, returning the radio to the clip on his uniform. 'But there has been a possible sighting of Frederick on the mainland. It's probably a false alarm, but I'm going to investigate. I will, however, return as soon as possible.'

'How could Freddie be on the mainland?' Anna took the words right out of Penny's mouth.

The cop grimaced. 'The chances are that it's a case of mistaken identity. But you never know ... Neil Nicholson's just off Grulin and is going to call in at the harbour, pick me up and ferry me over to Campbeltown.'

'Can't one of your colleagues check out the sighting?' Penny said. 'Someone who's already on the mainland?'

'All other available officers are attending the incident I referred to. We're a bit thin on the ground at the moment, unfortunately. But as I say, my colleagues and I will return to Faida as soon as possible, and the local volunteer searchers will be arriving at some point this afternoon.'

Penny looked at Anna, and Anna looked at Penny.

25

ANNA

Anna stood in front of the shop watching Bill stride off down the road to the harbour. When he'd gone, there'd be no one else on the island – just Anna, Alfie and Penny. She wanted to run after him, stop him, tell him –

Tell him what?

That she'd catfished Rod and lured the Clarkes here? That she had Freddie locked up on *Merry Dancer* and had just dumped Rod's body into the sea at Laimrig Head? *But I didn't kill him – Penny killed him and tried to set me up for it! Honest!* Bill would have no choice but to arrest Anna and cart her off to the police station. She'd be charged with Rod's murder and Freddie's kidnap, and Penny –

'I know who you are,' said Penny behind her.

Anna turned. 'Evidently.'

'Mum!' Alfie raced towards them from the second Land Rover. 'Did you find Dad?'

'Does it look like it?' Penny growled. 'I thought I told you to stay in the vehicle?'

Anna stared at her, this woman who'd just murdered her own husband and coolly tried to make Anna the scapegoat. Who abused her children. Anna wanted to snatch Alfie up and run hell for leather with him after Bill.

But what good would that do? Bill would look at her in his gentle way and tell her to put the boy down, give him back to his mother ... And when she tried to explain everything, would even Bill believe her?

Probably not.

Penny stared back at Anna, her thin lips lifting in a slight smile, as if she could read her mind.

'Can I get something from the shop?' Alfie pouted. 'It *is* open. I saw you coming out of it.'

'No, sorry, darling. You can have something nice when we get back to the house.'

As Alfie skipped ahead of them, Penny hissed at Anna: 'And then we can talk.'

Anna walked numbly with Penny to the Land Rover she'd been driving. She felt like she was trapped in one of those dreams where you know something terrible is going to happen but you're powerless to do anything about it.

She had to think.

She couldn't go to the police.

So what *could* she do?

As she started the Land Rover and pulled out onto the road she knew so well, she tried to calm her racing brain, to form a plan, but Alfie kept wailing from the back seat about wanting his dad, and Rod's face was all she could see. Those dead fish eyes.

Very soon, Penny was going to tell the police about the bus connection, in order to scapegoat Anna for Rod's murder. The police would probably find the body, and its location would be another strike against her rather than Penny. It was very unlikely that Penny would have known there was a handy cleft in the rocks just there for hiding inconvenient corpses.

Anna would definitely be the prime suspect.

'Shut up, Alfie!' Penny suddenly yelled, and the boy immediately went quiet.

In the rear-view mirror, Anna watched him biting his lip, his sweet little goblin face anxious. Anna had to tell Bill what Penny was doing to her children. There was no question about that.

The sky had cleared and the machair was bright green in the sun, sparkling with a million tiny jewels as light hit the raindrops clinging to the grass. A pair of oystercatchers flew up as they passed. If she opened her window, she would probably hear a lark sing. And in this same world existed a human being called Penny Clarke, sitting here by Anna's side.

At the house, she parked in the yard and got out and walked round to Penny's door.

'You're not going to get away with this,' was all she could think to say.

Penny smiled as she got out of the vehicle. 'Oh no? Poor Anna. Poor mad Anna. Your husband and son were killed, and now you've killed Freddie and Rod – an eye for an eye, was that the idea?'

'Freddie's not dead.'

Penny seemed not to have heard her. '*You're going down for this!* There will be traces of your DNA on Rod's body, you know, wherever you've stashed it. And when I tell your friendly neighbourhood cops that we're the Clarkes of Peaks Transit, that you lured us here to get revenge –'

'Do that, and I'll tell them where the original duty roster is.'

That shut her up.

The idea had just popped into Anna's head from nowhere. And now the words were tumbling out of her. 'And *you'll* "go down" for killing *seven people!* Rod hid the original paper copy of the roster. He got it out of the recycling and hid it away. And he told me where.' She leant forward. 'So you'd better keep your mouth shut about me catfishing Rod, and you'd better forget trying to set me up for his murder, or I'll tell the police where that roster is. And I'll make sure the families of the other people who died on your bus know all about it, about how they died because you were determined to squeeze as much profit as possible out of your drivers, and then covered up what you'd done. They'll be out for blood. It'll be a media circus, and this time there'll be no wriggling out of it.'

'*Maybe not!*' Penny spat at her. 'But if I'm put away, it'll only be for manslaughter. *You're* going down for *murder!*'

'Oh, really? I'll tell the police that you killed Rod because he was about to come clean about everything. I'll tell them I only took Freddie to give you a taste of what I've gone through.' Freddie, of course, would tell a different story, but Penny wasn't to know that. Not yet, at least. 'Freddie's alive and well, if you're at all interested.'

Penny's lip curled. 'You expect me to believe that?'

'I don't care what you believe.'

'You might not actually have killed Rod, but what happened to him is down to you! If you hadn't lured us here, kidnapped our son, got in Rod's head – I bet you were *so* supportive, weren't you? *Yes, Rod, you're right, that's the only way you'll get closure, if you go to the authorities and confess everything.* Never mind that he'd be ruining the lives of *his whole family!* You left me with no choice. For the sake of the kids, I had to make sure he never opened his mouth again.'

As Penny looked at her, Anna could almost see the same

thought running through her head as was running through Anna's.

She'd made a huge mistake in telling Penny about that duty roster.

Penny had killed her own husband to keep him quiet. If she hadn't baulked at that, she was hardly going to have any scruples about silencing Anna, now that she'd revealed she knew where the roster was.

Desperately, Anna tried to distract her. 'For the sake of the kids? Don't make me laugh! As if you give a damn about them! You don't even care whether Freddie's alive or not! Don't you want to know where he is?'

And now Alfie was out of the car, wailing, '*Muuuum!*'

But Penny was walking away from them both, across the yard towards the garage. Anna shot a look at Alfie. 'Go inside, Alfie. The door to my bit of the house is open.'

And then she hurried after Penny.

'You don't even care what's happened to Freddie, whether he's hurt –'

There was a flowerbed against the garage wall in which catmint and roses were showing fresh young growth. The front of the bed was edged with small rocks from the beach. As if in slow motion, Anna watched Penny lift one, wheel round and come at her with it, lashing out at her head. But then suddenly Alfie was there, running to Penny, crying and pawing at her fleece.

Penny, hardly glancing down at him, whacked him away with her other arm.

Alfie screamed.

Anna didn't hesitate. She punched Penny as hard as she could in the face.

Penny made a wordless noise and fell to her knees.

Frantically, hands shaking, Anna felt in her pockets for

the key to the Land Rover. Where was it? Where had she put it? Had she dropped it?

Penny was trying to push herself up.

Anna took a couple of steps back. She knew Penny would have the upper hand in a physical struggle. She was bigger and stronger than Anna. She knew how to inflict pain.

Anna grabbed Alfie and ran.

26

What was she looking at? Bumpy rectangles, dark grey and light grey and pale pink. There was a tiny piece of twig lying diagonally on one of them. She could smell salt and something rotten.

She blinked. One of her eyes felt swollen, and the movement sent pain shooting across her forehead. When she gasped, much worse pain exploded in her head.

She closed her eyes.

Better.

She was lying on something very hard.

The cobbled farmyard. Yes.

That bloody island.

It was important to move.

Anna ...

The bitch had hit her. Concussed her?

She opened her eyes again. Turned her head to look at the back of the house. Slowly, she sat up. Stood, shakily. Put a hand to her face. The area around her left eye socket was tender.

But she couldn't have been out of it for long, because she

could see them, Anna and Alfie, silhouetted against the sky. They were right at the top of the grassy slope above the beach, a couple of fields away. Anna had hold of Alfie's hand. As Penny watched, Alfie slowed and stopped, dragging against the woman's arm. His piercing whine drifted back to Penny.

That bitch!

How dare she take Alfie!

What did she think she was going to do to him?

And fucking Rod! Not only had he kept the original roster, but he'd told Anna where it was! Thanks to Rod, she was now going to have to go after Anna and finish her off, when all she wanted to do was lie down on that comfy bed upstairs and pull the duvet over herself and go to sleep. It wouldn't be a huge problem to find that roster when she got home. Rod was unimaginative – he'd have hidden it somewhere stupid and obvious.

No, her problem was going to be catching up with Anna. Normally, that wouldn't have been an issue. But as things were ...

She took a few experimental steps across the yard, each one like a jackhammer on the inside of her skull.

But she could move.

If she had to, she could run.

ANNA

Alfie plomped himself down on a rock and really went for it, bawling, his fists pressed to his temples as if he wanted to pummel at what was inside his head. For a helpless moment, Anna just stood watching him, becoming conscious for the first time that her right hand was throbbing painfully. She glanced down at it. It was swollen, the knuckles bleeding. She must have hit Penny hard.

The noise Alfie was making seemed to reverberate off every surface and must surely be giving their location away to Penny.

'Shhh,' she said, sitting down next to him and putting her throbbing hand on the back of his neck.

He flinched away.

'Oh, Alfie, I know it's horrible, what just happened. But we have to get to Freddie. You want to see Freddie, don't you?'

'I – want – *Muuuum!*'

'Your mum isn't safe to be around at the moment.' At the moment? She was *never* safe to be anywhere near a child.

'You hit her!'

'Only because she tried to hit me with a big rock. If she'd

hit me with that, she could have killed me. I had to defend myself.' She wasn't going to sugar-coat this for him. She didn't have the luxury of time to be gentle. 'Your mum is a dangerous person. Freddie has told me she hurts him a lot. He showed me all the bruises on his skin.'

The bawling increased in volume, and he started shaking his head, and then he was jumping up away from her and running, not back the way they had come but across the grass in a different direction, seemingly at random.

Anna ran after him, caught the back of his fleece and pulled him to a halt.

'Alfie, I'm sorry.'

'I want *Daaaad*!' The turnaround would almost have been comical if it hadn't been so completely heartbreaking. But this meant that Alfie hadn't heard Anna and Penny talking about Rod's body? Or if he had, he hadn't understood? Or was it just too terrible a thing for his little six-year-old brain to encompass? The image came into her mind of Rod swaying above the chasm as she poked at him with the broom. Tumbling free. Bouncing off the rocks as if he were a daredevil engaged in some sort of extreme sport.

She bit down on hysteria.

'Alfie. We have to go quickly to Freddie. Maybe your dad is with him.' The terrible lie almost stuck in her throat, but she needed him to cooperate and hurry with her to Bàgh an Ear. Penny had probably heard him. She could be running in their direction right now.

At the thought, she looked behind them, but the rise of the ground prevented her from seeing back towards Engster.

'Dad is maybe with Freddie?' Alfie's voice wobbled.

'Maybe. Come on, now. You really don't want your mum to catch us when she's this angry, do you?' *Angry*. That was how Freddie had described Penny and was presumably the language she used to justify what she did to them. She told the boys they had made her angry, as if it was all their own fault.

Alfie shook his head, looking down at his trainers.

'It's going to be okay,' Anna said gently. She found a tissue in her pocket. 'Would you like me to wipe your face?'

After a brief hesitation, he nodded, turning his face up to her and closing his eyes in a trusting way that clawed at Anna's guts. She wiped his eyes, his nose, turned the tissue to a dry place and wiped his cheeks, his snotty upper lip, chattering the while about how Freddie was looking forward to seeing him and had been missing him, which she suspected was true, although Freddie would probably never admit it.

'Now, Alfie, I need you to run with me as fast as you can.' She shot a look back up the grassy slope. Still no sign of Penny, but she could be just on the other side of that low summit.

Anna had no plan other than to get off the island with the kids. To get them away from Penny and make sure they were safe, in the short term. In the long term – well, she would think about that once they were all on *Merry Dancer* and skimming across the sea to the mainland. She would take the boys to Fiona and Gareth in Oban. Tell them everything. Call Bill and, when he arrived at Fiona's house, repeat it all to him.

What else could she do?

Water. She needed a drink of water, and then she'd go after them.

In Anna's kitchen, she ran the tap and filled a glass and drank it down, thanking her lucky stars, as she so often did, for the quick mind she'd been born with, which had got her out of so many scrapes in the past.

Anna was heading across the island, not back in the direction of the harbour. Across to where her boat was moored? She remembered Anna talking about that to someone, the cops or the searchers or Rod. Her boat was on the east side of the island. South-east.

If Freddie really was alive, where better to keep him?

But why hadn't Anna taken the Land Rover instead of going on foot?

Silly woman.

What a shock she was going to get when she arrived on the other side of the island to find Penny there waiting! Penny was sure she'd have time to get out to the boat, get Freddie and set up an ambush before Anna and Alfie arrived.

She filled a water bottle from the shelf over the sink and

headed back out to the farmyard. Already her head was a lot better. She felt energised. Up for this. She could still turn this around if she played it right.

She opened the driver's door of the Land Rover. No keys in the ignition – it was too much to expect to be that lucky. She knew it was possible to hot-wire a vehicle, but had no idea how.

Maybe Anna had dropped the keys during their confrontation?

But a quick scan of the cobbles proved fruitless.

She returned to the kitchen, to the row of hooks on the wall above the dresser, on which hung an array of keys. They all had labels tied to them: 'Creel Cottage', 'Garage', 'Small Store'.

No Land Rover keys.

Dammit!

Where would she keep the spare keys to the vehicles? If she was anything like Rod, they'd be shoved to the back of a drawer somewhere, and it would take a major search of the whole house to locate them. When Rod had locked his keys in the car last year, it had literally taken Penny all day to find the spare.

Okay.

A change of plan was needed.

Think, Penny, *think*!

Water bottle in hand, she left the kitchen, crossed the big guest living space to the glass doors, pushed them open and shouted, 'Fuck off!' at the crows that were lurking in their usual sinister way at the edge of the decking.

Ow, her head!

She took a swig of water and headed off down the track to the beach. It was a gorgeous day now. The wind had dropped and the sun was shining. The sea was like a millpond. But my God, she'd be glad to see the back of this place!

At the big beach, she took the path that led over the grass to the smaller one and the little stone shed. When she turned the doorknob and pushed at the old wooden door, though, it didn't open. She shoved at it in frustration, and to her surprise it gave a little under her hand. It was just warped, she supposed, and sticking at the jamb.

She pushed hard, and it came suddenly open and she staggered forward, groaning as her right foot hit the floor and set the jackhammer off again. She grabbed a couple of oars from the rack on the wall and chucked them into the red inflatable.

At university, she'd done a bit of rowing – not on the team or anything, just for the exercise, but she'd been good at it, as she was at all sports. She'd enjoyed the mindlessness of getting into a rhythm and concentrating only on the power of her body, the buzz of the adrenaline, the boat zipping through the water.

This boat was a little squidgy under her hands, and if she'd had the time she'd have stopped to see if there was a pump. But it would serve her purpose well enough. The island was only a mile wide. It wasn't going to take her long, with the sea flat calm, to get round the south end of it to the cove where Anna's boat was. She might not beat Anna and Alfie to it, but she was confident that she'd get there before Anna was able to put the next part of her plan into operation, whatever that was.

Kill Alfie?

Perhaps Freddie was on the boat, but dead? Anna had said he wasn't dead, but she couldn't trust a word that came out of that madwoman's mouth. The thought of Alfie, her baby, in such danger almost had her panicking. But she had to keep a clear head.

She pulled the boat down the sand and into the water, and clambered aboard.

In other circumstances, this would have been enjoyable. The water was crystal clear and she could see right to the bottom, to the sand and the rocks with seaweed waving above them. The bench seat was a little damp from having been in that dank shed. Penny wiped it with a tissue and took up her position. As soon as she set the oars in the rowlocks, the technique came back to her.

The boat began to surge through the water.

Had Anna called the cops? Had she told them that Penny had tried to kill her?

No matter. The bruises on Penny's face would tell a different story. Penny would say that Anna wasn't in her right mind – which would surely be obvious given what she'd done to Freddie – and none of what she said could be believed. Penny would tell them that Anna had crowed about it, what she'd done to Freddie, what she'd done to Rod. And then she went psycho and tried to kill Penny and Alfie too. If the kids got through this, they'd fall in line with whatever Penny told them to say.

The boat was fairly bowling along now as Penny hit her rhythm, stretching over her knees, flipping the oars so the blades sliced into the water, pulling back.

She actually *was* almost starting to enjoy this – pitting herself against the elements, against that bitch, against the whole world. People were always doing their best to thwart her, but Penny always came out on top in the end.

She wasn't being big-headed. That was just the sort of person she was.

29

ANNA

Unlike Freddie, Alfie seemed fearful of the water. As Anna rowed, he sat very still in the stern facing her, little hands clutching the sides of the tender, eyes wide as he looked first one way and then the other at the sea all around them. A slight onshore breeze had got up since they left the beach and there was a bit more of a swell.

'The boat's moving!' Alfie suddenly yelled. '*Dad! Wait for us!*'

Anna turned to look. All that had happened was that *Merry Dancer* had drifted over her anchor and swung round, head into the wind.

'It's just the change in the wind direction. The boat has moved on its own. It's still anchored. It's not going anywhere. See? It's stopped now.'

'It's stopped now,' Alfie repeated softly to himself, his gaze still fixed on *Merry Dancer*.

'There's lots of nice food on the boat,' said Anna to distract him. 'Crisps and chocolate and cakes.' Were there cakes? Maybe not. 'Lots of nice unhealthy stuff! Unless Freddie's eaten it all.'

This raised a slight smile. 'Dad likes cake.'

Oh God. 'And what's your favourite unhealthy food?'

In a small voice: 'I had too much chocolate. I was sick.'

And then his goblin features were collapsing, and he was crying again, tears and snot running down his face, down his receding chin and onto his neck. Anna rested on her oars and found the damp tissue. She handed it over and he took it from her almost eagerly – but instead of using it, he just clutched it in one hand and closed his eyes, as if trying to distance himself from where he was and what was happening to him.

'Soon be there,' she said, although actually she was dreading their arrival on *Merry Dancer* and Alfie's realisation that Rod wasn't, in fact, on board.

They were safe now, at least, from Penny. Anna kept her eyes on the shoreline, but even if Penny were to appear there now, she couldn't hurt them. They were far enough out, and close enough to *Merry Dancer*, that they would reach the boat before she could swim out here.

As the tender approached the yacht, Alfie scanned the cockpit, the side decks, the bows. 'They're not here!' he wailed, staring at her in horror.

What did he think? That she had lured him away with a lie, meaning to do something terrible to him?

'Freddie's in the cabin,' she hastened to reassure him. 'Look! There he is!'

Thank God, Freddie's face had appeared at one of the cabin windows. He grinned and waved, and as Anna brought the tender up to the stern, Alfie was suddenly scampering up the ladder and over the hatch to the lazarette, through the cockpit and onto the side deck, where he knelt to stare in at his brother, a smile transforming his features. '*Freddie!*'

Anna quickly secured the tender, wincing at the pain in her hand as she manipulated the ropes. She hurried to unlock the cabin hatch, and then Alfie was half-falling down the ladder in his haste, jumping up on Freddie, who laughed and put his arms around him in a hug. 'Hi, Stinkypants!'

'Is Dad here?'

'Uh, no. Why would –'

'Okay, boys,' Anna interrupted with false brightness. 'We're going for a bit of a sail, so life jackets on. I think there should be a smaller one in here that will fit you, Alfie.' She opened the locker opposite the galley.

Freddie put Alfie down and frowned at Anna. 'Why are we going for a sail?'

'Slight change of plan, Freddie.' She held out the life jackets to him. 'Can you help Alfie put the smaller one on? Once we're underway, you can both come out on deck. Or not,' she added hastily, imagining what might be going through Freddie's mind.

But he nodded slowly, taking the jackets from her.

'Everyone has left the island except your mum,' she said briefly. 'She tried to hit me on the head with a rock.'

Freddie's eyes widened and then narrowed. She expected him to ask all about it, demand to know why everyone had left and where his dad was. But all he said was, 'Okay. So we have to get out of here.'

'And then when we're back on the mainland, we can sort things out.'

'With the police?'

'Yes.'

Freddie nodded.

30

PENNY

The sea was choppier around the fingers of rock that stuck out into it, and at first Penny gave them a wide berth. But she soon worked out that the current was faster there and was running in her favour. If she kept close in to each miniature headland, the sea swept her round it, almost like the boat was surfing.

It really was quite fun.

Maybe, when everything was back to normal, she could get into this as a hobby. One of Rod's friends, Jonathan, was a keen sea kayaker. She could join the club he was in.

Jonathan was recently divorced. A lawyer. Just a common or garden high street solicitor rather than anything high-powered, but still. He probably made good money, judging from the exorbitant fees her own solicitor had charged her just for some advice about a potential divorce. The hourly rate had literally made her gasp when she'd seen it stated, quite blatantly, on the invoice.

The palms of her hands were sore now. She was probably going to get blisters.

And her head was still thumping. It didn't help that she

kept having to look over her shoulder to check where she was.

She was approaching another headland, this one longer and higher than the others, with a flat grassy bit on the top. One of those old forts, no doubt. She steered for the point of the headland, looking over her shoulder from time to time to check she was still on course. And then she felt the boat skidding under her as it was pulled into a current, and just in time looked round to see white horses breaking on a reef just metres away.

Her left arm seemed to respond automatically, heaving on the oar to bring the boat round and away from the reef.

That had been close.

But now the current was sweeping the boat past the rocks and spitting it out into another bay. She turned on the bench seat to get a look at it.

Bingo!

There was a sailing boat sitting in the middle of the bay.

And there was Anna – and Alfie! They were getting aboard from an inflatable like the one Penny was rowing. Would they look round and see her?

No. Alfie was crouched on the deck looking in through one of the windows. And now they were going inside the boat, Anna's dark head disappearing down into the cabin.

Now was her chance.

Penny grasped hold of the oars and pulled, sending the boat shooting across the bay.

Freddie was contemplating his younger brother. 'Alfie, you have to behave yourself on a boat. You can't just go running around. You'd better sit down, and I'll make you some food while Anna gets us underway.'

Anna couldn't help but smile. Freddie was already picking up the correct sailing terminology.

'But we have to wait for *Daaaad*,' whined Alfie.

'I'm not sure where your dad is,' Anna said briskly. This was at least partially true. His body may, by now, have been swept out to sea. 'I'm afraid we can't wait.'

'Are we going to get in trouble?' Alfie asked Freddie. 'Mum tried to hit Anna with a rock, and then I grabbed her, and she pushed me, and Anna punched her right in the face! I want Dad.'

'We'll see him soon,' Freddie asserted confidently. 'And we're going to live with him from now on.'

Anna's heart contracted.

'It's wrong that Mum hurts us,' continued Freddie. 'The police won't let her live with us if I tell them the truth.' He glanced over at Anna.

'You're not going to live with your mum any more,' she confirmed.

Alfie looked up at her anxiously.

Would relatives take them in? Or would they end up in care? If that happened, might they even be separated?

'It'll be okay,' Freddie assured his brother. 'It'll be better. What do you want to eat? Look, there's loads!'

She couldn't stop the tears prickling as she watched the two of them examine the food on offer, Alfie's hand reaching for a crisp from the packet Freddie held open.

'Okay, boys, you stay here, and I'll hoist the anchor.'

She climbed the steps to the cockpit and stood for a moment, looking back at the shore but not really seeing it, rehearsing in her head what she would say to Fiona, to Bill. The important thing would be to make sure someone went to the bird sanctuary straight away and retrieved the evidence from Rod's locker: evidence not only of the Clarkes' wrong-doing regarding the accident, but of a motive for Penny to murder Rod to keep him quiet. The very fact that Rod had kept the original duty roster would point to his being likely to confess everything at some stage, and would lend weight to Anna's version of events rather than Penny's.

Would Bill take her away then and there, lock her in a cell for kidnap, for attempted murder? Or would she be arrested, charged and released on bail?

How could she ever have contemplated *killing* those two children in there?

Her mind reeled as she thought back to the moment on the cliff at Sgorr Gobhar when she'd been reaching for Freddie's hand; to the moment here, in the cockpit, when she'd grabbed him and hauled him to the side of the boat. Had the person who'd done those things really been *her*? Even as they were happening, both those moments had felt unreal, like weird dreams in which she was part of the action but somehow also removed from it, watching herself. She supposed it had been the only way she could have hoped to go through with it – if she could somehow become detached from herself, as she'd been detached from the rest of the world these last two years.

And yet she hadn't been able to do it.

She hadn't.

The idea of revenging Broc's and Tam's deaths, the anger that had burned in her whenever she thought about the Clarkes, had just been something to hold onto as the tsunami of grief had threatened to sweep her away.

It had never been more than a fantasy.

She'd pretended to herself that Freddie was a make-believe child, a nasty little brat from a cautionary tale, but in the moment she'd been about to push him off the boat he'd sprung to life as a real boy – just as he had on the cliff at Sgorr Gobhar as she'd looked at his hand, at his little fingernails ... Even if Rod hadn't suddenly turned up, she would never have pushed him over.

She took a deep, fortifying breath of mineral-laden air as her eyes focused again on her surroundings.

There was something in the water.

It was the tender, bobbing away towards the shore.

Damn. She couldn't have secured it properly.

But there was something not right.

It was the *blue* tender. Which should still be in the boathouse at Traigh Bheag.

She was looking down at the stern, at the red tender still tied up there, when hands clamped down on her arms and she was spun round, and now she was looking into a face that was more like a mask, contorted and unhuman and swollen, with staring, popping eyes, blonde hair straggling out behind it in the wind.

'Bitch!' Penny spat, and Anna reeled away, stumbling, falling back against the wheel.

Penny grabbed her again, grunting, muttering to herself, her hands suddenly around Anna's throat. Anna tried to break her grip, she clawed at her hands, at her wrists, her arms, she tried to reach her face, but Penny was too tall, her arms were too much longer than Anna's.

She tried to wriggle free, but there was nowhere to go.

The hands around her neck were squeezing, squeezing –

Too strong –

She kicked out at Penny's legs, and as Penny instinctively moved back, her grip slackened and Anna managed to twist to the side and elbow her in the stomach. Penny released her and Anna scrambled away, making for the cabin hatch, but now Penny was on her again, slamming her down on one of the benches, her hands back around Anna's throat, and this time it was as if those fingers were made of iron.

Anna couldn't breathe.

There were grey splodges everywhere, sounds receding ... The calls of the gulls, Penny's rasping laugh –

And then suddenly there was air in her lungs and she was gasping, and Penny was staggering away, Freddie clamped to her back like a little limpet, his hands in her hair, his face stiff and determined.

Penny shouted, punching behind her, catching Freddie a clout on the side of the head, but he hung on. Anna was on her knees, gulping air. She managed to heave open the locker under the bench just as Penny snatched the grappling hook from the stern and swung it in a wide arc, up and behind her. Once, twice, *thunk, thunk,* she whacked at Freddie.

He finally let go, tumbling down the steps to the cabin.

'No!' Anna heard herself shout.

She saw her hands in front of her face, lifting the flare gun.

She felt the pain in her hand and the kick as she fired, point-blank, into Penny's body.

Penny disappeared.

One second she was a woman and the next she was smoke and fire, orange and yellow and red and blue flames dancing and roaring, and then she was a woman again, arms flailing.

A scream ricocheted round the bay.

Anna had never heard a sound like it. It seemed to come out of the fire itself, an unearthly shriek that ripped at the air, at Anna's ears.

And then the fire woman was gone.

And now Anna could move. She staggered across the cockpit and looked down into the water. A wisp of smoke rose from the waves and was gone. She could see a dark shape sinking, and into her head flashed all the research she'd done on the cold shock response.

After that scream, Penny's lungs would have expanded, trying to suck in air, and they'd have flooded with water. And so she was sinking like a stone.

'Mum!' wailed Alfie from somewhere, and Freddie's voice said harshly, 'Stay here!' and then he was standing next to Anna, his cherub curls dishevelled, his beautiful face stern.

'Don't,' he said.

Anna hadn't even realised that she had straddled the guard rail. Freddie grabbed her; pulled her back into the cockpit.

'Leave her be,' he said.

For a long moment, Anna just stared into his blue eyes.

And then she nodded.

P ain. She was pain.
And yet she could feel herself detaching from it, going somewhere beyond, somewhere it couldn't touch her.

No.

No. She had to fight.

She had to kick.

She had to *breathe.*

The light was going, she was sinking, the world was somewhere up there and she was down here drowning and that couldn't happen.

She kicked against the water and her whole body convulsed, and she wanted to scream again but she had to hold on, she had to hold the tiny amount of air she had left in her lungs and then her head was breaking the surface and she had to breathe but for a long, terrible moment she couldn't, until more pain wrenched inside her and air was tearing into her chest.

Pain. All her nerve endings felt like they were still on fire, as if the fire was still raging all over her face, her shoulders, her right arm. Her right arm didn't work. Her right shoulder was just *pain* –

But she was alive, and she would get through this.

The sea must have put the fire out before it could do too much damage.

And now she was able to look around her, treading water, keeping her nose and mouth just above the surface of the swell that rocked her, that threatened to pull her back under, that sent icy shivers through her body to alternate with the pain.

The yacht was right there, almost in touching distance, and she could hear them, her kids, Freddie and Alfie. Alfie crying. Freddie speaking.

Freddie.

He had done this.

He'd helped that bitch against *his own mother*.

For the first time, she let the thought she'd been repressing for so long come screaming to the front of her mind.

Freddie's evil and he always has been.

Right from the second he was born, she had seen it. She'd been in denial all his life, and look where that had got her.

But she couldn't do anything about that now. She was too weak. It was all she could do not to shout and yell with the pain. Her right arm was useless. The only thing she had to concentrate on now was surviving this.

A little way from the yacht, the blue inflatable rocked on the waves.

She took a huge gulp of air and made herself sink back down under the sea, kicked with her legs, clawed at the water ahead of her with her left arm and let the right dangle at her side. When the pressure in her lungs was too much, she resurfaced, gulped more air, checked the position of the inflatable.

Back under.

Kick.

Claw.

Endure.

Repeat.

And now she was near enough to the inflatable to grab it with her left hand and quickly, quickly work her way round its side, so it was between her head and the yacht. She couldn't see the yacht any more, apart from the mast sticking up, which meant they couldn't see her.

If they happened to look this way, all they'd see would be the blue inflatable carried along by the waves towards the shore.

It was easier to lie on her back, her body stretched out under the boat, her left arm hooked over its fat inflated side. She had the strength only to kick for a few seconds before she had to stop and rest. Then kick. Then rest.

But she was doing it.

The inflatable, helped by the tide, was gaining on the land.

And the yacht was moving too. The engine had started, and it was moving out of the bay. Anna was kidnapping *both* her kids and there wasn't a thing Penny could do about it, other than hope justice caught up with her in the end. For that, and for Rod. Anna might not actually have wielded the frying pan, but it was down to her that Rod was dead.

Finally, finally, she was at the beach.

Her feet hit the sand and she flopped into the shallows. Crawled up out of the water, pain exploding, and now she could yell, she could scream, and there was no one on the island to hear her.

She lay on her back and sobbed, and then screamed, and then sobbed.

The holiday cottages.

She could rest up in one of those, take all the time she needed to heal. No one would be looking for her – she'd be presumed drowned, her body washed out to sea. She could raid the shop and stock up on supplies, maybe use that trolley thing to get them to one of the cottages near the harbour.

She'd have to get herself there on foot, but there was no rush.

There was no one else on the island.

ANNA

Anna stood at the closed door of the room she hadn't entered since Tam and Broc had died. She'd thought about this room constantly in the time she'd been away from the island – a month on bail, when she'd stayed with Fiona and Gareth, and a month 'at Her Majesty's pleasure', as Mum called it, in the women's prison. And every day of the week she'd been back on Faida, she had come to this door and stood here and remembered what Fiona had hissed in her ear, on the day the whole family, Mum and Dad and Uncle Henry, Fiona and Gareth and Deirdre, had picked Anna up at the prison gates.

'You can do this.'

Meaning, she supposed, life.

The rest of her life.

Fiona had been absolutely fantastic, from the moment Anna had turned up at her house in Oban with Freddie and Alfie in tow, gabbling about Rod and Penny and insisting that Freddie needed to be checked out at the hospital immediately. That done, Anna had told Fiona, Gareth and Bill everything – up to and including what had happened with

Penny on *Merry Dancer* – and Bill had called Sergeant Stewart. The four of them had awaited his arrival in Fiona's lovely conservatory overlooking the breathtakingly beautiful Firth of Lorn with its backdrop of islands, near and far – Kerrera and Mull and Lismore. The scene was an ever-changing tapestry of light on the water, clouds massing and moving away overhead, ferries and little boats busy on the sea lanes.

Fiona had sat by Anna's side, squeezing her uninjured hand so hard that it hurt too, while Gareth and Bill had occupied two of the wicker chairs, legs stretched out, contemplating the view.

Eventually Anna excused herself to check again on Freddie and Alfie, who, exhausted, had been put to bed in one of the spare rooms, curtains pulled against the strong evening sunshine. The room was still quiet, the two of them zonked out under the covers, the cut on the side of Freddie's face cleaned and closed with butterfly strips. Thankfully, he seemed none the worse, physically at least, after their battle with his mother.

'What's going to happen to them?' she asked Bill as she returned to the conservatory.

He lifted his shoulders. 'That will be a question for social services.'

'Someone needs to tell the boys – about their dad.'

His face was kind. 'Aye, but that person shouldn't be you.'

She nodded.

Her sister stood, and pulled Anna into her arms.

When Sergeant Stewart arrived, Anna was arrested and taken to the police station, where she spent three hours answering questions and giving her statement. She told them about the original paper copy of the duty roster Rod had hidden in his locker at the bird sanctuary. She told them what he'd confessed to her, and that she was sure he must have told Penny about his confession, and she'd killed him and attempted to kill Anna to stop the truth coming out.

Anna didn't hold anything back. But when she came to the part where she'd almost pushed Freddie overboard, she had to stop as the enormity of it filled the windowless little room, seemed to press on the walls, to press on her head so she couldn't think, she couldn't contemplate it, what she had so nearly done.

She was charged only with abduction 'for the moment', as the detective interviewing her said ominously.

She was assessed by a psychiatrist and released on bail, on the condition that she stay with Fiona and Gareth in Oban.

In the event, there were no further charges. Freddie and Alfie backed up her story of self-defence against Penny on the yacht. Rod's body had been found in the cleft, and there had been an unexpected breakthrough to back up Anna's version of events. The police had asked about CCTV on the island, and she'd told them there was none, although there were a few motion-activated cameras that Broc had set up for wildlife watching. On the footage from one of them, there was a clear image of Penny throwing a pair of yellow rubber gloves into the sea, timed just after Rod must have been murdered. Microscopic yellow particles from the same type of glove had been found on the handle of the frying pan she had used as a weapon.

As Anna had admitted everything, there had been no trial, only a plea hearing at which the judge had sentenced her to two months, which meant she would be released automatically after she'd served one month in prison. It had helped enormously that Freddie had insisted on making a statement, which had been read out in court by Anna's lawyer.

'Anna isn't the kind of person who could have gone

through with hurting me. Mum and Dad killed her little boy and her husband, and Anna was sad and lonely and she was lashing out at the people who had done that, but in the end she would never have hurt anyone. And she didn't. She gave me nice food and books and a hot water bottle. I told her what Mum did to me. Mum killed Dad and then she tried to kill Anna and she punched me and hit me with a grappling hook and Anna had to fire the flare gun to stop her. It wasn't Anna's fault. Anna probably saved me and Alfie's lives, because if Mum had killed Anna she might have killed us too, because she was really, really angry.'

The judge had said that Freddie's victim statement had weighed heavily with her in her sentencing decision, as had other statements from local people as to Anna's previously good character. She had talked about the effect on Anna of Tam's and Broc's deaths, and her desire for revenge against the people responsible who, it seemed, had escaped justice.

'While I am in no way condoning anyone taking revenge of this sort, and most of all against an innocent child, I accept that this was, in the defendant's own words, a "fantasy" that she would never actually have carried out – although she came pretty close. Nevertheless, a custodial sentence is warranted in view of the fact that she abducted a ten-year-old child and put him, albeit momentarily, in fear of his life.'

Freddie.

What a remarkable boy he had turned out to be.

Broc, she thought, would have liked him a lot.

She turned the doorknob and pushed open the door.

In the slanting early morning light, dust motes danced. The room had that unused air about it that reminded Anna of the attic in her childhood home. It smelt of warm, dry old wood and neglect.

In the middle of the room was a battered old pine table with the paraphernalia of an artist: a pot of brushes, a bottle of turps, tubes of paint, a plate that had been used as a palette, rags streaked with browns and blacks and oranges and greens. In the middle of the table was a tiny, half-painted wooden bird – a warbler of some sort?

The whole of the wall opposite the window was shelves, on which perched peewits and magpies and chaffinches and blackbirds and every other kind of bird you could think of ever visiting Faida. In pride of place in the centre of the middle shelf was Norman Hoodlum, his feathers painted glossy black and soft grey, his eye seeming to shine with the dab of varnish Broc had added, triumphant to have thought of this genius idea.

It had started on Broc's eighth birthday. Tam had worked secretly, in the workshop next to the garage, on a piece of oak he'd found washed up on the Singing Sands, transforming it into the shape of a duck. He'd presented this to Broc over the breakfast table, after he'd opened his other presents, along with a box of paints. 'See, you can paint it whatever colours you like.'

But Broc had been adamant that it must be accurate. It must look like a real mallard.

She walked slowly along the shelves and picked up that first creation, the rather stiff mallard, the plumage crudely painted, the colours too primary, too brash. Dust came away on her fingers, and she kept running her hand over it until it was clean. She would have to get a duster, a wet cloth, the hoover ...

Over the years, you could see the progression they had each made, Tam's carving becoming more fluid, more life-like, Broc's painting likewise. The little warbler on the table was a masterpiece in the making.

She picked it up.

It was a wood warbler, its back and the top of its head a matte greeny-grey, a darker line across its eye 'like a bandit's mask,' as Broc had once said. The throat and chest would have been yellow. The belly, somehow rendered soft and feathery by the skill of Tam's hand, would have been white.

Gently, she set it back down.

What was was hard enough. *What would have been* was still unbearable.

She left the door open behind her and descended the stairs to the kitchen, turning her mind to all the mundane tasks she needed to do. Today, she decided, would be a day of physical work, of cleaning.

On Friday, she would leave the island again to spend the weekend with Fiona and her family. In the meantime, there was plenty to keep her occupied. The holiday cottages all needed a deep clean to get them ready for when she started to take bookings again. And there might be some minor repairs to be done, a list of jobs for tradesmen. She needed to check there were no missing slates on the roofs, no dripping taps, no problems with the boilers or the central heating systems or the chimneys.

Harbour Cottage, with four bedrooms, would take the most time.

She'd start there.

In the kitchen, she loaded up the pink plastic caddy with cleaning products and cloths. The locked cupboard in each cottage had a vacuum cleaner and a mop and so on in it, so she didn't need to take anything else with her.

Harbour Cottage was set back from and slightly above the harbour and sheltered by a belt of Sitka spruce, so it wasn't visible from the road. She turned up the track and parked the Land Rover on the gravel in front of the cottage. It was the typical two-storey Scottish house, with a window on either side of the front door and two dormers in the roof separated by a little metal skylight. The floor plan was T-shaped, with the stem of the 'T' sticking out the back and not visible from here.

The red flatbed trolley was standing by the side of the house.

Had Gareth or Bill, perhaps, been here to get a head start on the list of repairs?

A strong westerly was agitating the sheltering band of spruce trees, and Anna thought again of Broc and his horror of them. Their branches seemed to reach for her, flung out and back by the wind.

She hefted the caddy and crossed the gravel to the front door, pulling the keys from her pocket. But when she tried the door, she found that it was unlocked. She must have forgotten to lock it when she was pretending to search the cottages for Freddie with the Clarkes.

She walked into the hall, a long space leading through the house to the kitchen at the back. As she passed the door to the sitting room, she glanced inside.

What the hell?

The room was in a state of disarray, a pillow and duvet on the sofa, dirty plates and mugs on the coffee table and the floor, an overturned glass on the rug. Food packaging tossed about the place. She was just taking all this in when she became aware of movement.

A glinting movement, right in her line of vision.

In the room, but not in the room. She was looking, she realised, at her own reflection in the glass of the big picture on the wall opposite.

But Anna herself wasn't moving.

There was someone behind her.

She was already turning, already lashing out with the caddy as a knife sliced down at her back.

The knife left the hand that held it and arced away across the hall. A kitchen knife, Anna registered with some detached part of her brain, one of the set she had bought for the cottage a few years ago.

And then she was lashing out again, at the wild, snarling face coming at her, and as the caddy whacked into it there was an animal sound, a howl as cleaning products flew everywhere, clattered to the floor. And then Anna herself was screaming, the sound juddering from her as she hit out with the caddy again, at that face, almost unrecognisable, raw and puckered and haloed by tangled pale hair.

Penny.

Lying, now, on the floor.

She was filthy, the once-white fleece a patchwork of stains, blackened and rusty with old blood where the flare must have hit her. The right side of her face was angry red, tight-looking. Anna stood over her, breathing hard, still gripping the caddy.

The knife.

She should get the knife.

It was over by the wall. She swooped on it; held it in her right hand, pointed down at Penny, the caddy grasped in her left like a shield. But Penny wasn't moving. And under her head, a pool of blood was expanding outwards.

She must have hit her head on the flagstones.

'Penny,' said Anna, nudging the woman's leg with the toe of her shoe.

Penny's eyes flickered open.

Police.

Air ambulance.

Anna needed to go to the café and call 999. But she couldn't look away from those boggling eyes, the rage in them, and now an answering rage was tearing through her and she found herself squatting on the floor, hissing right into Penny's face:

'You will never, *ever* see those boys again!'

Penny's mouth opened, but no sound came out.

'What kind – of a mother – does what you did to them?' Anna could hardly get the words out for the emotion welling up, like a physical blockage in her throat. 'They're safe. You'll never – be allowed – anywhere near them – again.' And suddenly, as the anger swept through her again, the blockage in her throat was gone. '*Everyone knows what you did!*'

Penny was trying to speak.

In the gloom of the hallway, Anna watched her struggle to form words, the muscles of her jaw, of her neck, jumping. In the end, she managed to speak quite clearly.

'Dad. My dad – knows?'

Anna smiled. 'Of course he does.'

Later, when Penny had finally stopped breathing, when she was just a dead body lying there in the hall of Harbour Cottage, it occurred to Anna that she had missed her chance to say something about Tam and Broc.

But what would she have wanted to say?

To this woman: nothing at all.

WHEN SHE FINALLY REACHED BILL ON the phone, she didn't tell him what had happened, just that she needed him on the island urgently. 'Get Neil to bring you. Tell him you're helping me prepare the holiday cottages for guests.'

He arrived within the hour. As Neil and *Ocean Rose* were departing the harbour, he turned to her.

'Well, now, Anna. This is all very cryptic.'

'I know. I'm sorry. It's – Penny. She's here. She tried to kill me.'

'What?'

Anna almost smiled. It was a rare thing indeed, to get a reaction like that from the unflappable Bill.

'She's dead. I – She came at me with a knife. I hit her with the caddy and she fell and smashed her head on the flagstones.'

He grasped her shoulders in his big, steady hands. 'Are you all right?'

As tension left her body, as if he were somehow drawing it out of her, she realised that it was one of the things she had missed most over the last two years: ordinary human contact.

'I'm fine. The knife didn't touch me.'

'And she's *definitely* dead?'

Anna nodded. 'She's in Harbour Cottage.'

They walked there in silence, and Anna waited outside in the fresh air while Bill went into the house. She supposed Penny must have broken in at the back and then used the set of keys kept on a hook in the kitchen to unlock the doors from the inside. Security had never been something they'd had to worry about on Faida.

Bill was in there a long time, or so it seemed. When he came out, he was rather white-faced, but otherwise as outwardly composed as ever. They stood, the two of them, looking across the Sound to Jura.

'She's obviously been holed up in there all this time,' said Anna. 'She must have crossed the island on foot after somehow making it to the shore. How on earth did she manage that, in the state she was in? That flare – it exploded against her body ...'

He shook his head. 'Incredible. She must have been in a considerable amount of pain.'

'I guess she hid in Harbour Cottage while you – the police, I mean – were retrieving Rod's body and processing the crime scene in the café ... There would be no reason for any of you to go into any of the cottages.'

'No, there would not,' he agreed.

'And then when you'd all gone, she used the trolley to get food from the shop. But why did she hide? She couldn't have known she'd been caught on camera disposing of the gloves, so why not take her story to the authorities? As far as Penny knew, it would be her word against mine. And I was already compromised by ... well, luring the Clarkes to Faida and kidnapping Freddie. There was every hope, surely, that I would be the one going down for Rod's murder, not Penny.'

'But there was the duty roster,' said Bill. 'She must have known that you would tell us where Rod hid it, and that would be the final nail in the coffin for Peaks Transit. She must have known she would be brought to justice for what she did, for the deaths of seven people on that bus.' He narrowed his eyes as the sun suddenly came out from behind a cloud. 'I would say she intended leaving the old Penny behind. For all the world knew, she was dead. She may well have planned to reinvent herself as a completely different person.'

That made sense.

Anna sighed. 'But before she did that, she wanted revenge on me. As she saw it, I'd destroyed her family. She must have planned to attack me at some point, maybe when I came to the shop ... But I walked right into Harbour Cottage, right into her lair ...' She shuddered.

He nodded. 'She was a very dangerous woman. No blame will attach to you, Anna, for what happened here.'

'Maybe not,' she said slowly. 'But I don't want Freddie and Alfie to know about this. If there's an investigation, it will all come out, won't it? That she holed up here waiting to kill me? For over two months, without any medical attention for her injuries.'

'Aye.'

'Those boys have been through enough, Bill. Surely it would be better for them to think she died instantly and her body was swept out to sea?'

For a long moment, he said nothing, and she thought he

was going to shake his head and say that, in his capacity as a
police officer, he couldn't countenance being a part of any
such cover-up.

But he nodded.

They buried her in the machair. Bill did most of the
digging, the sleeves of his shirt rolled up to his shoulders,
sweat soaking into it, but he didn't remove it as he might have
done if she hadn't been there. Afterwards, he showered in the
old farmhouse, and she gave him a shirt of Tam's to put on.
He appeared in the kitchen wearing it with a diffident look,
but it was fine. It seemed right that he should have it.

She smiled. 'It suits you.'

It was time to give the rest of Tam's clothes away too.
Perhaps his brothers would like some of them, and his other
cousins.

They cooked themselves a simple meal of pasta and
tomato sauce and vegetables, and afterwards they took coffee
and biscuits through to the sitting room. As Bill walked into
the room ahead of her with the tray, Anna stopped on the
threshold. She wasn't used to having company in here, the
scene of so many happy times, snuggled up on winter
evenings watching Agatha Christie or playing board games
long after Broc really should have been in bed.

Bill set the tray down on the coffee table and glanced
round at her, but instead of commenting on her tears he just
handed her a mug of coffee and started examining the paint-
ings on the walls. There was an eclectic mix of pictures –
atmospheric Victorian seascapes and watercolours of birds
and animals and her own family's work, mainly her mother's
quirky cityscapes and portraits. But the one Bill homed in on
was a painting on the wall by the window, positioned to
protect it from direct sunlight. It was a little watercolour of a
man standing in a river, wooded hills rising above it, a flock of
birds in the pale blue sky. In the corner was 'River Garry,

Pitlochry, CH, 1947'. CH for the painter's name, Charles Hislop, Anna's great-uncle.

'Aye, this was Tam's favourite,' said Bill. 'He told me that, once.'

Anna leapt hungrily on this new piece of information about Tam. 'Did he say why?'

'Because it's such a peaceful scene. Looking at this picture, he said, you'd think the world was a peaceful place and had never been otherwise. But it's 1947. Just months after the end of the War.'

Anna looked at the little fisherman, and thought of Tam standing where they were now, contemplating him too. Thinking about all the Highland soldiers who'd seen action in so many conflicts.

What had that fisherman witnessed?

What had he suffered?

What had he lost?

But maybe that was the whole point of this unassuming little painting. Maybe that was what Bill, in his gentle way, was trying to tell her.

There is still this.

In 1947, there was still the river on a long summer's afternoon, and the quiet hills, and the birds flying over them.

THE NEXT DAY, after she'd waved Bill off at the harbour, she returned to Harbour Cottage to start the process of obliteration. She had refused Bill's offer of help. He'd already done more than enough. And she wanted to do this alone.

She'd brought washing soda and a stiff bristle brush in addition to the products she usually kept in the caddy. As she scrubbed at the hall floor, radio blaring to try to distract herself from what she was doing, it was Freddie and Alfie she thought about, not Penny.

After Anna had been arrested and taken away, the boys had stayed on with Fiona and her family for a few hours until their aunt and uncle had arrived.

'You should have seen Freddie's little face! He obviously adores his auntie, and she him. Ursula and Will are really lovely,' Fiona had assured her when Anna had returned to the house on bail. 'Rod's side of the family, not Penny's. Ursula is an occupational therapist, and Will is a paramedic. They don't have kids of their own. Ursula has been struggling to get pregnant. They'd actually started to think about adoption.'

Ursula had sent Fiona a photo of the boys in their garden a few days later. It was an action shot of Freddie and Alfie playing football with a tall woman who looked a bit like Rod – the same lanky frame and unruly hair. She looked like fun. And the house was gorgeous, really chocolate box, with a thatched roof and overhanging eaves. Penny had mentioned something about an inheritance of Rod's. Presumably the sister had used hers more wisely and wasn't short of a bob or two.

A couple of weeks ago, Freddie had sent Anna a letter from Devon, laboriously penned in his childish hand but, she wasn't surprised to see, without any spelling errors. He told her that he and Alfie were going to live with their Auntie Ursula and Uncle Will 'forever'. They had a new puppy 'and he's really naughty, even worse than me,' and he hoped that Anna might come and visit them.

That couldn't happen, of course.

Ursula and Will wouldn't let Anna within a hundred miles of the boys, no matter what Freddie said, and that was as it should be. But she knew they'd be fine. The last sentence of the letter had stated simply, 'They love us.' And then he'd signed off, 'From Freddie.'

It still brought tears to her eyes to think about it. He'd

gone straight to the heart of what really mattered – not the house or the puppy or even being physically safe.

They love us.

Freddie had seen the very worst of what human beings were capable of. No – he hadn't just *seen* it, he'd experienced it first-hand, and she supposed that was going to be an issue for him all the rest of his days. But he would be happy now, she hoped, with his nice auntie and uncle. And, if Anna had anything to do with it, he would never learn the truth about his mother's death.

She sat back on her heels and contemplated the space where it had happened.

She smiled.

'Karma, Rod,' she said to the empty house.

BACK AT ENGSTER, she poured herself a long glass of orange juice, fetched the box of food scraps and sat out on one of the plantation chairs in the hot midday sun. Soon the Hoodlums descended, all five of them, swooping down onto the grass. Norman marched towards the decking with the purposeful swagger that always made her smile.

'Well, Norman,' she said, and he regarded her with his clever little eyes. 'Here you go.'

She tossed him some nuts to start with, and Norman changed from a strut to a bouncing hop to make sure he got to them before his offspring. Then Monty and Morag tucked in. They might officially be 'helper' crows, but their family feeling didn't extend to feeding little brother Freddie before themselves.

She would have liked to have written back to Freddie and told him she'd named the new crow after him, but that wouldn't be a good idea.

Freddie hopped up to Norman and started shrieking.

There was no other word for the raucous young-crow noise, beak open wide to reveal the bright red inside, which served as a target for Norman to shove the food at. The shrieks got more and more frantic the closer Norman came, until they morphed into a glugging noise as the food was crammed into Freddie's beak and he necked it, only to resume shrieking immediately afterwards.

Norman looked round at her, as if to say, *Typical.*

'Now here's a treat, Norman,' she said, and, moving slowly, placed three eggs side by side on the decking. Then she sat back down and watched.

It had been one of Broc's favourite things to do, to give them an egg.

They're so funny!

First there was the problem of the shell. Norman stood over one of the eggs and eyed it consideringly. He knew it was too big to fit in his beak, so he pulled back his head and whacked at it until he'd made a hole, carefully removing bits of shell to enlarge it enough to be able to stick his beak in and gobble up most of the yolk. Then he pushed his lower beak inside the egg and clamped his upper beak over the shell so he was grasping it.

Now came the tricky part.

He picked it up and walked carefully to the dish.

He dropped the egg into the water.

At this point, Broc would be shaking with suppressed laughter.

Why do they do *that? What a* mess!

The wisdom of dunking raw egg was, it had to be said, not clear. The whites dispersed in the water, turning it cloudy, and Norman then perched on the edge of the dish and tried to scoop it up in his beak.

Why not just eat it from the shell?

She had no answer to that. Bill's theory was that Norman

was hoping that the shell might soften enough in the water to be palatable, but surely the crow must know by now that that wasn't going to happen?

'Just one of life's mysteries, eh, Norman?'

What had the Hoodlums thought, in her absence? Had they feared that, like Broc, she wouldn't be coming back? And now, every time they swooped down and saw that it was still just Anna, were they disappointed? Were they hoping that Broc might one day also return?

Sometimes she found herself imagining them, the two boys, Broc and Freddie, sitting here together watching the Hoodlums. Broc would never have what Freddie had, all those years stretching away into adulthood, but his short life had been happy. There had been nothing to cloud it. She thought of Broc's smile, sunny and uncomplicated and full of an eagerness to embrace all that the world had to offer, because he had known it only as a happy place.

He'd been a happy boy.

And maybe that was something she needed to think about more often.

As suddenly as they had arrived, the Hoodlums took off, flapping away south along the line of the beach. Freddie was still cawing raucously. On a whim, Anna stood and followed them, down the track through the machair to the Singing Sands. It wasn't ideal conditions for it, but she scuffed determinedly at the sand with her shoes and was rewarded with a small squeak.

She turned her face up to the sun.

She would spend this weekend in Oban with Fiona and Gareth and Lily and Moira and Hamish. For so long, she had felt she was being disloyal to Tam and Broc if she admitted there was anything in the world that was good. How could there be, if they weren't in it? She had avoided seeing and even thinking about her nephew and nieces these past two years.

She imagined Broc smiling, digging at her with his gentle humour.

You have to maybe forgive them for not being me.

MUCH LATER, in the softening light of the long summer evening, she sat in the old farmhouse with the door open to the hall and the front door open to the garden, to the scents of catmint and roses and the tang of the sea. If she closed her eyes she could almost hear them, Tam and Broc, chattering and laughing as they walked back up the track from the beach. Maybe Broc had found a particularly smelly bit of driftwood and Tam was trying to persuade him not to bring it home.

At the fading of the day, when reality blurred into unreality, into dreams, into the what-might-have-been, she knew that they would always come back to her, and that she would always be here waiting.

Here's the old cottage, here the open door;
Fond are our hearts although we do not bare them –
They're yours, and you are ours for ever more.

FROM JANE

As a reader, I love novels in which my perceptions of the characters change. The idea with *The Lost Boy* was to take this to an extreme. I wanted to start off with a character, Anna, plotting the worst of all crimes – the murder of an innocent child. Over the course of the story, the challenge was to make the reader sympathise with her and maybe even like her a little. I'm not sure if I have succeeded in this, but it was fun to try!

The island of Faida is imaginary, but inspired by happy (and murder-free) holidays on various islands on the west coast of Scotland. There is a remnant of temperate rainforest on the island of Eigg in which my friend Jocelyn and I experienced what we still refer to as our 'ordeal' – we took a path that turned out not to be meant for humans and ended up on a precipitous slope, crawling our way over and under branches while attempting not to slip off the muddy path to our deaths (okay, *possibly* a slight exaggeration!). Like many ordeals, this proved to be great material, and I lived it again with Anna in that Fairy Forest scene.

So, my first 'thank you' has to be to Jocelyn for failing to navigate us onto the correct path. (I'm blaming Jocelyn, although I expect she'll claim it was my fault.)

Next, thank you to my mum Grace and sister Anne for reading the first draft of the first chapter and providing invaluable feedback at that early stage. (The word 'shocking' was used, but I chose to take that as a positive...) My brilliant writer friends Lucy Lawrie and Lesley McLaren read the whole manuscript and improved it no end with their ideas and comments and mistake-catching. Lesley put a cat amongst the pigeons with her annoyingly accurate knowledge of tachographs, necessitating my trawling through an HGV drivers' forum for ideas on how to disable them. (I only hope the police never have cause to check my browsing history!)

Lesley and Lucy also suggested that the book should include a map of the island, which has been beautifully drawn by Claire Milto. Thank you, Claire, for patiently incorporating all of my bizarre requirements.

The text was very carefully edited by Jodi Compton and proofread by Pauline Nolet – I'm embarrassed by all the mistakes you found but very glad you did so! Thanks to multi-talented Claire for formatting the text and preparing it for publication, and to Claire (again!) and Garret for all the mysterious marketing wizardry you do.

And thank you, as ever, to Brian Lynch for many in-depth plot and character discussions and for steering the whole thing in the right direction, and also for some great editing. Just one example – there was a sentence at the end of the first chapter that I just couldn't get to work no matter how long I agonised over it. 'That will do,' I said to myself at last, although I wasn't happy with it. I didn't mention this problem to Brian, but a comment miraculously appeared in the manuscript with a suggestion for rewording that I knew immediately was right. I'm very lucky to have so many talented people helping me with my writing.

Finally, I'm extremely grateful to all of you for reading my books and allowing me to fulfil my dream of becoming an author. It's even more fun than I thought it would be!

www.janerenshaw.co.uk

Reviews are so important to us authors. I would be very grateful if you could spend a moment to write an honest review on Amazon (no matter how short). They really do help get the word out.

ALSO BY JANE RENSHAW

INKUBATOR TITLES

THE CHILD WHO NEVER WAS

WATCH OVER ME

NO PLACE LIKE HOME

THE STEPSON

THE LOST BOY

JANE'S OTHER TITLES

THE TIME AND PLACE

THE SWEETEST POISON